YOU LOOK SOMETHING

ADVANCE READING COPY

You Look Something
an indigenous coming-of-college-age novel

Jessica Mehta

Pub Date: April 7, 2020

ISBN: 9781948018746
248 Pages, 5.25 x 8
$14.99, Trade Paperback

CATEGORIES:
FIC043000 FICTION / Coming of Age
FIC059000/FICTION/Native American
FIC027230/FICTION/Romance/Multicultural

DISTRIBUTED BY:
INGRAM, FOLLETT, COUTTS, MBS, YBP,
COMPLETE BOOK, BERTRAMS, GARDNERS
Or wholesale@wyattmackenzie.com

Wyatt-MacKenzie Publishing
DEADWOOD, OREGON

PUBLISHER CONTACT:
Nancy Cleary
nancy@wyattmackenzie.com

**This is an Uncorrected
Pre-Publication Review Copy Only**

JESSICA MEHTA

YOU LOOK SOMETHING

an indigenous coming-of-age novel

Wyatt-MacKenzie Publishing

DEADWOOD, OREGON

YOU LOOK SOMETHING

an indigenous coming-of-age novel
Jessica Mehta

ISBN: 978-1-948018-74-6

Library of Congress Control Number: to come

Wyatt-MacKenzie Publishing
DEADWOOD, OREGON

Wyatt-MacKenzie Publishing, Inc.
www.WyattMacKenzie.com
Contact us: info@wyattmackenzie.com

For all the Native teenagers, the indigenous 20-somethings, the self-proclaimed misfits searching for a home and the finding of someone "like them" amidst all the post-Colonial chaos. We are here. We are looking for you, too. It really does get so much better.

1

I SHOULDN'T HAVE been there, I knew. But I faked it real hard. Even *I* thought I passed for a minute, that the boys were sneaking glances because I looked so damned good. Not because they were sniffing out that I didn't belong. But maybe they'd let me know that by slipping a finger under my skirt to the wetness instead of pushing me off the campus curb like they ought to. Okay, I'll be honest. I didn't even really know how I got there, or who let me in. I was twenty years old, way too old to be a college freshman, but that gave me some kind of warped upper hand because it meant I was so much closer to being able to legally buy alcohol than anyone else.

Four years prior, I was living in a car with my high school boyfriend, Ben. That was before the abuse eked out of his words and slipped into his fingers. His knees. Straight into my throat that one time on the bathroom floor. Ever since I'd turned thirteen, I let my grades slip and my skirt hike, and my mom just totally gave up, going batshit crazy when my dad left. That was when I was almost sixteen. Thank god the freedom of a car was already parked in the driveway, paid for with sweaty summers scooping up bubbly nachos at the race track so the old, leering men could plop orange stains down their shirts.

Still. I didn't know what the difference between a college and a university was, what exactly a scholarship was, but the idea that I would go to college had been lambasted into my brain right alongside endless drills on shapes, spelling, and rudimentary math ever since I was a toddler. My mom, she wanted a redo of her life through me. She wanted to go to college. To be pretty. To be smart. Be thin without having to subsist on nothing but lettuce leaves, mustard, and Kool-Aid for three days before the binge set in. That's why, when the Indian started to show in my hair and it went from plat-inum to brown real fast in kindergarten, she fell apart crying in the kitchen while unscrewing the bottle of laundry bleach. I didn't look like an angel anymore, and the Chero-kee she'd prayed to see when I was inside her took her by surprise. There wasn't a drip of my dad's swarthy, beige buffalo skin showing in me. She retaliated with chemical burns on my scalp and had to slather my bald spots in extra strong sunscreen the rest of that summer.

And now (can you believe this?) here I was. On a real college campus, the biggest one in Oregon. Muted, crunchy leaves underfoot and everything. Ben, he'd only been gone for six months, but he ducked away fast because he'd already pinned another young, stupid thing in his sights. She was sixteen and he was twenty-three, and her being a minister's daughter made her ironclad-closed thighs smell that much sweeter. He only begged for sex twice after we'd broken up since she was too scared. I was a bit impressed at how quickly he gave up. I thought I'd be disappointed.

Why I chose this college, this campus, this dorm room, this *everything* was why I chose, well, everything. It was easy. I knew about it, it was in downtown, and it was so massive that surely they'd let me squeak in, and squeak I did. I had all the pity cards, some extras tucked up my sleeves and bonus ones shoved down my boots. Considered independ-ent by the federal government due to "abandonment by both parents"? Yep, and the college knew that meant an endless flow of grants and student loans to back up every poor decision I was sure to make. (I, on the other hand, didn't really "get" that part of the benefit.) First generation student? Got that. Low income? Naturally. Tribally enrolled Cherokee girl? Oh, hell yes. I was the poster child of diversity, especially since they didn't ask for pictures to see I didn't look Indian at all, and in some lights, I even looked pretty. (College departments love that shit. Love to plaster it in their brochures and pleas for money to annoyed alumni.) I should have been set. But I was dumb and saw thousands of dollars pooling into my brand new student checking account, and it was so damn cozy in the blindness. It was the first day of freshman year and I was already twenty thousand deep in student loan debt, with a flippy salon cut and color, itchy Abercrombie wool sweater, bootcut jeans from Express, and sometimes when I passed the windows of the student center I almost even looked skinny.

"Hey! With the cute hair, hey!" A murder of girls with flat-ironed hair and too much lip gloss let one out of their fold to chase me with a bright purple flyer. "Recruitment starts on Thursday," she said. "You should come." She was hapa with slightly protruding teeth in a moon-pie face that worked for her at nineteen. She'd be fat for sure by thirty.

"What recruitment?"

"Sorority recruitment," she said, her practiced smile twitching. I wanted to tell her she could stop smiling. Her buggy, tired muscles made it hard to keep looking in her eyes. "Formal Panhellenic recruitment begins on Friday, but the information session is on Thursday."

What the hell was Panhellenic? Formal? I didn't know, but images of matching hoodies with telltale Greek letters from the movies began to wail a siren's song in my mind. I mean, I'd tried this before. My first year in high school, I made it onto the cheerleading team. Yeah, yeah, I'll give my mom props for that one. She'd spent years shoving me onto every stage she could find. School plays, jazz dance, folk storytelling, clown school (seriously), beauty pageants, and modeling open calls. If she could get someone, anyone, to validate that I was special that meant she was special too. I nailed that cheerleading façade because I could act like I knew I belonged there. I didn't, of course. I only lasted a year. By the time the following tryouts came around, my mom had hounded the cheer coach daily for weeks, begging to make sure I was kept on. I didn't find that out until it was too late, and my mom broke down sobbing that it was all her fault. It was. I was the strongest base they had, but not strong enough to make dealing with a psychotic mother worth it.

But this? This I could do. I'd left the saboteurs back in Central Point, and this was the big city. Nobody knew how alien I was up here.

"Yeah, sure," I told Hapa, slipping the flyer into my bag.

"I like your hair," she said. "What's your name?"

"Thanks. Julia." As she walked back to the booth, her flat butt in too-tight jeans, I realized my mistake. I should have complimented her too.

My dorm room was a single, evidence that my sprinkling of agoraphobia had won this time. I knew I should have gone for a shared room, forced myself "out there." Made myself sleep an arm's reach away from a strange girl who was probably thinner, prettier, and not nearly as awkward as me. Maybe some of her rightness would have transferred to me by osmosis. Like when I mistook her toothbrush for my own, her spit and foodie bits would crash into my stomach and turn to muscle. To energy. And I'd be just a little bit more normal like her. It hadn't worked yet, not with my best childhood friend Amanda at least, but that didn't mean it would never work.

But that's not how it played out. For starters, all the shared dorms in the one traditional building the campus had were booked months before I slinked in as a last-minute student. Well, technically, I was a transfer student. I picked up a few community college credits while getting my high school completion program at the local two-year school.

That got me out of tight freshman deadlines, taking the SAT, and a bunch of other bullshit teens who went to prom and didn't sleep in cars got to muddle through so they could feel like they'd lived something. No. They hadn't lived anything. How could I think I could make them mistake me for one of them?

It didn't matter, because a single was all that was left and one the size of a semigenerous closet was all I could afford. And I didn't give a shit. I could touch both walls from my twin-size bed, and there was an odd sink in the corner even though the whole floor shared a bathroom down the hall. I took that first student loan check installment and bought a nylon comforter with bright green leaves printed on it. Around the pedestal sink, I wrapped fake plastic vines and white twinkle lights. I even bought a candle, one of those expensive Yankee ones. In my tiny oasis, I wanted to feel warmth and smell Baking Snickerdoodle Cookies. Comfort. Like I lived somewhere wildly beautiful.

It didn't help after my first hangover. It was my twentieth birthday, just four weeks before the hapa chased me down for my Rachel cut I got five years too late. I'd never had more than a sip of warm beer, and that from my dad while I watched him weld makeshift tables in the barn out back. I'd been living with Amanda 'til classes started. Now, she was seven months pregnant and looking for an apartment with her sometimes-coked-up newly minted husband, Chuck, in Kansas. I had the keys to my dorm but hadn't unpacked the Official New School Stuff yet. Instead, I was camping out in Amanda's empty apartment, so bored I challenged myself nightly to see how many times I could get myself off.

Kayte, she was the most beautiful girl I'd ever seen in real life. We worked together at The Limited. I'd been there three years, hidden in the back because I was fast to fold but couldn't talk right to people. Kayte was out front, making goal every month. She was at least six feet tall with gold skin and honey-green eyes. She was white-ish, or something, and kept her perfect-ringlet, dark auburn curls clipped just one inch long. She smoked with a vengeance and mainlined coffee, but somehow her flawless teeth stayed porcelain white and she always smelled like the sweet kind of sex. And she was loud. God, she was loud, as if her beauty weren't enough to make you fall at your knees.

I think she felt sorry for me. Or maybe she really did like me a little, who knows. But when I asked her at work to take me out for my twentieth birthday, that I had no one else (she'd seen the ugly Ben breakup), the kindness in her ponied up. "You want to drink?" she asked.

"I don't know. I've never really drank."

"Seriously?" she asked. Who would lie about that? "Okay. I know somewhere that doesn't card."

I didn't know what Lowbrow meant, but that's the name of the bar where she took me. Her and her "best friend" Max, who was so obviously in love with her it made me sad. Sadder after the first cocktail. I didn't know what to order, so they did it for me. Sex on the Beach tasted like juice gone bad, but by the third one, it was just pure sweetness. By the fifth, it had snuck a cigarette between my fingers. I was suddenly and somehow in a car, and I could hear Kayte laughing somewhere far away. I tried to keep the cigarette from resting on the car's carpet, I really did, but it was just so heavy.

Kayte bottle-fed me like a child, leaning the front seat all the way back so my head was in her lap as she curled up in the backseat like a purring cat. The little bottle of whiskey in her purse that she rested against my lips didn't taste like I thought it would. It tasted like water. Just water.

I'm assuming they dropped me off. I don't really know. I have flashes of stubbing out the cigarette in the car carpet. I hope I did a good job, but either way, she never said anything about it and acted normal at work two days later. I woke up in the dorm room spooning the green comforter that was still wrapped in its square, plastic container.

In the morning, my brain had swollen so big it didn't

fit in my skull anymore. I knew about hangovers, but this couldn't possibly be a hangover. This was death, circling like a vulture. Not knowing what else to do, I called Ben's mom. She'd technically, kind of, become my legal guardian a little bit. Just to help with insurance.

"I think I drank too much," I told her.

"Drink a lot of water and go find some bread." The walk to the Safeway four blocks away was a stabbing reminder of the pain at first, and then it became soothing. The bread, it soaked up the alcohol like it was soup. Like my stomach was a ceramic bowl. That. That had prepared me for a sorority. Hadn't it? Hadn't I condensed four years of what should have been high school experimenting into one blackout shitstorm of a night?

The fourth day of classes, I shuffled down the hall to the coed shared bathroom in my new shower slippers that pinched my feet. It looked like it was designed for senior citizens with sprawling beige plastic seats and handlebars in each shower. How did people do this? Keep two towels dry, their little bottles of shampoo, conditioner, face wash, and shaving cream always full? My towels were instantly soaked, and my underwear felt on display dangling like a flag over the shower rod. From the sinks, I could hear boys grunting at each other in post-adolescence depths.

Get in, get out. I'd never taken long showers. Actually, I hadn't taken a shower at all until Ben, unless you count the ones at the public pool. I preferred baths, the ones where my mom would dribble blue food coloring into the water to hide the rust color from the old well. And cheap, slimy bubbles from liquid dish soap. What was relaxing about standing while you washed your hair?

Luckily, I had a plan. I'd left my room carefully unlocked, the door just barely balancing against the frame. When the deep voices left and only the hiss of one other shower filled the room, I pulled my dirty clothes back on, sans underwear, and raced to my room. The one five doors down with the door wide open. Fuck. My wallet.

I'd left it stupidly on my desk, and it was gone. Along with the fake ID Amanda gave me when she turned twenty-one. We looked nothing alike, but she swore it would work—she told the DMV she lost hers and voila! Two IDs. My credit cards. Well, those were maxed out anyway. The debit card to my student loans. Oh, my god. My student loans.

"Excuse me?" The boy at my door looked fresh out of an ad for joining the military. Big opal eyes, skin clearly bronzed from real sun, and perpetually hard nipples pressing through the tight, thin cotton. "Is this yours?" he asked, holding up my wallet.

"Yeah. Yes! Thank you."

"I found it in the bushes outside." In that moment, I didn't find that explanation strange.

It was empty, except for my Blockbuster card and tanning membership. In the mirror above my useless sink, my reflection showed me what he'd seen. A girl going soft, hair wrapped tight in a towel so she looked like a raggedy unicorn. And no bra, the wetness from the shower making a deranged clown face across her middle.

"THIS IS AN UNTRADITIONAL campus, and we're untraditional sororities," said the super traditional, slip of a thing with virgin hair that couldn't possibly have a single split end. Her eyes shone and she scanned everyone's faces. On one side of me, a petite girl with a face generously kissed with freckles kept playing with her knotty hair. On the other side, a blonde with a fishlike face and pantyhose. Did college students wear pantyhose? "In fact, we're all about diversity," continued the Panhellenic President of the year. I'd come to learn Panhellenic was some kind of overarching organization for a lot of Greek sororities and fraternities. It forced sororities to recruit kind of together on campus, trying to even things up. "African American, Hispanic, Asian. Even Native American," the Panhellenic President said.

"What a crock," said the brunette next to me. And I smiled, not because I necessarily agreed, but what else was I supposed to do. Was she Native? "I'm Zadie," she whispered, tugging at the name tag she'd picked and curled into flaky bits on her thigh.

"Julia," I said. The Panhellenic President turned in our general direction, a disappointed frown on her face. You don't talk when they do.

"Anyway," Panhellenic President said, "the first event is

tomorrow at five sharp. We'll meet right outside, in the lobby of the student union. You'll be split into groups and be escorted by a Panhellenic Representative from one party to the next. At the end, you'll complete comment cards and begin deciding which house is the best match for you! It's all part of the 'pref' process. Any questions?"

A girl with an obvious makeup foundation line across her jaw raised her hand. "So, like how do you decide who gets in where? Does everyone get in?"

"It's a secret process that ensures fairness," said Panhellenic President. "There aren't really any *guarantees* that everybody will get in, but we do our best to match every house with the best new recruits for them."

Everyone tried to look like a lady as we filed out, shoulders back and Dooney & Bourke purses in place. "That was ridiculous," said Zadie.

"You not coming back then?" I asked her. She shrugged.

"It looks good on scholarship applications," she said. "I mean, I'm a transfer student, so I'm starting my sophomore year now. I was already at OSU for a year, but that . . . that was a nightmare."

Did she want me to ask her why? I didn't know, and too soon my window had passed. So I just nodded.

"I'm in the outdoor club. I lead kayaking groups in the summer," she said. "But scholarship committees want diversity, you know? Which, *clearly*, sororities have plenty of. Plus I don't know anyone here."

"Me either," I said. "So . . . which sorority do you think you'll pref?"

"Probably the least crazy one. What, Phi Zeta Zeta? The one that doesn't have the Stepfordian Panhellenic President in it, that's for sure." Who the Panhellenic members belonged to was top secret until Bid Day, the day everyone found out which house—if any—they got into. But it was obvious who went where. The pretty girls, the put-together ones, the ones who looked like fresh-scrubbed alphas with otherworldly manicures, they were clearly Alpha Pi Omega.

APOs. The others? PZZs were the outliers. I wanted to be an APO so bad. Then, with that accolade, I would surely be ushered into the world of Normal. Mixers, Catholic School-girl parties, and all the Greek-letter-emblazoned swag my student loans would let me buy. I could tell now, Hapa was an APO. They may as well have rolled out the welcome mat for me already because she, she *adored* me. She was my in.

But I needed to stack the odds. Instead of tanning just twice per week, I committed to every single day. I knew I could do it and get brown fast. That beautiful kind of brown where people stopped me on the street and asked, "What are you?" The Indian crept into the tanning beds with me, curled up against me like a sorry lover. It made my skin flawless. Made me look thinner. Exotic.

I'd been doing it since I was eleven and my mom guilted my dad into buying a home tanning machine. We could only afford the kind with one panel, so you had to tan thirty minutes on your stomach, then flip over onto your back. My mom set it up in their bedroom with a big fan on both ends and the television on the floor so daytime talk shows kept you company.

"Can I tan too?" I asked her after she'd tried it out the first day. Her eyes ricocheted all over me, her thoughts leaking into my head. *She should have been darker. Where's the Indian baby I was supposed to have? There's not a whisper of Chero-kee in her.*

"Okay," she said. "But just ten minutes this first time." Ten minutes did nothing. After thirty minutes, I emerged rosy cheeked and smelling like the good kind of burning flesh.

"Can I do it again tomorrow?" I asked.

"Just don't wear it out," my mom said. "There's some sun accelerators in the front room if you want. But use it sparingly. It's expensive." I was the only girl in sixth grade who looked like I arrived daily from Hawaii. At fourteen, my mom decided the at-home bed wasn't strong or fast enough, and sprung for a tanning membership at a place that was walking distance to my high school. Within one month, it was a shared membership and that was my new after-school activity, trekking to the tanning salon in platform Mary Janes and thigh-highs to bake beautiful into my too-pale skin. When someone asked what my secret was, I was proud to say a tanning bed. That's what rich people do.

So, yeah. Spending even an hour a day in a tanning bed leading up to recruitment would seal the deal. They wanted perfect skin, golden limbs, and a girl who could afford an unlimited pass at a downtown (downtown!) tanning salon? That was me. The student loans would pick up the tab.

Sorority recruitment parties aren't like in the movies, and not a single person said anything about my perfect complexion. First of all, only APO had a house near campus. To keep things fair, the "parties" were both held in conference rooms in one of the campus's most dilapidated of buildings. I also heard both houses got the same, paltry budget. Waiting in the lounge, I got put in the same group as Zadie. She'd dressed up for the event, or her version of it. No rips in her jeans, her ropy mess of hair in a low ponytail, and what had to be her crispest North Face jacket. Me? I was there to impress. An A-line flowered skirt, skintight cashmere sweater, and knee-high leather boots. "What do you think these parties will be like?" I asked her. The blonde fishface butted in. "My cousin? She's a Delta Delta at some place in Alabama. Or maybe Tennessee, I don't know. She says they're crazy."

"Okay," said Zadie.

"I'm Stephanie," said Fishface, holding out her baby-small limp hand. "I work at Nordstrom. The *downtown one*," she clarified, lest we think she trudged all the way out to Washington Square in the suburbs.

"Well," said Zadie, "I just hope they end on time."

"Ladies," said the Panhellenic President, signaling our group to go into the APO party. "You have forty minutes. Enjoy."

As we filed into the fluorescent-lit conference room, the cheering was already spilling into the lounge. Part cheerleading, part campfire songs, and 100 percent laughable, the APOs were lined up in matching brown vests and cowboy hats. Streamers hung from the ceilings and quiet country music played in the background. Themed parties were a chance to show off their personality, party skills, and creativity. That's what they said. They'd done a lot with a little budget and not much of a room. All of their makeup was flawless, their cute little pigtails way too darling. The refreshment table was lined with petite chili cups—they even made a western mess of a dish look dainty. Chips and salsa, "cowboy crunch" popcorn, and soda in little glass boots awaited us while they finished their sing-song chant. "Woo!" they all screamed as their stomping came to an end, and immediately they were on us.

I saw Hapa head straight for a girl with waist-length black hair, while a redhead with muscular arms came my way. She had brown eyes, not blue, and brown was the only way a ginger could be beautiful. "Julia," she said, reading my nametag. "I'm Heather." Even in the moment, I didn't know what we talked about. Classes, majors, hobbies. Somewhere in the murkiness, I know I mentioned I worked at a salon. "Oh, you work?" she asked. "I . . . sometimes work. In the summer." She was younger than me, I could tell.

Seamlessly, nearly without my noticing, Heather slipped away to be replaced with a new APO. This one had a brown bob forced into the cutest little pigtails I'd ever seen. Her teeth were everything I ever wanted, complete with the tiniest of gaps in the middle. I felt like I was speed dating, and this one was particularly hot. I didn't have what it took to win her over. None of them wore watches, but I didn't know until much later that they weren't allowed. It might make recruits think the sisters were bored if they looked at their wrists. How they knew when to switch, I didn't know.

The time moved way too fast, but I didn't make any huge blunders. I don't think. It was awkward to eat or drink anything. What if a kernel get stuck in my throat or the soda fizz got into my nose? But those things kept my hands busy, so I used them as comforters instead, like a child and their beat-up stuffed animal.

"Ladies!" said Panhellenic, suddenly emerging in the doorway. We were never girls. We were women. Or, technically, "ladies." She clapped her hands lightly. "It's time for the next party! You'll have five minutes in the lounge so the houses can regroup, then I'll take you to Phi Zeta Zeta.

The lounge exploded with comparisons, all riding high on adrenaline rushes. Compacts were pulled out of bras, lipsticks refreshed and the reviews started to pour in.

"Oh my god, their decorations were *so cute*. Weren't they so cute?"

"They all looked so good! I couldn't pull of that vest. I don't know what I'll do if I get in and have to wear one!"

"Oh, I'm sure they liked you. You're *so nice*, how could they not?"

The only familiar, nongushing face I saw was Zadie's, who was perched in an oversized vinyl chair staring out the window.

"You survived the first flogging," I told her.

"I once took a bunch of mushrooms at a friend's place, then we hid in her barn. I saw spiders everywhere. So this was nothing," she said. I'd never tried mushrooms. Or anything else.

"It's time!" Panhellenic announced. I stood behind Zadie in line. Why even bother going to this next party? I was an APO all the way, I totally knew it.

As we dutifully piled into the room, they were already singing. They had matching outfits too—theirs was a pirate theme, but it looked like everyone put together their own costumes. The eye patches and hats weren't all the same. "Pirate's booty" popcorn, "ale," and "scurvy-fighting fruit salads" were on the table. But something just seemed off. They weren't as lively as the APOs, as into it, or nearly as pretty. Did I really have to spend forty minutes in here?

I went on autopilot as the first PZZ approached me. Her laugh was too forced and her eyes kept darting around. There was a single, long black hair at the bottom of her chin that I couldn't stop staring at, and we had the exact same conversation I'd just had with twenty other girls. Sorry, *ladies.*

We swallowed up Panhellenic's farewell speech, got the schedule for tomorrow, and were prepped for "Pref Night," where we were supposed to wear all white and it would be a more solemn affair. Apparently that's where we'd learn a few public facts about each house and get serenaded with a ballad. Whatever. After that, Sunday, was Bid Day. That's when the next four years of my new life would start to unfold.

Or unravel. Pref Night was a little cultish, a little freakish, and members of both houses were tripping over their own tears as they shared stories of sisterhood none of us could relate to. A few of those dressed in white teared up too. I never understood empathy.

I was as polite as I could be to PZZ, but really I didn't want to waste anyone's time. "You looked bored," Zadie said after Pref Night, as we both hid our yawns behind hands that had been gripping sparkling cider all night.

"I was."

Saturday night, post-recruitment, and I was on lockdown. We all were. Panhellenic couldn't technically tell recruits to stay in, but they made their own and let it be known. If they saw you at a party, passed you on campus, or even sat next to you in class, sorority members couldn't speak to you. Otherwise, it might look like they were showing a preference or had the opportunity to get to know you better than others. Really, it meant that if you partied together, a shared love of bad decisions might be the foundation for the newest class.

It was already two weeks into classes, and I hadn't studied once. I skimmed the chapters in the books, wishing I could absorb the information in some easier way. As soon as I applied to college, I declared myself an English major. But wait, should I? Just because I liked reading and writing? Criminal justice, that seemed pretty badass. And I always thought I'd work really well around dead people. The crime scenes and bodies wouldn't creep me out thanks to a lifetime of horror movie conditioning, and I wouldn't have to deal with nearly as many talkative people. So criminal justice it was, decided in the middle of freshman year after wasting too many credits.

I already knew I was failing. What the professor said in the intro course made sense, but then she'd pose questions that had nothing to do with what I swore she just said. It might as well have been, "Fact: Melanoma is the deadliest and most common type of cancer. Now tell me the best way to make beef wellington." I couldn't follow. I just couldn't.

Plus, I knew it was still early in the quarter, so she was being kind. But a C on my first paper? I could bullshit better than a C in any class. And that requisite pre-algebra class was getting to me. I was bad at math. Not "Oh, my! Math sure can be cantankerous" bad, but dumbshit hillbilly bad. It terrified me. I could get one equation at a time, and by themselves they made sense sometimes. But when it came to tests, where I had to know which equation to use where, my brain fell apart. I needed at least a D minus to stay in school. And it wasn't even college-level math.

So I committed to a Saturday night spent studying. Except I couldn't. I mean, I read the chapter for Criminal Justice I was supposed to, I'd already blasted out the one-page essay for Intro to Writing all new students were required to take, and I'd already cheated on my math homework by looking at the answers in the back before I really let my own marinate. I couldn't exactly undo that. So I called Ben.

"Hey," I said. "What are you doing?"

"Nothing. Lisa's closing tonight."

"Wanna go to Shari's for pie?"

"Okay."

It was stupid, and I didn't want him back, but Ben was a shot of familiar after I'd been in the wild for too long. Plus, all he talked about was Her, so how bad could it be?

"She's perfect," he said, scooping peaks of meringue into his pinched, cherub-like mouth. "Well, not perfect, you know. But close. I mean, she's *really* beautiful."

"She should be. She's sixteen."

He shrugged. "She doesn't act like it." Why did I ask to see him again? "Anyway," he said, pushing his plate away and grabbing mine. "She wants, like, one of those pea coats for her birthday. Want to help me shop for it? I'm going to Washington Square next weekend. You can try them on and I'll just buy a size or two smaller." Fucker.

"Oh. Yeah. Sure."

Great things are supposed to happen on Sundays. Rest, or I think god talks to you if you've bought into that. Maybe all the shame from the past night gets washed off you if you shower at just the right time. I never did (buy into it or shower right), but I remembered Sunday mornings at Sunday school when my mom figured it was better safe than sorry. I liked making the paper lambs with their little cotton ball bodies. When you threw them away in the bathroom bin, it was like you'd sent them home.

"Under your assigned seat," said Panhellenic slowly, after we'd all found the chairs with our names on them. "You may find an invitation card. Please, check now."

Blindly reaching under my chair, I felt the card. It was creamy and thick, a good sign of a rich house. Tearing into it, I let the gasps and happy noises, sad noises and gulps fall around me. *We're pleased to invite you to join your new sisters of Phi Zeta Zeta!*

What the fuck? No. This was wrong. Wrong, wrong, wrong.

In the row ahead of me, a big girl with arm flab so massive she could take flight began choke-sobbing and ran out of the room. There was no envelope in her hand. Up front,

Panhellenic shook her head sadly, disappointed at such a poor emotional display. "Now, it's time to guess which house we all belong to before you go meet your new sisters!" she exclaimed, pasting that smile back onto her lips.

From the other side of the room, Zadie's eyes found mine. She raised her brows, putting one hand over her eye like a pirate. "Ahoy, matey?" she mouthed. I nodded in defeat. At the least, at the very least, I would have her.

3

"ARE YOU GOING to that thing?" Zadie asked, her hip bones digging into my thighs as she sprawled across my lap in Stephanie's backseat.

"What thing?"

"You know, that white party thing. Next Friday."

"You mean the black sorority party?"

"I don't think you're supposed to call them 'the black sorority.'"

"Well, sorry, I forgot what their letters are. What are they?"

"How am I supposed to know!" she said.

"I think it's Omega. Omega something. Right?" asked Stephanie, squinting at the MapQuest directions we'd printed out in the university library, hidden between the sheets of a random science book so it would look like we were using official school library supplies for school classes. Nobody answered Stephanie.

"I don't know," I told Zadie. "It's like a couple thing, and I'm not a couple."

"Well, neither am I. Anymore. Thank god—or not, since I'm going to hell and all."

It had been a month since Bid Day which, I have to admit, ended up with a softer blow than I'd first thought. Like an open-palmed smack instead of a fist. After getting our requisite matching shirts, inexplicably navy blue with a white moose and Phi Zeta Zeta on the front (I hated that the "zeta" just looked like a regular "Z" and not a weird Greek letter—how would anyone tell I was in a sorority?), we were herded to an "alum's" house in West Linn to get handed roses, play stupid games that seemed a little less dumb without the pressure to impress, and sing songs. The best part was learning all the dirty songs. "We are the Freshmen," "I'm a Little Tea Pot," and a nasty Gilligan's Island twist. And we were all gifted a "big sister." But not really because there were none, so we got volunteer big sisters from another campus instead.

Okay, here's the deal with this particular PZZ chapter. This year was their last chance. Nobody was *supposed* to talk about this, so everyone did. Apparently two years ago, some of the sisters got stupid drunk at Meet the Fleet and made a sex tape with a bunch of sailors. In their PZZ letters. I don't know how many "a bunch" is, but it sounded like a lot. And it was a huge scandal. National wanted to pull their charter, which is Greek speak for "the national, overarching PZZ organization wanted to end the chapter on this campus for good." Then a sole surviving member, Amber, volunteered to organize recruitment with a bunch of borrowed sisters from a different campus a few hours away, and now here we all are. Funny. None of this was mentioned during rush. (Sorry, recruitment—it turned out "rush" had bad connotations these days. Like circling the fat and making girls watch porn, naked while straddling basketballs to shame the one who soaks the ball first. That kind of stuff.)

Maybe if the whole sailor gang bang thing was brought up in between Pirate's Booty, I might have been a little more impressed with them.

The other thing that had happened in the past month? Zadie and I wiggled closer. Maybe some of her magnetism would rub off on me, right? It was a stupid word for her kind of beauty, "magnetism," but that's exactly what it was.

She wore not a whit of makeup, barely brushed her hair, and her durable shoes and out-of-date jeans were for comfort. Nothing more. And she didn't need any more anyway. Men were drawn to her, tails wagging and chins on floors. She was totally oblivious. But she was also still seething over Dave.

"Dave is very, very sad about that, you know," I told her.

"Yeah," she said. "Maybe he'll toss me down a ladder from his high-horse perch in heaven."

Dave was Zadie's first college boyfriend. They fell into each other at the Big School four hours away, and dropped out together too. Dave was a Bible-thumper, Zadie an agnostic in deep foreplay with atheism. But she grew up in a small town and had dealt with so-called Christians before. Then Dave got down with god real deep.

Zadie and Dave lived together in a little basement studio in Southeast Portland. Or they used to. Zadie worked at a doggy daycare as she waited for classes at her new school to start, our school, and Dave had transferred to a local Christian college. As it happens, living in sin is okay. But only if you've both been saved. The sex had already dried up, but Zadie was comfortable enough. Then one day, amidst bickering over whose shit was splattering all the way up to the toilet seat cover, Dave said, "You know, it just makes me sad. Very sad. I'm disappointed that we won't be in heaven together."

"And why's that?" Zadie had asked.

"Because you'll be going to hell." That was it for Zadie. She stuffed her good long johns into her CamelBak and hiked right up out of that little den they'd created.

I didn't tell her much about Ben. It was weird to announce something like "I was *abused*," because that ushered in questions. Looking at the vomit I'd spewn up for the past four years with him in fresh daylight was embarrassing. So I just said, "My ex was an asshole." After all, it was true. So, really, Zadie and I were in the same, so far booze-laden, rocky but fun "we're about to go overboard" boat. Both single and totally okay with it. Which is why we were quick to let Stephanie, another "new sister," drive us to the Chi Alpha fraternity party in her dead grandmother's chortling maroon Buick.

"Maybe you can find a date tonight," I teased her, her hip bones pressing bad into my pelvis.

"Right. Fraternity guys are totally my type."

"I know, I know. I'd never date one either. Then you'd have to see them all the time."

"Some are hot!" said Stephanie, oblivious that she wasn't in the conversation.

The "fraternity house" was actually an old, rambling Portland bungalow that was owned by one of the guys' uncles. He kept it as an investment property, but finally let Steven (current CA president) rent it out. Immediately, it had been kitted out with a pole in the basement, a decrepit ping pong table for flip cup, and an ancient green couch with cushions that were sagging like sad, little deflated breasts.

"Hey! You made it!" Steven said. He looked like he should be grown, but the acne wouldn't let him. At nearly six feet five and thin, he had no choice but to hover. And his voice, laughably deep, didn't match the rest of him. "Keg's in the kitchen. Hard A downstairs."

Zadie and I darted into the kitchen with its unforgiving fluorescence to linger over the warm keg and see if we knew anyone.

"You guys. You guys." Melanie was perpetually stoned, ticking "stoner new sister" off the PZZ dream list. Already, her eyes were swimming in red and she had that sleepy smile that washed over her when she was feeling alright. "Where've you been? I almost left," she said, rubbing her hand along the knotty frame of the kitchen door.

"We've been here for an hour," I told her, Zadie shooting me a look.

"Oh. Oh, I didn't see you," Melanie said. "I'm losing my

buzz. You wanna smoke?"

"Sure."

I'd never smoked pot in my life. I wasn't against it; it had just never come up. Besides, Stephanie was driving and the little clusters of people looked vaguely familiar. "You gotta . . . you gotta hold it in, like. You know? Hold it in your lungs as long as you can," Melanie said.

God. This was a lot easier than cigarettes. Smoother. The gray smoke snaked down my throat and coiled, warm and safe into my middle. "Dang, girl. That's good!" Melanie said. I imagined in the '60s she would delight in taking people on their first acid trips.

I took two hits. Maybe ten. The joint got sticky in my fingers, and when I turned my head, my eyes didn't follow fast enough. And I was *thirsty*. God, I needed a drink, *any* drink. People were moving too slow, and so was I. Why was I so painfully aware of every little detail?

Making my way down the stairs, Flipper was mid-game and already the oversized pitcher was half full with discarded PBR. "Yo!" said some guy who had a touch too much caveman to him. "We need another. You in?" Why the hell not.

I'd never played before, but I was good at it. Like, really good. The trick is to wet your flipping area with beer before each round commences. That way the cup rim sticks to it when you flip it. So you can suck at flipping and still win. Even so, the rest of my team was terrible, and I helped chug a disgusting concoction of cheap beer and spit as everyone snapped photos with plastic disposable cameras.

I was stoned. And drunk. But there were suddenly bags of Taco Bell upstairs (I don't know how I found out). It tasted like Dave had carved off a little piece of heaven and dropped the shavings right into a crunchy taco shell.

"So. I have some friends. Some guy friends," said Melanie the next day at "our" big round booth in the student dining lounge. Whether you got there at eight in the morning or two in the afternoon, at least one PZZ was there. "You know. If you guys want dates for the white party."

"Ugh," said Zadie. "I really don't, but we can't be the only ones solo. What are they like?"

"They're nice!" Melanie said. "Seriously. One, Matt, I went to high school with. The other one. Preston, I think? I don't know, but he's Matt's friend and should be cool."

"What do you think?" Zadie asked me.

"I guess. I mean, it would be nice to dress up and every-thing." *Please let's go dress shopping. Please, let's go dress shopping. I'd never been to prom.*

"Awesome!" Mel said. "I'll set it up."

We got ready at Aliya's place, a big black girl who slid into Bid Day because she was 1) big, 2) black, and 3) had a two-year-old daughter her mom cooed over like it was her own. She was diversity gold too. I should have liked her more. But she had a mean laugh and looked at me like she knew more than I'd told her. She lived with her mom in a manufactured home that smelled like chemical flowers, and the nine of us ordered pizza before the boys arrived.

The boys. Zadie was getting Matt, I was getting Preston, and neither of us had even seen a photo. The white party was actually a white, black, and silver party, so you got to wear any dress with one or all of those colors. I'd found a black slip of a dress with a white cowl-like contraption flow-ing down the back. I'd never gone to a real high school dance, but I imagined the same energy of that teenage mile-stone was buzzing tonight.

"They're here!" Melanie called. She glommed onto her own stoner of a boyfriend before ushering two polar oppo-sites toward Zadie and me. It was like the *Weird Science* movie, and I got the tall, lanky unattractive blond one.

"This is Matt," Mel said to Zadie, pushing the just-a-little-Latino-looking one at her. Zadie gave him her fake smile. I knew it by now.

"And this is Preston," she said, smiling encouragingly at me.

"Hi," he said. "So . . . I know what you're thinking."

"What's that?"

"I look familiar, but you can't place where." That wasn't what I was thinking, but now that he mentioned it, he was right. He did look familiar. He held up his hands, "I'll make it easy for you," he said. "It's Andy Dick."

Yes. Yes, it was.

Zadie and I lasted at the white party for an hour, making awkward conversation with guys we didn't know around a table that was too big. "One of my old high school friends is having a party up by Twenty-Third," she offered suddenly. They were? "You guys wanna go?"

That party didn't even last thirty minutes after we got there. Cops were called, cops pounded on the door, cops outwaited us while about forty underage drinkers clung to each other in the basement, shushing each other while the early drunks let the walls hold them up. I heard some people got MIPs, and maybe they did. But by the time the herd of us trotted out of the basement, the cops just wanted to go home. Or back to patrolling. Whatever they were doing, so they waved us on.

"I'm going home," Zadie announced as her one pair of heels sunk into the grass outside. When she was done, she was done.

"Okay," I said. "See you Monday," and she wandered off toward her car, Matt trailing unsure behind her.

"It's just midnight," Preston said. "You want to go anywhere else? Or home?"

"Midnight?" I asked. It was. It was midnight on a Friday night, and I was in a beautiful dress with some boy whose last name I didn't know. He was ugly, but sweet. Like a bulldog. "I've never been to Canada. You wanna drive to Canada?"

"Now? Tonight?" he asked. He didn't look at me like I was crazy. Why wasn't he giving me the crazy look? "I . . . guess?"

"I'll drive," I said. I had a Hyundai Elantra whose steering wheel—the actual steering wheel!—had fallen off into my lap between Ben and school. My dad, who had reappeared with a new wife, new life near Salem, shoved it back together.

"Okay. Uh . . . can we just stop by my mom's first? It's in Southeast. I just need to get some stuff." God, okay, fine. Whatever.

We snuck into his mom's old Victorian like we weren't supposed to be there. How did I even know this was her house? What if it was some random house? Preston took a bigger wallet than what he had and a VCR. "Why are you taking a VCR?" I whispered as a wiry cat hugged against my shins.

"I don't know. Maybe we'll get bored?"

Here's the thing about Oregonians. We don't pump gas, we don't like to pump gas, and we forget we have to past the state border. Preston and I sat in my little blue Hyundai for ten minutes in the middle of rural Washington State at two in the morning before figuring out nobody was coming. I let him pump. It was cold out there. I should have brought something besides a formal dress.

The first few hours, winding through the dark, were laced with magic. We were doing something stupidly dangerous. *I* was doing something stupidly dangerous, forget this blond stick figure beside me. When the pink began to creep up over the evergreens, I was over it. What the hell was I thinking?

"Hey," Preston said, suddenly awake, "just twenty more miles to the Canadian border!"

Hell, we were almost there. Might as well.

Getting into Canada is easy. It's getting out that's a bitch. We spent just one day in Vancouver, BC, and I paid for the room at the Howard Johnson. Would he expect sex? Did I have to since I paid for the room and half the gas?

Yes, but thankfully it was over quickly and I felt sorry for him anyway. I hadn't been with anyone since Ben, so it's not like I had a very high bar. Afterward, we walked to the video rental store down the block and got an '80s action movies to feed to the VCR. We shouldn't have bothered taking his mom's—the hotel already had one hooked up to the TV.

"I brought some weed," Preston said, digging a little bag out of his pants. "You wanna smoke?" If it would take me somewhere else, yes. I'd smoke all day. Instead, it just made the time with him stretch longer and me hyperaware of his bulbous eyes. His clammy skin on mine. But I had to hold his hand and pretend he didn't disgust me because I'd dragged him all the way up here.

At the border line again the next morning, we were stopped. There was a german shepherd on a short leash three cars back. "Where's the bag?" I whispered to Preston.

"What bag?"

"The *pot!*"

"Uh . . . the glove box?"

"Fuck! Hide it."

"Where?"

"Figure it the fuck out," I smiled to him as a Mountie lumbered up. From the corner of my eye, I watched Preston cram it into the crevice where the windshield met the doorframe.

"Passports?" the agent asked.

"Passports? I don't have a passport . . ." I said as Preston pulled his out of the oversized wallet.

"You need a passport to go to the US."

"We didn't need one to get in!" I said. *Stop yelling at the cop*

He raised his brows, making them wiggle like a cartoon. "Don't need one to get in."

"I . . . I have my driver's license. Is that okay?"

"That's only valid in the US," he said.

"But the US is right there," I said, pointing to the land of freedom as the dog inched closer.

He sighed, the eye roll palpable. "You know what? I actually don't have time for this. Just go. Just go, and don't come back to Canada without a passport."

"Thank you, officer," I said, willing sweetness to spill from my words as I drove away. "Oh my god, oh my god, oh my god, can you believe that?" I asked Preston, who kept reaching like a protective mom toward the crammed-in baggie.

"That's insane," he said. "Why didn't you bring your passport?"

Preston called me for two weeks straight after I dropped him back off at what was, apparently, really his mom's house. When had I given him my number? He and Zadie were the only ones who shook my cheap Target landline phone designed to look like an old-fashioned one. I started screening and skipping voicemails when I heard his familiar lilt. Especially after that last message.

"Hey . . ." he began. "It's Preston. I'm just, uh. Wondering? If, uh, when I could get my mom's VCR back? She's kind of really upset about it." No. I was keeping the VCR. I didn't even want it, but I wanted to see him again even less. There was a Blockbuster having constant sales just three blocks away, so I began buying and hoarding anything remotely interesting.

"You stole his VCR?" Zadie asked at the PZZ booth on Monday. Mel just shrieked with laughter.

"His *mom's* VCR, okay? She has like this enormous house. I'm sure she can afford it!"

"So, it's like your payment for sleeping with him? I can't believe you did that by the way."

"You slept with Matt!" I said.

"Yeah," she said. "But I was *drunk*."

"Vancouver? That's not that far. My uncle lives in Vancouver," said Stephanie. Nobody told her we were talking about Canada, not Washington.

SHIT. NONE OF my size eight jeans fit anymore. Halloween was creeping up, and we were all in a mad rush to look equal parts whore and creative. A Creative Whore. Maybe I was getting fat. No. No, I had been a size eight ever since I could remember, sprouting to my full five-foot, six-and-a-half height at eleven years old, C-cup breasts, exploding hips and all. It was the goddamned oven of a dryer in the shared laundry basement. I mean, I hadn't changed what I ate, and in an effort to look the ever-ready manly drinker, I only had beer during drinking games and otherwise went with whiskey and diet coke. Diet coke I could manage when it was, for once, the most appetizing flavor in the cup.

"Who are you going to be?" asked Stephanie as she scaffolded on the MAC pigments, one by one, to her face with no angles.

"I don't know. Lara Croft?" She was hot. Guys thought so, anyway. And it seemed like an easy costume, not that I'd ever seen the game or movie.

"The Tomb Raider girl? She's so sexy," said Stephanie. "I think I'm just going to wear one of my corsets and leather pants. Get angel wings or something." One of. This was the girl who owned numerous corsets and pairs of leather pants just because she could. She was the quintessential butter-face, the perfect body but a face that held no punches when telling you the insides were empty.

"Yeah. Where are we meeting?"

"I dunno. I think, like, Donna's dorm in Ophelia?" Ophelia. The university named the one "official" dorm room after a random Shakespeare character. Now Ophelia, *she* was a whore. Full of naked, stinking bodies and their fluids. But Donna? Donna was clean. A virgin. Seventeen years old and already in college. She'd moved here from Russia at thirteen only to lose her accent and adopt a voice like a six-year-old that put all the guys on edge. She sounded like a child, legally still was one, and dangled that over-ripened cherry over all of them like a conductor's wand.

Donna hated me. I don't know why, but most girls do. Maybe it's because I'm so quiet, or they can feel me watching them to understand who they are, like hunters stalk their prey. I want to tell them, "Shh, it's okay. It's okay. I just want to know you, not bury a bullet in your skull." But I couldn't—that would be weird. At least Donna didn't hate me outright. But the recesses of her pupils let me know.

"You know what Donna's gonna be?" I asked Stephanie.

"I think, like, a rave zombie she said?"

I didn't actually care.

Halloween night on an oversized urban campus is wide-legged begging with potential. By the time we clunked up to Donna's in the too-high heels we'd ditch before midnight, already four students had had their stomachs pumped. The ambulance might as well just idle outside. Donna's face was expertly whitewashed, kohl smeared beneath her eyes and her waist-length hair in a tight ponytail. Like Stephanie and all the other naturally skinny girls, her soft belly was distended with the night's alcohol. They didn't look fat like that—they looked feminine.

Me, I'd gotten a fake ponytail from the salon where I'd just started working, braiding it clumsily to try and look like Lara Croft. Okay, I stole it. Well, kind of. After half-heartedly going to beauty school before Ben went real bad, I was non–board certified by the state cosmetology board and knew enough about the industry to slip into a retail position. I told women with too much time which shampoos to buy based on which ones we got bonuses for during that month. I acted like I cared about OPI's latest cutesy names. And I found out about the rules. If anything's returned, even if it's sealed, it can't be resold. It gets dumped, or employees can take it.

That was pretty awesome. And when I realized that it wasn't very hard to throw an item into the "returned" box for a few days to make it seem legit, that they'd never bother to actually cross-check the return log to see if a return was real, I couldn't help it. Slowly, I started collecting things. First, things I really wanted, then things I couldn't even use. I had over 100 nail polishes, three huge boxes of shampoos, some for black hair, and now I was working on nail accessories. I even had a stylist-grade pair of shears (not scissors), because why not?

"You guys look *so* good," cooed Donna. *You're fat*, her eyes told me. Nobody else heard. Really? I hadn't been called fat since ninth grade, when some little bitch of a sixth grader asked me, "Why do you wear those shirts that let your stomach hang out like that?" After that, I tucked in all my shirts.

"Oh my god, *you* look *so good*," said Stephanie.

Donna gave her tinkle laugh. "I like doing theater makeup. Anyway, I was thinking the plan should be go to that Delta Tau's apartment. Ken, was it? It's just a couple of blocks away, and he told me he has access to the rooftop." By now, seven of us were huddled in Donna's cramped room that smelled like lavender. Her roommate was out of town, so we took over both beds, smearing makeup and shoe dirt onto the pillows.

"Ken's super hot. Like, really hot," Stephanie said. That was the (first) night she fucked him, and how she got the nickname Springs. *Creak, creak*, goes the springy mattress.

My alcohol tolerance had built up fast, and not even a quart of one-fifth of straight Malibu rum did much. There were some nights, I'd learned, I just couldn't get drunk no matter how much I tried. How much I drank. I might as well give up, but then I'd have nothing to wrap my fingers around.

All of these new boys, I barely recognized anyone. There was the glorious, beautiful, should really be gay Juan. It's like he didn't even know what he looked like. "Hey, hey," he said as he pulled my arm in Ophelia's expansive lobby. "You look amazing! You know my name?"

"Yes." Everyone knew Juan's name.

"What is it? What's my name?" he asked, his too-white teeth shining.

Fuck. I hated saying people's names. Always had. It felt too intimate, and it made them real. "Juan," I said.

He bounced away in his white toga that juxtaposed that gold-dust skin like new, bright trim. "She knows my name! She knows my name!" he yelled into the night, the fake vine in his gelled hair trembling.

"You gonna turn that gay boy straight," whispered Aliya, suddenly at my side with her thick forearm against mine. She hadn't dressed up, just wiped a slick of lipstick across her bulbous lips and called that effort good.

"He's not gay," I said.

"Coulda fooled me."

Ken had set up his apartment—so big compared to the dorms it looked like an estate—with one clear intention in mind. Getting everyone as fucked up as possible. The veteran couches and fall apart chairs were lined up with their backs against every wall and window. The kitchen counters were so littered with Solo cups, liquor, and beer that you couldn't tell if the grout was dirty, even if it was. In the middle of the otherwise vacant living room was a single chair, the kind we sat in during boring lectures. It had clearly been stolen from an unattended classroom.

"What up?" Ken said as he opened the door. Draped

over his shoulders was a polyester Dracula cape, and light-up horns rested on his head. Stephanie's face instantly lit up, a little fish watching food crumbs get dribbled into her bowl. Her angel wings were working out so well. "If y'all aren't at least five deep, you've got some serious catching up to do."

"Let's play I Never," said Stephanie. God, not this again. I wished Zadie was there, but she'd given up Halloween for a weekend of rafting and camping.

Actually, I really liked I Never. It was a way to show off that quiet didn't equate to boring. I had done stuff. Serious stuff. Because who could prove otherwise?

I've never kissed a girl. Drink. *I've never had a threesome.* Drink. *I've never done anal.* Should I drink? Was that too whorish? Fuck it. Drink.

"Guys, guys, guys," said Stephanie, curling into Ken's crook like she belonged. "Let's play Truth or Dare." She'd already flaunted what she'd done (everything). And what she hadn't done (nothing). Just like me. But I Never was safe. Truth or Dare was dangerous. Truth or Dare had me creeping to the kitchen to pour the longest drink anyone had ever seen.

Peeking around the corner, I could see Stephanie was mid–lap dance for a tubby Guatemalan who got a mean face when he was drunk, but never said a word. She shoved her ass in Tubby's face, pushed her tits into Tubby's crotch, but kept glancing at Ken. In the corner, Aliya had squashed some poor boy beneath her so hard, all you could see were his stick legs protruding from her generous thighs, his worn out, slip-on Vans dangling like they wanted to jump.

"Aliya, you should let that poor boy go," I told her, squeezing in beside her. She'd keep me safe from the game. When she rolled off him, he sat up in a pink prom dress, the stretchy kind everyone wore in 2000 with the sparkles that shed. A shaky smudge of eye shadow was wiped across his lids.

"He's a prom date!" Aliya said with her guttural laugh,

and he smiled so you could see where the lipstick he'd had on went—all over his teeth and likely into Aliya's searching mouth. Beneath the poor makeup application, if you looked beyond the dress, he looked a little like Elijah Wood, dark hair and the craziest blue eyes. And his teeth. They looked like mine would have if my parents hadn't sprung for a full set of veneers when I was fifteen (Dad with his good insurance and Mom devastated if I looked anything but perfect). He was cute in a little boy way—not like I wanted to fuck him, but like I wanted to protect him.

"He likes it!" Aliya said. "Don't you, Ezra?" He just nodded, too drunk to speak.

The next morning, we carried our heavy heads to our booth and gorged on pancakes, hash browns, anything to sponge up the alcohol simmering inside us. "God, I feel like death," said Stephanie.

"Your head or your twat?" asked Aliya.

"Oh, uh, hey." And suddenly Ezra was there.

"Hey," said Donna, her little-girl voice too piercing for my head rush.

"What, you didn't get enough last night?" asked Aliya.

"Oh. I got plenty," said Ezra. Then he looked at me. "You were Lara Croft, right?"

"I tried to be."

"It was good!" he said. "The costume, it was good."

"Uhm, thanks?" He couldn't even talk last night, so how could he remember costumes? "Hey, Steph, let me out. I have to be somewhere." Everyone was quiet except for Stephanie dragging her leather pants, the same ones from last night, out of the booth. And Aliya as she chewed through burned french fries.

Ezra followed me out. "You live on campus?" he asked.

"Yeah. The Maria." Why was I telling him where I lived?

"Oh. Cool. I'm in Ophelia. Do you . . . do you want to get lunch sometime or something?"

"Or something." It wasn't a question. *No, I do not. I don't find you attractive, and Aliya was just licking your saliva out of your mouth last night like a dying dog.*

"So, can I get your number?" he asked.

"I don't know. Can you? If you really want it, you'll figure it out." Turning away from him, that little jolt of a thrill pulsed through me—that power surge that was getting harder to suss out. I didn't look back because not a sliver of me wanted to. It was all very cinematic.

But find my number, he did.

Ezra and I began dating immediately. Our first date felt all official. It was at a bubble tea place on campus where he told me about growing up in Mitchell, Oregon (I'd never heard of it), his full-ride engineering scholarship, and the high school girlfriend who'd broken his heart. I didn't really care, and I answered his questions because it was better than sitting in silence. For being so short and his calves half the size of mine, that strangely deep voice kept throwing me. So it didn't feel strange, like the kid I was babysitting suddenly took out a wallet and paid for the cheap food.

I was terrified of crushing him the first time we had sex, so four, five, six drinks worked wonders. "Your boobs are amazing," he told me. But that's just because I demanded to keep my bra on. Goddamn, they *did* look pretty phenomenal all pushed up. And he was uncircumcised—only cleaned himself well on rare occasions. Wrapping my lips around my teeth, the questions would bubble in my head like champagne. *Is this pre-cum, old cum, or piss I'm tasting? Is he purposefully lasting longer than he could? Just keep going, and you might get out of actually fucking this time.*

"You guys are really cute," gushed Stephanie when she'd see us, me in his fraternity letters and his holding doors open for me like I was a cat scratching to get in.

"Yeah. Thanks," one of us would say. There *were* cute moments, like when he gave me the *Army of Darkness* action figure, showing me he actually listened. I felt owned, in a good way, like a pet whose master's name and address were clearly etched on the collar tag.

"You want to go to Mitchell with me for Christmas?" Ezra asked.

No. "Sure." *I don't want to meet your family. Just let me be safe here, in our own little world, a little longer.*

"I was thinking, we'd drive in late on Friday night. You'll like it there. It's quiet."

"Do I seem like the kind of person who likes the quiet?"

"Well . . . yeah," he said, looking confused.

I should have argued, should have fought harder for a more normal homecoming. He angled the old, white Jeep Cherokee through the Painted Hills as snow grumbled down, weaving over the buried yellow line. "Can you, like, stay in the lane?" I finally asked. I saw death coming. It was a big, redneck-lifted Chevy. Or maybe a semitruck hell-bent for The Dalles.

"This is how everyone drives here," he said. But he started keeping to the right while slowing down dramatically, setting his already thin lips in an even thinner line. In his snowboarding jacket, he rolled down his window completely. My jacket was packed in the back.

"It's freezing," I finally said after twenty minutes of snow slapping inside.

"Shoulda wore a coat," he said. The complaining Jeep finally rolled into Mitchell at three in the morning. His mother's house, a century-old bed-and-breakfast with colonial leanings, was the grandest in the tiny town. But then again, Mitchell only had two stoplights so it wasn't that big of a feat. Peppering the driveway was a menagerie of old and rusted cars. How many belonged to family and how many to paying guests, I didn't know.

We snuck up to the third floor like cat burglars, into the tiny room his mom had reserved for us. It smelled like dust and old people, and the bed sighed deeply beneath the quilts. Outside, the darkness. It was so oil-black, so thick not even the stars could struggle through with all their points and helium.

In the morning, Ezra was gone. How had I slept through him getting up? I didn't sleep through anything. Pots smashed against each other in the kitchen, an angry mating, while the smell of eggs and sausage wafted upstairs. This was it, I had to make a grand appearance, down a spiral staircase and all, and totally alone. I'd packed my best "meet the parents you don't want to meet" outfit, the skinniest jeans I still fit into (size ten) and a green wool sweater with Abercrombie deer on it.

His family, including five of the six "kids," were already arguing at the lengthy pine table. His mom, a tiny thing, scurried from cast-iron pot to cast-iron pan, her mediocre black bob of a wig a little skewed. Half the kids, they all looked like Ezra, short and squat with perfectly circular faces. He was the oldest of "his" generation. Ann was next in line, and a senior in high school. The sadness in her chocolate eyes made her beautiful. "She's the one who beat cancer," Ezra said, and Ann blushed. She'd had Hodgkin's lymphoma in junior high, the scars and tiny blue tattoos from treatments peppered across her collarbones. Betty, she'd had been given an old woman's name, and maybe that's why she looked so wild. She wasn't pretty, and her big arms told that she was prone to fat. Her freckles that she was likely to get real red when she yelled. The other two kids, they were from his mom's third of four marriages, I didn't quite catch it (she was now on her sixth). Magda and Leah, they were named after the bible and were thin hippies.

"There she is!" Magda said, the eldest of them all at thirty-six.

"Hi! Hi, honey, come on in," said his mom. "Do you want scrambled eggs? Sausages, links or patties? They're all from local farms. All organic."

"Uh, yes, thank you. Both, please." His mom smiled, the sticking-out little mole beneath her right eye fluttering. She had teeth like a British person, perpetually coffee stained, but something about her was lovely.

"So," said Betty as I sat down. "You're a freshman too, right? Why are you so old then?"

"Betty!" said Leah, shaking her head but smiling.

"I'm twenty," I said.

"Yeah. And Ezra's eighteen."

"Well," said their mom, leaning over me to scoop gooey, not totally done eggs onto a chipped plate, "that sounds perfectly legal to me!"

The long weekend was, I suppose, what family Christmases are. For normal people. Betty threw a full-fledged tantrum, kicking and everything, on Christmas day for a reason nobody could figure out. His mom put oranges in everyone's stockings, even the one she'd made for me that clearly didn't go with the rest. There was an okay dinner and lots of mulled wine (my first). I had a fantastic excuse to not sleep with Ezra, hiding behind respect and modesty, not to mention the tattle-telling bed. And the day we left, he gave me a late gift wrapped in a tiny jewelry box.

"Don't worry," he said. "It's not a ring."

It was the spare keys to the Jeep, and they curled into my palm like a tiny skeleton. A little piece of death. "I can't drive a stick shift," I said. I'd tried, really. At fourteen, my mom forced me behind her friend's little Fiat Spider and spent fifteen minutes raging and crying at me when I kept killing the engine. "How fucking stupid *are* you?" she'd yelled so intensely her voice was giving out. "Any fucking *retard* can drive a car!" That was the last time I'd tried.

"I know," Ezra said. "You're either going to learn now and drive us back, or we're staying."

I learned in ten minutes. It was easy. He didn't yell, didn't say I was stupid. When I needed to change gears or push harder on the gas, he just told me to in that same, steady monotone he always had.

My little campus mailbox was throwing up letters when we got back. A lot of junk, and those bills from the credit cards Ben had opened in my name to treat himself. A thousand dollars overdue to Nordstrom, $500 to Banana Republic. I couldn't really blame him—after all, he'd asked-told me he was going to do it. But I'd heard that if you didn't pay for a certain amount of years, it would drop off your credit report naturally. Like antlers shedding in the woods. But then there was that one letter. The one with the campus insignia and from a department I knew wasn't good. The Office of the Registrar, Admissions Division.

Dear Ms. Julia Turner,

You have not successfully passed MTH98, the contingency for admission during the 2001-2002 academic year. As such, we regret to inform you that your admission status has been revoked. Please withdraw from any classes you are currently registered for to ensure no penalties, fees or tuition will be applied to your account. Should you have any questions, please contact my office.

Happy holidays,

Andrea Wochit.

5

"JULIA, IT'S NICE to meet you. I'm Ann." She was a wire of a woman, the type born to play a nonspeaking librarian's role, so it was strange that she could talk. The kind I knew was a caramel bonbon of a woman, not requiring much to melt her shell if you squeezed it tight enough. Still, I was brimming with nerves, and nerves made me say dumb things. Do ridiculous things that kept me from getting what I wanted.

"Thank you for meeting me," I said. I'd worn my most grown-up outfit, even though and even with all the spandex it was getting too tight. It was stretchy slacks I couldn't afford, a blazer that cost over one hundred dollars, and a white button-up shirt you couldn't tell had yellow deodorant stains if I kept the jacket on. I'd bought it for my dad's wedding to Kalin two years ago in Reno. He'd worn his good cowboy shoes, she a maroon mini dress. Her son so grown he was going gray, Lyle, stood by her side and we all pretended they hadn't torn apart their marriages for one last romp. In the wedding photo, I looked like a lesbian.

"Of course, of course," Ann said. "Although I'll be honest, I'm not sure I can do much for you. The policies, you know, they are what they are."

"I understand."

"Well, then, what can I do for you?"

"I wanted to talk to you about the contingency. I mean, I understand it now of course. But, you see, it's only been twelve weeks. Since I started." That was true. A rarity in the state, the campus operated on a quarter system which made tests come at you faster, grades whip at you like they were made of leather straps.

"I realize that, but you were admitted under this contingency. Without SAT scores, any kind of discernible GPA because of your graduating from a community college high school completion program, without any kind of references . . ."

"I know, and I know the university was very generous. It's just . . . okay, I'll be honest. I had no idea what I was getting into. I mean, I'm the first person in my family to go to college. One of the few to even get a high school diploma. I just, I don't know what happened. But I promise you I won't let it happen again."

Ms. Wochit's eyes were flying over papers I couldn't make out upside down. They were full of marks, white out and Post-its. "You are . . . were . . . majoring in criminal justice. Is that right?"

"Yes, ma'am."

"And what made you decide on that?"

"I'm not really sure. I . . . well, first I had put down English as my major. But that just seems, I don't know, not very reasonable? In terms of getting a job? So, you know, criminal justice seemed like it had a better foundation."

"Julia, a lot of students don't have a clue what to major in. Especially as freshmen. Many don't declare one at all until the end of their sophomore year, and others change it a dozen times during their first year. Honestly, looking at the grades—beyond the math—you don't seem to enjoy the field." She could tell that from grades?

"Maybe not. I don't know. It's just been one term."

"And it was the first term. The easiest."

"So . . . what should I do?"

She sighed, pinching the fold of skin between her eyes like a man does when he's overburdened. "If I were advising you, as a student who was trying to plan their next quarter's course load, I would tell you to change your major."

"To English?"

"Probably. Your grades in your composition and rhetoric classes are top. But that's not what we're here to do."

"So, there's nothing I can do?" Fuck, my voice was starting to tremble. I'd never cried in front of anyone who cupped so much power in their pruning hands.

"No," she said. "But there's something I can do. Look, technically I can override this 'expulsion,' if you will. But I rarely, rarely do it. And the few times I have, I've regretted it. Are you going to make me regret this?"

"No, ma'am."

"Okay. Okay, I'll let you have one more quarter. That's it. You need to pass this pre-Algebra, there's nothing I can do about that. But, I'll tell you, all you need is a D minus. That's enough to satisfy the school's systems. And you *need* to choose a better major. You're not going to make it with the path you're on. You got it?"

"Yes, yes ma'am. Thank you."

"You're welcome," she said, standing and holding out her veiny, fat-free hand. "Don't make me regret this one. Good luck."

I didn't tell Ezra. I didn't tell anyone. Who was stupid enough to flunk out of college the first term largely because of a math class that wasn't even college level? Instead, I changed my major that same day. English it was. I was signing up to be a cliché, and a broke one at that. But at least maybe I'd like the classes. And the pre-algebra? There were twenty classes to choose from. Most were taught by seniors or grad students in the math program who needed to teach remedial math in order to satisfy their own arbitrary requirements. What I needed was a man—one with a white-sounding name. They'd be easier to manipulate, beg and prod than someone from another country, another culture with sturdier ethics. Certainly easier than a woman.

Nate Brown. He sounded good. Safe, probably young and malleable. The hard part was figuring out who the hell he was with such a bland name. Google was just starting to inch out the likes of AOL search, making the whole online stalking possibilities more of a crapshoot than anything else. Here. Nate Brown, first-year master's student in mathematics education. His thumbnail picture showcased a skinny guy with a pockmarked face and homemade haircut. Good, he wasn't attractive at all. Had he been, I wouldn't have been able to flex my own prowess over him. I signed up for his class, even though it gave me only twenty minutes between my newly plucked Lesbians in Literature course.

"You're taking math again?" Ezra asked as we compared schedules.

"Not *again*. The next one." He didn't need to know.

"Oh. Why? I thought you hated math."

I shrugged. "Thought it might be good to do. And I changed my major. English."

"I figured you would."

Here's the thing about math: I can get it. Really. It's just that one at a time is *all* I can get. For the first two weeks, I thought some miracle had blossomed in my brain, and all those little numbers and squiggles were falling into place. But at our first test, when we had to figure out which ludicrous formula was best to solve some other absurd problem—like how many chocolate bars a cow could eat after sharing some with their pig friend—it all fell apart. I got a D, but barely. And I knew it was the easy one. Even doing all the homework and forcing myself to go to every class, I was cutting it too close.

"Hi, can I talk to you for a minute?" Nate looked part surprised and part so very pleased. Most of the students always started walking out of his class before their bags were even zipped.

"Sure! What can I help you with?"

"Math is . . . really difficult for me—"

"Oh, that's not true! You know, a lot of people think that, but they just haven't been shown the best way to learn for themselves." Oh, god, he was one of those.

"Right, okay. So, anyway—"

"I can recommend some on-campus tutoring for you, if you want extra help. Or do you have a specific problem I can help you with?" Fuck. I would have to say yes to both. Otherwise, he'd never believe I'd tried.

I chose one of the few problems I actually got, so I could play dumb and then pretend that he'd miraculously solved my math stupidity with his teaching genius. After he'd explained how to figure out how much fencing Rancher Bob needed to pen in his chickens using this oh-so-easy formula, he was radiant. And I felt sorry for him.

"Thanks!" I said. "And can I get the information for the tutoring, too?" As if I needed to ask. Finding free help on campus, staffed by enslaved labor by way of students desperate for easy credits, was the only simple thing about this place. But I let Nate write it down in his scratched up, doctor-like handwriting because it would make him feel good. And attach that good feeling to me.

Four weeks and a fluttering of failed tests, complemented with flawless homework, later and it was time to set up the next stage of Project Nate. I hate waiting, so this was the hardest part.

"I just don't understand," he told me after class, shaking his head sadly. "You've been going to the tutoring?"

"Twice a week," I said. I'd gone once. But when I realized nobody tracked your admission, I stopped.

"I don't know," he said. "I don't know."

"Is there anything else I can do? Maybe—" *Please say no. Please say no.*

"I don't . . . I don't know." Was that all he could say? "I mean . . . okay, here's the deal. I'll make a deal with you. Okay?" Okay? He was asking my permission now? He'd squirreled away into the corner I wanted easier than I'd expected. "You, uh, you keep doing solid homework. Come to every class. Participate when you can. And, uh, I can promise you a D."

It was that easy.

Sorority elections were coming up, and these ones were for real. In the fall, there had been a crazy rush to get everyone assigned to something—anything. Corinne, a girl who only showed up for the most boring and required of events, had somehow weaseled her way into presidency. Donna was her biggest supporter, and together they spent Sunday night meetings mooning over Corinne's massive engagement ring. She'd been engaged to her high school boyfriend, an ogre of a guy named Joseph four years her senior, since she was fifteen. It was his grandma's ring. When she wasn't perched in her special robe overlooking us all with her pinched-up mouse face, she was monologuing about the upcoming summer wedding. I, along with Zadie and a handful of others who didn't paint on smiles every meeting, weren't invited. "There's just simply not enough space!" Corinne would crow, and we'd nod like we ever wanted to go in the first place.

"Are you running for anything?" Zadie asked as we slipped onto the now-familiar barstools of The Slaughtered Goat, which had become "our" gay bar in the crusted-up Chinatown. We were there at least two nights a week. Usually much more.

"I dunno. Maybe Archivist? I like taking photos."

"Ugh, I'll have to be *something*, you know. Hopefully they just let me be Recreational Chair again. That way I can just invite you all rafting, camping or whatever and everyone can say no like always but I'll still fulfill my 'duties'."

"Do you know who's running for president?" I asked. The overly strong whiskey was already beginning to soften my insides, loosen up my heart.

"Didn't you know? Corinne is running again."

"Again? Are you serious?" What the hell? I mean, a few

months interim was one thing, and she'd forced her way into that. I'd heard she'd surreptitiously gone person to person, quietly gathering votes to "overthrow" the one, lone, remaining member, Amber, who had saved the entire sorority from extinction. Of course, I didn't know that for certain. Corinne had never approached me for the mutiny, that was for sure. But when Corinne had succeeded and snatched the presidency in her pink little hands, Amber had skittered away and it was like nobody noticed. Corinne and me, we'd sensed the enemy in each other from the start.

"Yeah. I mean, actually. Some of us have been talking. Stephanie, Aliya, you know. The non-Corinne bootlickers. We think, maybe, maybe you should run?"

"Me?" Yes, thank you *god*, Zadie. This was it. Being in the sorority itself, it hadn't gotten me much. I was already kind of over getting to wear those weird looking letters— especially since the Zetas just looked like capital *Z*s. It had gotten me a boyfriend I didn't really want, but he was a nice and cozy little safety jacket for a while longer. I could only imagine what a whore I'd be if I didn't have a flimsy excuse for not fucking everything I saw.

"Why not? You'd do much better than Corinne. I think you'd be good at it."

"I don't know. Maybe. Everyone else thinks it's a good idea?"

"Everyone I've talked to. You know who that entails." I did. It was the majority, but just barely. "But, you know we have to make nominations on Sunday. So are you up for it?"

"Yeah, sure. I mean, just don't let Corinne know about it. Not 'til Sunday."

"Oh, we won't. We all want to see the look on her face."

The nominations for all the chairs, all the lesser positions, took over an hour. Come *on*, Corinne. She was stretching out the minutes until the presidential nominations, so sure of her domination. Like she was teasing out the orgasm precipice to make it last longer. Actually, I couldn't imagine her and Joseph in bed. I'd been to their house once, a cookie cut-out of an *Edward Scissorhands* of a neighborhood. They'd already hung the chuppah they'd bought for the wedding over their bed. She thought that was naughty.

"And now, I'd like to welcome nominations for that of president." Donna's hand immediately shot up. "Donna?"

"I'd like to nominate Corinne!"

"Aw, thank you, Donna! That's such a nice surprise. Of course, I'll accept. Now, for voting—"

"Hey. Corinne?" Zadie said. "Aren't you going to ask for other nominations?"

"Zadie, please use Robert's Rules of Order if you want to speak."

"Kind of too late for that now."

Corinne rolled her eyes. "Okay, fine. Any other nominations? Now, if we could—" Aliya's hand waved in the back. "Aliya, do you need something?"

"I'd like to nominate Julia."

"For?"

"President . . ."

"Oh, I'm sure . . . Julia? What's your response?" Corinne asked.

"I accept," I said, nonchalant like I hadn't been expecting it.

"Really? Okay." Corinne stopped talking. Nothing stopped her from talking. It forced the quiet advisor, on loan from a nearby campus, to step in.

"Now, ladies, anymore nominations? Now's the time. No? Okay, please write down your top pick for all of the vacancies on the paper I'm passing out." The advisor, Alice, was so quiet you had to try real hard not to step on her.

"Alice? Alice? Is there any way some of us can vote for a person twice? Because not everybody is here—" Donna began.

"No," Alice said. "You get one vote."

All I could hear was the scribbling. Scribble, scribble, scribble as our fates were jotted down.

"Seriously?" Ezra asked. "You won?"

"Yeah. Isn't that crazy?"

"I bet Corinne was pissed."

"She tried to hold it together. But already I heard she's requested alumni status. It's because she's getting married and doesn't have time for the 'frivolity of a sorority.' Aliya swears she was crying in the hallway. But I bet you anything she's going to try to become the advisor or get on some other kind of board."

"I don't know. I think she'll slowly just fade away."

"One can hope. It seemed like Donna was madder than Corinne was."

"Well, she lost her leader. Minions don't really know what to do when that happens. She can either start to play nice, or she can disappear, too."

"Yeah. Did you know she's dating Juan now?"

"Does she know he's gay?" Juan and Ezra were fraternity brothers, and although Juan was far from "out," it was by now an unspoken thing.

"I doubt she cares. She's clinging to her virginity, and he's totally okay with that."

"What a couple," Ezra said. As if we were one to talk.

"My landlord's selling the place," Zadie told me. I was sad for her—she loved that little slip of a bedroom she called her own.

"That sucks."

"Yeah. It's almost time for you to tell the school if you want to renew your room, right? I was thinking, you want to get a place together? Maybe at the Swan, a two-bedroom?"

The Swan was technically college housing, but really just a massive skyscraper of old apartment building bought by the campus. Twenty-four stories of nothing but college kids in big-kid apartments.

"That would be awesome!"

"I know! I already have a bunch of furniture we can use. We just need a couch, I think. My last day is May 30, if you can move in June."

"Yeah, for sure." Even if it wasn't "allowed" to break my lease four weeks early, even if living with your best friend was the stupidest thing you could do, I was going to do it. "The Swan, you know, they allow some pets. I want to get a snake, like I had when I was a kid. What do you think?"

"Sure. As long as you're the one feeding it."

6

I named her Eden and found her like you do all sins—the newspaper. She was a ball python five feet long and twenty years old, unheard of for snakes. Zadie, Melanie, and I drove for miles down a gravel road, Melanie's BMW chewing through the curves with ease. Eden's owner had rescued her the same way he did all two hundred of his snakes, by being the first to show up when the police were shaking their heads over a black market find. An escape artist, she'd slithered between the drywall in the abandoned apartment when her smuggler had fled. The other snakes had starved to death, wriggled onto the streets and been flattened one by one. But Eden, she tucked into a warm space by a pipe and waited. Now she would be mine.

Her foster father wasn't surprised when she was out of her terrarium. "She escapes all the time," he said, pulling a tiny white mouse out of his pocket and tossing it towards the ceiling of his barn where an unearthly green snake snapped out of a fake tree to snatch it. "Bubble gum," he said.

"What?"

"See the gum down there?" he asked, pointing at the pink webs across the floor. "She went through it when she got it. We'll find her." She was hiding in an old work boot, clear brown eyes searching and tongue wagging back and forth. Whatever my smell was, she accepted it, and for fifty dollars she belonged to me.

But all that was after I found out I was almost fat.

Snakes cost money. The feeder mice, the heating lamps, the special rocks to help with their shedding, and of course, the terrarium. Even with taking summer classes to squeeze out a little more student loans, I was desperate. I'd been awarded work-study for next year and had been placed at a nonprofit called Oregon Literacy, but that didn't start until September. I didn't know what a nonprofit really did (or how they made money with no profits), but the grad student who matched us with jobs said that since I was an English major and this was a literacy organization, it was a good fit. I had no idea what I'd be doing. Then Melanie told us about plasma donations.

She did it in high school to pay for her weed, back when her parents thought itemizing her allowance would keep her from getting high. How much you got depended on where you were in the donation cycle, but up to sixty dollars was doable. That was sixty dollars for getting hooked up to a machine for an hour while your blood got sorted and you got so light headed afterwards a single drink would get you buzzed. We all did it, but at the first appointment you had to tell whether you shot up, frequented prostitutes, were gay, got a tattoo recently—and you weighed in.

I couldn't remember the last time I'd been on a scale. Probably in high school, and I knew I'd weighed 145. Yeah, I'd been to the doctor since then, but they didn't say your weight out loud, and it was easy to look anywhere but at the numbers while the nurse held your bag and you wondered how much your jeans weighed.

To buy Eden, I paid in blood and found out I weighed 198 pounds. What the fuck.

I mean, I guess 198 wasn't *quite* fat. It was almost fat. Two hundred pounds, *that* was fat. And I'd eaten that day, but I couldn't remember what. I think pizza from Pizza Schmizza and a chicken salad. Maybe it was a can of that hot chili I liked and a full sleeve of crackers. I don't know. Ezra had gone back to Mitchell for the summer, so I didn't need to hide my eating ways from him. Not that I did, much, anymore, but still. For the plasma people, that was good. The more you weighed, the less likely you were to pass out. And I had the rarest blood type of all, AB negative, so they were opening up the cash register before I even shoved my shoes back on that were kicked off by the scale. I needed to cut down on something, I don't know. The drinking? Probably. No more beer, just straight hard alcohol. Maybe some diet soda mixed in. The new Coke Zero wasn't too bad. Yeah. It had to be the alcohol.

But there was always stuff. Things. Happy hours, Zadie and her french toast in the morning, somehow slipping it into her petite little frame like she was swallowing air. We'd moved onto the twelfth floor, one of the highest. The apartment was big and old, a relic of the '70s with an amazing bookshelf built into the hallway. I got the big bedroom because I offered to pay more, and there was enough room for Eden's new terrarium. Zadie found a senior selling a couch in the same building, and he even had an old waffle maker he gave her because he was smitten on sight. She got him to haul it up four flights of stairs by himself, then disappeared back downstairs with him, sweaty balls of twenties in her jeans. She didn't come back for three hours.

"What's on your face?" I asked her when she finally returned. By now, Melanie and Stephanie had come over, but Mel was out of rolling papers. Digging through the boxes we hadn't unpacked yet, I had found a package of stale Twizzlers. Just cut out two holes on one end, one for the weed, one for the carb, and you got licorice-flavored smoke. We were high as hell.

"What?" Zadie asked, the red burn on her chin shining.

"Is that . . . is that rug burn? On your chin?" Melanie asked.

"Oh my god, it is!" Stephanie said, twirling together the cheap spaghetti and butter she'd go throw up in ten minutes.

"It is not!" Zadie said.

"Did you seriously sleep with couch guy? He knows where you live!"

"He's moving out," Zadie said, reaching for the ashy Twizzler.

"But why?" I asked. I knew Zadie's type, part teen model and part wild outdoor man. Couch guy was bland and mild in every possible way.

"I don't know," she said. "He was nice to us."

"But what did he *do* to you?" I asked. We all knew, we'd all had it. That whisker burn from men with hair too thick.

"*Nothing.*"

Stephanie began giggling into her pasta, and Melanie was partially distracted from deseeding the cheap weed. "I know what happened," I said. "He was going at it from behind, pushed your face into this lovely carpet, and yelled, 'Down, bitch!' That's why you don't want to tell us about it!"

Zadie didn't deny it, and for the rest of the summer she was Down Bitch.

Ezra called most days from his mom's landline. There was no cell phone availability out east, and for that I was grateful. He'd picked up the same job he'd had in high school, doing IT troubleshooting for local high schools. I'd stubbornly decided it was chic to not have a cell phone, but it was also an excuse to never talk to him. Until he started asking for phone dates.

I have to admit, it was easier with him with all those miles between us. I could forget about his chewed up nails and gappy teeth. How I could see the top of his head, and how much I hated his shoes.

"How's Eden?" he'd ask.

"Fine. Good. She keeps getting out and knocking over

the plants when she's climbing down. So we have to follow the trail to under the couch or wherever." I didn't tell him about how, some nights, she'd escape and sneak into bed with me. Sense my heat and wrap herself around a leg or arm, fast and tight, to suck my warmth for herself.

"So I was thinking, since my birthday is on a weekend this year, maybe I'd come to Portland for it?" Was this a question?

"Oh. Okay! What do you want to do?"

"Just hang out," he said. I'd have to sleep with him.

His nineteenth birthday. He shared it with Harry Potter, and I was embarrassed to know that. Last year, we'd made a deal. I'd read the first *Harry Potter* book if he read one of my favorite books. First, I tried *I Know Why the Caged Bird Sings* on him, but when he'd only read ten pages in one month I realized it was fruitless. Instead, I gave him *The Metamorphosis*. He said it was "okay." But *Harry Potter*, my god. It was torturous. So I surprised him with tickets to the midnight showing and prayed the movie was more tolerable.

I can pretty much sleep with anyone with the right amount of alcohol. Brownouts, that's what they call them. God, what I'd give for a blackout. Why were only the most shameful things I did the ones that came firing back at me at random the next day? Peeing on a bench in the Park Blocks, only sometimes remembering to pull down my panties before fluffing out my skirt. Giving the so fat he could barely stay stuffed in the closet president of Ezra's fraternity a lap dance. Kissing Stephanie.

It was normal, right, girl-on-girl action in college? GOGA. At first, we dreamt up up flimsy excuses during games of Truth or Dare, but it then became bargaining fodder with the boys. I'll make out with Melanie if you guys buy us a fifth. She was my first. With tongue at least. And it's clichéd, but she was soft in a way I'd never felt before. The plumpness of her lips, the lingering sweetness of old gum, the knowing that there'd never be a chin burn from her. Zadie, it happened in our new apartment. I don't remember what we were bargaining for. One of the guys to clean our toilet, or maybe a ride to the river because my car was getting too cranky to stand the heat. She hesitated, pulled away, until I said, "Just do it," and she did. But she laughed in my mouth, and I could taste that it was wrong. For all the wonder the men saw in her, that was an intersection we couldn't stop at.

Stephanie was the worst. Springs. I figured with all the fucking around she did, at least she'd be good at it, but it was like kissing a corpse. Just like her eyes, in her mouth there was nothing. She didn't anticipate; there was no meaning between her teeth.

Still, sometimes. Sometimes. I thought about a woman, faceless, when Ezra was between my thighs.

His birthday weekend, a group of us got shitfaced in the apartment and climbed onto the fire escape to chainsmoke unfiltered cigarettes. I don't know if it was the weed or if I'd just been born with iron lungs, but I could smoke like I was made to. Ezra's own smoking habit he'd picked up in high school. It was the femme version of chewing, which is what most of the cowboys he'd been raised with did. Juan was there, posing with Eden as she explored his sand-colored chest. She loved people and ate anything, the opposite of what her breed was supposed to be.

"What do—what do—what do you want to do? After college?" Juan asked me as Ezra staggered back to the apartment. I had no idea. I'd never even thought about it. This, it was supposed to last forever.

"I'm not sure," I said. "Honestly . . . nothing."

"Nothing?" he asked.

"I guess . . . I mean, I know it sounds weird, but maybe be a housewife."

"It's not weird," said Juan. "It's the hardest job. My adopted mom, that's what she did." His mom was white, had saved him from Chihuahua when he was four years old. I'd seen photos of him with dusty feet and too-big shorts when he could hardly walk. A beautiful little lost thing. "So, with Ezra?" he asked. That was the real question.

"I don't know. Sure." Ezra was a good guy. He was smart—brilliant, actually. And he'd make decent money, right? A computer science degree and all? His family liked me okay, and it was an automatic huge family. I saw all the hell the others went through, Zadie with her constant influx of men she never kept more than a night, Stephanie with them all making creaking noises behind her back. I could do a lot worse.

"I have to tell you something," Zadie said when I got back from my summer class. It was Greek Mythology and it was destroying me. I could barely understand the professor, her voice was so thick with accent.

"What? Are you pregnant?"

"Worse. For you. You remember . . . remember how I'd applied for that program?" Shit. She was leaving.

"Yeah . . ."

"Well, I got it. I got in. Nine months in Australia, and I have to move out September first." All I could think about was what I was going to do. I didn't want to go into this new year without her. And how the hell was I going to pay the rent? We were locked into a year lease, and had only been here less than three months. The selfishness was flowing thick in me, but I couldn't stop it.

"Oh. Shit. Well, I'm happy for you? I'm just—"

"There's more. Please, please don't be upset."

"Wha—what? Upset about what?"

"I didn't tell her. Okay? I just . . . I mentioned this whole thing to Melanie, because we were at lunch when I got the email. And she . . . fuck. She told Stephanie. And Stephanie said she'd move in. I'm *sorry*! Okay? I mean, they both know everything! I didn't say anything to either of them since, and it was just the morning, but I don't know what to do."

Stephanie? I guess it wouldn't be that bad, right? I mean,

she's dumb as hell but she has money. Always talking about her rich family back in Minnesota. "The same place *Fargo* was filmed!" she would say. And when the fall quarter starts, we'd both be busy, right? It was just nine months.

"I'm not mad," I said. "I mean, she's not my top pick, but I guess . . . I guess it's doable."

"I am *so* glad I'm going to be on the other side of the world when all this shit goes down."

Zadie and I, we had August birthdays fifteen days apart. Both Leos, and we combined them something terrible. Ezra's mom had offered a group of us the little house behind the sprawling bed and breakfast. It was usually booked by hunters, but in an effort to bring her son a touch of something more to the summer, spending my twenty-first birthday in the middle of nowhere made sense. It was free, there were a dozen of us, and we could drink. A lot.

Ezra's president, Cody, called shotgun because he couldn't fit anywhere else and licked his fingers to Custom's "Hey, Mister" on the road trip mix tape I'd made whenever, "I'd like to eat her like ice cream, maybe dip her in chocolate" rang through the car. Nobody knew how old he was. Or his middle name. By getting him really drunk and tracking him down as he slept naked in the bathtub during fraternity parties, we'd narrowed it down to "about thirty-four years old." To the rest of us, that made him a grown-up.

"I'm gonna have to keep my eyes open at night so you all can still see me!" he said. Nobody in Mitchell had seen a man this black before. Cody was, rightfully, terrified.

It was Zadie's last hurrah, and I felt bad. Making her come to Mitchell like this. But it's not like I wanted to spend the weekend at Ezra's either. I did feel bad. When we arrived, Ezra had made me a cake by hand. He didn't know you needed to let the cake cool before icing it though, so the icing had melted off into a slush pile at the bottom while leaving the top shiny and bald.

There was nothing to do in Mitchell. At all. We'd all

made half-hearted efforts to talk about floating the river, fossil hunting, or seeing the painted hills, but when it came down to it we just got high and drunk. When the sun went down, we played Kings and when it was my turn to make up a rule, brilliance struck. "Whenever anyone speaks, you have to grab your junk and say, 'And I want Stephanie to suck on this.'" Something was wrong with Stephanie, though, and she didn't think it was funny. But that didn't stop everyone from doing it.

Ezra and I, we were the only ones that got a bedroom to ourselves. When the sun goes out in Mitchell, the black is a gooey kind of ink that you can't see through. Your eyes don't adjust, the blackness just seeps deep into your irises filling them all up. I'd eaten too much to get proper drunk, but the night made up for it. I could straddle him and pretend he was someone different. Something other. *Just don't talk, don't talk, don't talk*, I willed him. Let's be other people.

In the indigo, I wasn't fat. I didn't have that tucked in part over my bellybutton like a bread roll. Like I'd worn a belt way too tight my whole life. My nipples didn't point straight down because my tits were too big and too saggy. My upper arms didn't jiggle while I pressed into my knuckles on either side of Ezra's head, determined not to touch him more than I had to. At least when he came, he came hard. Hard enough to hit that space inside that made me go off.

I'd been bad. I'd looked when the nurse wrote down my weight in June when I went for my pap smear. I was twenty-one and weighed 235 pounds.

7

"JULIA. We're moving to North Carolina." My dad's voice was dipped in syrup. Maybe it had happened when he'd killed his mother coming out of her, all the sweetness she'd had left in her she coated onto him. His birth, a surprise, orphaned all three of his older siblings and turned his dad crazy. The midwife hadn't known what to do. It was a home birth on the reservation, and manslaughter was a gamble you took with birth.

"Okay," I said. He rarely called, not since he'd asked me to sign off on emptying the college fund my maternal grandfather had left me when he'd died. My dad, he'd gone through that $80,000 in six months.

"You should come," he said. "Visit. Kalin and I, we got a set up at a big mansion in the mountains. Cherokee country. We're gon' be caretakers."

"That's nice."

"Maybe open that chili parlor, even."

"I have school, you know."

"I know, I know that," he said. Frustration crept up his throat quick when you didn't do what he wanted. It was harder for him to charm when you couldn't see his fiery green eyes, the ones he'd gifted me.

"And, like I told you, you know I'm president this year.

Of the sorority. So . . ." *Tell me I'm good. Just tell me that.*

"Alright, alright. Well, don't you have a break for Christmas? Maybe then?"

"Maybe. We'll see." We'll see. It's what he always told me growing up when I wanted something and he didn't want to say no because it would cause too much trouble.

Being president, it wasn't hard at all. Corinne had, as Ezra expected, quietly drifted into the little shell of a life she'd dug out for herself. Through Donna, we all heard about elaborate wedding plans. It was going to be a winter wedding, and her bridesmaids were all distant cousins because (except Donna) she had no friends. Donna had staged the equally elaborate breakup with Juan before the fall semester started, with both of them greedily agreeing to "just friends" since they never fucked anyway. But, honestly, that whole presidency thing? It was really just following the rules to lead meetings then letting the vice president, a mouse of a thing named Stacy, do all the work. Stacy only came to meetings and random required outings, just enough to put Sorority VP on her resume. I didn't even know her last name.

"We should go," Ezra said. I was high and he wasn't, proving for the last time during the summer that taking even a hit made him vomit vehemently. We were devouring an entire box of those super soft, incredibly thickly frosted cookies.

"Where?"

"To North Carolina. To see your dad," he said. He liked my dad, the handful of times he'd met him. But everybody liked my dad, especially when he was drunk. He was the fun drunk, the one jumping in the pool and flirting just right with all his friends' wives. I was like my dad when I drank.

"I don't know. From what I heard, it's literally in the middle of nowhere."

Ezra shrugged. "Couldn't be worse than Mitchell."

Well. That was true.

Come November, I'd settled into some kind of rhythm resembling normalcy. Thanks to the generous offerings of writing and literature classes, my GPA soared up to a 4.0 easily that quarter. *This is, quite possibly, the best paper I've ever read*, gushed one professor in an African American lit course. The whole sorority thing had calmed down as Donna settled as far away from me as she could, burying herself in Russian Club activities and new, safe boyfriends that (like Juan) didn't eye her hymen like a sundae topping. Zadie emailed and sent postcards from Australia which, it turns out, is the only country that adores American accents. But she went all the way there to fall for a boy from California.

His name's Mike, she wrote. *He's amazing. Real, true amazing. We baked pot brownies, but nobody knew you're supposed to get the THC out in the butter I guess, so we just baked a bunch of buds into them. They tasted disgusting, but they got us all high for three days straight! We took a train to the beach, but I don't really remember any of it.*

"Let's do it," I told Ezra. "Let's go to North Carolina for winter break." Tickets were overpriced, but I had a $10,000 limit on a credit card and fresh student loans.

I hadn't seen my dad since the first quarter of college, that time I raced down to Salem when my car started shaking. Maybe it was because he'd felt bad, maybe it was because he was so flush with my grandpa's money, but he bought me a car right then and there. It was being sold for nearly nothing from the local Enterprise, and it was a Honda instead of a Hyundai, but it didn't shake like a scared, hunted thing. Two weeks later, I got it chained to the tree outside the apartment by campus security because I was too lazy to move it around the block to avoid tickets.

We weren't huggers, my dad and I, but we both faked it. "Hi, hi, hi," said Kalin, and I had to bend down to her. My dad always bragged about how she "didn't weigh even 100 pounds," and any ounces that put her over the edge were from makeup and hair products. She dyed her '50s bob an unbelievable black and kept her lips permanently lined in fire engine red, the quintessential aging housewife. Already, I could hear how the drawl had sloshed its way into her voice.

"Good to see you," Ezra said, taking my dad's hand. He gave Kalin that awkward half hug, butt sticking out so crotches can't get too close.

"How was the flight?" she asked. The polite, useless questions starting already.

"Fine," Ezra and I answered in tandem.

We had flown into Asheville, the closest city to Hemp Hill, and it took nearly three hours to get to the mountain range where the mansion perched. At the bottom of the hill, a little three-bedroom cabin was lit up like a jack-o'-lantern. "See that brick work, there?" my dad asked, pointing to the little pile that held up the mailbox. "I did that."

My dad, he didn't care about Ezra and me sharing a room. He was okay with him, said I'd found a good one. Really, though, after Ben—who my dad had yelled in a rare fit of rage, "He's using you! Are you too stupid to see?"—my dad would have been happy with anyone who was safe. Plus, he and Ezra could smoke together.

"We'll take you up to the house tomorrow," my dad said. "It's getting too late now. Kalin can cook tonight, or do you want to go out? There's a little bar in town . . ."

"Let's go out," I said. Anything, anything for a distraction.

For the most part, I'd stopped looking at pant sizes. I'd come to the conclusion that size twenty was it. It was a nice round number, even though it was huge. But it wasn't *quite* morbidly obese, right? Size twenty-two, now *that* was obese. The pair I had with lots of spandex in them, they were the last new pair I'd bought. It was weird, I knew the size of the pants. I knew the last number on the scale. But when I looked in the mirror, I looked the same as always. It was the photos that threw me. Who *was* that fat girl? In one of them, I was crouching on my knees with thirty sorority girls behind me, and it took me five minutes to realize who and where I was. I was twice the size of any of them.

But it didn't matter tonight. Who the hell did I have to impress in a town of one hundred people?

My dad drove like he was already drunk down the winding dirt road. Maybe he was. The kind of country I hated was on the radio, old John Denver. He sang along like always, looking at me to make sure I was rolling my eyes. When I was little, we'd spend every Saturday and Sunday morning racing from one garage sale to another. He'd buy me the big breakfast plate from McDonald's with the Styrofoam-like pancakes, extra syrup, and those incredible sausage patties. "I love you a bushel and a peck. A bushel and a peck and a hug around the neck." Those are the words he used to sing to me. I never knew it was a Doris Day song. The only voice I associated with it was his, deep and full of the South. Now, he sang along to "Country Roads," and I rolled my eyes like I should when he looked at me, the last remnants of the only dance we'd known.

"Your dad's a good singer, you know," Kalin said. I hadn't felt her eyes on me, felt naked that she'd been searching me.

"Yeah. Right."

"Really. Just because it's not your kind of music." Whatever. A few miles away, fluorescent twinkling lights fired up the night. The bar looked like an abandoned barn, but there were at least twenty cars in the parking lot.

Sex and the City had just wound up season five before Ezra and I came, and on campus we'd all been assigned characters. I was a Samantha, though I didn't know why. After all, thanks to Ezra, I couldn't fuck around. Well, I *could*, but I would have felt shitty about it. So I don't know how or why I got that assignment. Still, it let me know what to order in this hellhole of a bar to make it clear—in case anyone was wondering—that I didn't belong here.

"Can I have a cosmopolitan?" I asked the bartender. My dad and Kalin were at the table, domestic beers already ordered. Ezra was outside smoking. Not a damn person but the bartender could hear me.

"A what?"

"You know. Vodka, cranberry, martini glass—"

"Ain't no martini glasses here."

"Okay . . . how about Sex on the Beach?"

"Don't got that," she said. She wasn't going to dismiss me, but she wouldn't engage either. This was no fun.

"Okay. What do you have then?"

"Beer. Got a redheaded slut."

"A what?"

"It'll get you fucked up."

"That, then." Actually. It didn't taste that bad.

"Your dad and I, we've been clogging," Kalin said as I sat down.

"What's that?"

"That's *real* country," my dad said. Kalin laughed.

"It's like the country version of what the Scottish do."

I watched my dad drink one beer, two, three and then I lost count. There were too many redheaded sluts sliding down my throat, and all of a sudden it was last call.

Kalin drove home while my dad rolled down the passenger window and hung his head out like a dog lapping up smells.

"You hungry?" I asked the room when we got back, but really I just wanted to eat. And see if I could capture some of what my dad and I had when I was little. Back then, all I'd known how to make was grilled cheese, and I made it for him every weekend when he stuck himself under a truck with greasy black hands. Brought it out to him on a paper plate with a pickle spear on the side.

Looking in every drawer for the right sized skillet and anything to flip the bread, I made four sandwiches, but ate two myself. I don't think Kalin had any. From Ben, I'd learned to coat the outside of the bread in both butter and mayonnaise to make it even better. It's how the restaurants did it, he said.

The next morning, we were shuttled up the hill to the big house. Even though I'd grown up lower middle class at best, and half white trash at worst, I was never impressed by big homes. I didn't really know how to be. I didn't know that wood-wrapped doorframes cost a lot more or that having lots of grids on windows meant they were expensive. To me, nice homes meant having more than one floor and a doorbell. That's what made houses fancy.

My lack of enthusiasm trickled onto Kalin, and I could feel her disdain as she pulled out a rag and bucket before going to work on the floors. Before meeting my dad, she worked for the local government and came home to a husband of over twenty years she didn't like but didn't totally hate, either.

"How do you keep your nails so nice?" I asked her as she scrambled about on all fours. I really wanted to know. They were always perfect, bright little cherries on her fingertips.

"You know, you could help," she said. I looked around, but Ezra had disappeared somewhere.

"That's . . . that's not my job." I had a job, didn't she remember? Working for that nonprofit after classes. It was mind numbing work, but at least I'd figured out what nonprofits do. And now that they'd figured out I could write, I was getting to write up grant proposals and newsletters instead of entering addresses that were probably wrong into Excel spreadsheets.

"You think you're too good for it?" my dad said. He could tiptoe around like a cat, was watching us from the doorway.

"It's just not my job, and not what I want to do." It was a standoff. I didn't particularly want to scrub the floors of strangers so a cocktail of humility and humiliation could wash over me, but it wouldn't be the worst thing. But it wasn't about that anymore.

My dad just stared at me with those same, hard eyes as when he'd thrown a glass ashtray at my head when I was fifteen and had a party while he and my mom were out. *Throw that ashtray now*, my eyes dared him.

But he just walked away to the *schlub, schlub, schlub* of Kalin's soapy rag as it raced across the French oak floorboards.

The two weeks sprinted by fast, thank god. There were estate sales to go to and long, long trips to home improvement stores. I'd always hated going to those stores with my dad, where he could spend hours choosing lumber and staring at the wall of nuts and screws. But here, the employees and cashiers looked like real cowboys, somehow tanned and taut even in the unforgiving North Carolina winter. They called me ma'am, and I liked it. I pretended Ezra was my brother, and kept my distance from him whenever we walked those long, concrete aisles.

At the airport, the awkward hugs went another round. "The next time I see you, you'll have a different name," my dad said. What? But he always said weird things like that.

Like that time I was ten, and he came home on a Friday night demanding helter-skelter that we all drive to the coast. That got my mom started. The yelling went on for thirty minutes, until she negotiated to at least leave in the morning.

We left at six, when it was still dark, and nobody realized it was a festival weekend at the beach and that every single hotel room was booked 'til we got there. Turning around after five hours in the car, my mom stewing in her own anger, my dad said suddenly, "Ferris Bueller's day off."

"What the fuck, Danny?" my mom said. "What the hell are you talking about?"

"I just thought it, so I said it."

"Your dad seemed different," Ezra said as we filed onto the plane. In some miracle, we'd been bumped to first class. It was our first time, and I'd heard they gave you champagne before the plane even took off.

"What do you mean?"

"I don't know. Just . . . different."

"It was just the first time you'd really been around him," I said. The champagne came fast and free, but my eyes were rebelling against the two weeks in the mountains. My contacts glued themselves to my eyes, and my lashes zippered together. I spent the entire flight looking like I was crying and unable to see the television screen. I wanted to give back the upgrade, save it for another time.

I could only go so long without buying new clothes, but I just couldn't go in stores. It wasn't so bad buying stretchy, XXL skirts and shirts. Yes, the letters were there, but they weren't as scary as the numbers. Twenty, twenty, twenty.

Oregon winters mean rain and slush, hoodies and jeans. Hoodies I could do, especially when I just wore Ezra's. The jeans were another story, and the few I had that fit were waterlogged and shredded at the heels.

And then there was Stephanie. For the first quarter, it hadn't been that bad. She was fun to party with, and we hosted parties every weekend. But she'd started to go wrong right before I left for North Carolina.

"I didn't pass," she'd told me in mid-December.

"What? One of your classes?"

"All of them."

"You . . . you flunked out of all your classes?"

"They're just so hard!" she said. "But it's okay. You know? Like, I'm sure it happens. I'll talk to somebody." But she didn't. She just started sleeping all day and disappearing at night, not telling any of us where she was. I didn't really care, because that way it felt like I was living alone. Sometimes, for days at a time, the only evidence of her was the traces of vomit she left on the toilet rim. Always pasta.

Back home, Ezra and I took the light rail, MAX, from the airport directly to downtown, then lugged our suitcases toward the campus when the streetcar sign said it was thirty minutes away. "Just go, go to the fraternity house," I told

Ezra. He'd moved in right before the trip, and I didn't want him around while I investigated what Stephanie had done while we were gone.

She wasn't there, but her remnants were everywhere. Her closet had thrown up her clothes all over her room and hallway. There were boots, dirty g-strings and jeans in piles and clumps in the bathroom. Dishes had spilled over from the sink to the countertops, the cupboard doors left open to showcase the empty shelves. Her fish, a beta, had flung himself out of the bowl and dried like a little leaf on the counter. I threw him into the mess of her room while Eden watched, tongue flicking against the glass from my bedroom. And it smelled, the whole place, like a blend of men's cologne and Burnett's flavored vodka.

On the coffee table, the one Zadie and I had found by the dumpster and dragged all the way up to the twelfth floor on a day when the elevator was broken, was a magnifying makeup mirror with a straight razor on it.

8

"DRUG ABUSE HOTLINE, this is Cheryl."

I had no idea what I was doing. I mean, clearly Stephanie had been snorting up all the money she had access to. But what else was there? It's not like I could go to the college housing staff—they couldn't exactly be subtle or anonymous when it came to approaching her or kicking her out. It would be obvious I was behind it. But maybe these people would know what to do.

"Yeah, hi. My roommate? She, uh, well I just got home from two weeks out of state and . . . I don't know where she is, but I think she's gone on a drug binge."

"What makes you think that?"

"Well, there's a straight razor and a mirror on the coffee table."

"Yeah, it's probably crack or cocaine."

"I know that. So . . ."

"How do you know her?"

"College. We're sorority sisters."

"Isn't there something the college or sorority could do?"

"I'd rather not go through that route. I mean, I want it to be anonymous."

"Good luck with that."

That was the first and last time I ever called a helpline.

J, How's Oregon? The sorority? It was insane here, celebrating Christmas on the beach. I've attached a photo of me and Matt. I can't believe how fast time's going! We got really drunk on NYE. I spent the whole night throwing up bright blue water in the toilet. Wish you were here, but I'll be back before you know it. My flight's scheduled for June, so just six more months. Matt and I are going to try the long distance thing. He's going back to San Diego the same month. –Z

Stephanie still hadn't returned, but I saw evidence of her sneaking around when she knew I was in class. And I started spending more and more time at Ezra's fraternity house to avoid her. He shared a bedroom, but his roommate was constantly in a new freshman's bed, so it was like we had our own place. After I'd cleaned up Stephanie's mess, washed all the dishes and shoved her clothes back into her room, it was hard for her to hide her presence. The random butter-lined bowl in the sink. The comforter I'd never seen before scattered across the couch (I pushed it down the garbage chute right outside the apartment). The razor and mirror never reappeared. But a note did.

Staying at cosins in Vancoover. Steph. She'd forgotten that she'd told me her cousin moved to Florida for nursing school.

It was time to get out. The end of January snuck up fast, rent payments and all. I covered Stephanie with my fresh winter term student loans and while in line at the college housing administrative building I found a loophole. You could, it turns out, apply to break your lease with no fee if your roommate stopped paying rent. You got bonus points if she'd also gone AWOL. All that was required was letting them send a letter to your shared apartment, and if the roommate didn't reply within two weeks, you automatically won. It was easy. I was always the one who got the mail anyway. When the letter arrived, thick and important looking, I fed it to the chute. Ezra and some of his fraternity brothers helped me move out on a Saturday that threatened snow. It was a day I knew Stephanie never dared try because she thought I'd be home. I left all her things and carried Eden around my neck so the moving truck wouldn't scare her.

That lasted for two days.

JULIA THE FUCK??? It was the first of seven emails from Stephanie on Monday morning. *Wheres the rest of my stuff. Where r u?* Delete, delete, delete. Finally, I made a filter with her email address so I wouldn't have to see those angry subject lines pop up.

I got moved to the front of the college housing waitlist due to my "unique and unfortunate situation." After two weeks in the fraternity house, where my feet stuck to the floors and the microwave looked like it had taken a seppuku to itself, I moved into a quaint little third-floor apartment with french doors, a tiny kitchen nook, and a weird revolving door that circled into a walk-in closet before leading into the bathroom. It had wood floors, picture rails, and crown molding from way back. I felt like Sylvia Plath, and it was perfect.

Rich with work-study money, student loans, and a generous partial reimbursement from the Stephanie Incident, I bought one of those queen mattresses off a cardboard sign on the highway advertising them for $200 complete with a box spring. Kansas had long since swallowed Amanda up, but I remembered her bed that pulled you in tight like a mother and how she made it happen with those egg crate foam bed liners and down-filled duvets instead of comforters. I didn't care that I spent over $300 on bedding alone, it was worth it for the sanctuary.

Ezra began staying over, seeking out a refuge from the constant noise of his house, and for a month we were close to happy. I would smoke a bowl, binge watch comedies whose lines I'd memorized, and he'd pore over *Dungeons and Dragons* books to prep for the weekend's game. It was embarrassing, being with someone who was into that. But at least it guaranteed he would be gone every Saturday and Sunday.

It was three in the morning, one week before Valentine's

Day. I don't know why I woke up this time. Middle of the night bathroom trips, smoking expeditions, late night dungeon master planning, I slept through all of it because I willed myself to. But Ezra was up, anxiety cloaked around him.

"What? What is it?" I asked.

"I have cancer," he said. "Right here," pointing to a space right below his collarbone.

"What? How do you know? Did you see a doctor?"

"No. I just—I just know."

"Okay, well . . . do you want to go to the hospital?"

"Yeah." Shit. He wasn't supposed to say that. It was the middle of the night. What was I supposed to do?

The hospital was a twenty minute drive away. He demanded to go to the one that treated his sister Ann all those years ago, even though there was the exact same hospital offering the exact same emergency services just a few blocks away.

It's not easy to see an ER doctor when your only symptom is a hunch. I curled up into the scratched waiting room seats and closed my eyes, faking sleep. Ezra just paced. When he was finally called in back, two hours later, the sun was starting to work through the windows. He was back in five minutes.

"What'd they say?"

"Nothing. I told them I had cancer. I showed them where it was. They said it's just a swollen lymph node."

"Well, did they order any tests? Anything?"

"No. They just said I have a cold or something."

We didn't tell anybody. Didn't change our Valentine's Day plans either, going to the Macaroni Grill where you could draw with crayons on the paper tablecloths like you were little kids but they still brought you big glasses of wine.

Two months later during a routine doctor's appointment, Ezra was diagnosed with Hodgkin's lymphoma. After a month of initial treatments, he'd start eight hours of chemo a day, Monday through Friday, followed by radiation.

It was the middle of the spring quarter.

"Julia." My dad's drawl always stretched out my name into three long syllables instead of the shortened two like most people say. "What you doing?"

He never called for nothing. "Getting ready for class. What's up?" Ezra and I, we hadn't told anyone about his diagnosis, not besides his family. It had only been a week.

"Uh huh. Uh huh. I, uh, have something to tell you."

"What's that?"

There was a scrabbling over the phone, muffled voices and shushes. "Julia?" Kalin's voice came on the line. "Your dad's not very good at this. He collapsed in the Wal-Mart parking lot yesterday morning."

"What?" Was he drunk? Why was she telling me this?

"We took him to the doctor and, well—"

"Give me the phone." His voice was deeper, louder, like the sometimes mean-like drunk he was when I was a child and he came home at five in the morning, pissing in closets because he thought it was a bathroom wondrously sprung up in the house.

"Julia, I have cancer. Liver cancer from hepatitis C."

"What—what does that mean?"

"The doctors say I have a chance. Hepatitis, it isn't that big a deal. If you catch it early and all. But they estimate I've had it for thirty years. Took 'em forever to believe I didn't ever do hard drugs!"

"Dad, dad. What does this mean right now?"

"Well . . . I'm stage four. That's what they say. Gon' do chemo an' all that. Gotta go back to Oklahoma for it. Indian hospital an' all. It's free."

"Do you . . ." Fuck. You can't ask someone what their chances are? The odds of living or dying? "I mean, how do you feel about it?"

"The cancer? I dunno. It is what it is, I guess. Always kinda knew I'd . . . well, nevermind. But really, I feel great. Fine."

"Danny," Kalin's voice shrilled from the background. "The doctors said you must have felt like you've had a raging fever for years!"

"Calm down," he muttered to her. "I just, just wanted you to know," he told me. "You think you could come for a visit? Maybe in the summer?"

"I don't . . . I don't know."

"Anything going on with you?"

I thought of Ezra. Of the summer classes I'd already scheduled online so I could sit with him for hours each day at the hospital. The doctors said everyone reacts differently to chemo, but it's common to be so sick you can't drive. I thought of the paperwork we'd already filed so Ezra could move in with me. You couldn't be a cancer patient in a fraternity house, and his family was way too far away to take care of him, even help him. It was me. It was all on me. I'd already filed for early alumni status in the sorority, apologizing for having to care for a boyfriend who had just signed up to have poison pumped into him on banker's hours. The approval went through fast, and the Mouse VP was already starting to take over presidential duties. The most daring thing I'd done during my reign was fuck Ezra on the ritual table before the Sunday formal meeting started.

"No. Nothing going on here." How do you tell your cancer-riddled father that, actually, there was something new? You had a matching cancer-riddled boyfriend with a nearly matching diagnosis date.

E has cancer? And your dad? Are you serious? How are you doing? Can I do anything? I'll be there next month. Zadie's letters and emails came whip fast. Amanda's emails were slower, baby brain making her typing falter. *Oh, god, I'm so sorry,* she wrote. *I remember how your dad would always bring us junk food in middle school. Remember that? I felt sorry he had to live with your mom.* "I remember." Like he was already dead. The doctors at the Cherokee hospital said he'd either recover in the next six months or be dead.

Kalin told me stories about the backwoods care. About how his hair, so so black and to his hips, had started to fall in the bathtub like drunks. "He looks like a biker now with his shaved head! Do you want to see a picture? Should I send you one?" she asked me over the phone. She talked to me now more than my dad did. He was usually too tired.

"No, it's okay."

"You know, I had to go back to work here. In Vian. I got a job assisting in a real estate office, so a lot of the times I drop him off for treatment in the morning. The other day, I left him—he was in a wheelchair—in the lobby where the nurse told me to. This was seven, eight in the morning? When I got back to pick him up at four, he was in the exact same place. Had tears all down his cheeks. They'd forgotten him. He'd been there all day, was too weak to move or get anyone. Those damn nurses, someone had to have seen him sitting there all day. They *had* to. Right?"

"I don't . . . I don't know."

"You should come see your father."

Summer term came, my A after A after A trailing behind me like a headdress. Nothing would be enough to pump that first term of college up to a 4.0, but I could get close. Now, it took no effort at all, as natural as pissing. All those writing classes, required essays, I just wrote about cancer. Or what it was like being whitewashed, passing as white when I felt the Indian history pulsing through my blood. "Bet you wish your card said that," my dad had laughed when I was ten, comparing his tribal card from the Cherokee Nation and Bureau of Indian Affairs to mine. His said "Full Cherokee Indian." Mine said "1/2." Who wants to be half of something? Whole was so much better. Half-assed, half-hearted, half-dead. The professors ate it all up, left dribbles of my misfortunes on their chins.

"You know," said one of my poetry teachers, clutching my forearm after class. "You don't have to answer this, but your writing? Is it . . . true?"

"Yeah. I mean, mostly. I leave a lot out."

"I certainly hope you're getting a lot of scholarships then."

The thought had never occurred to me.

Summer classes were full of online composition courses and the most far flung lit classes I could find. They were all done without much thought, and the Wi-Fi at the hospital as Ezra was tubed up to the poison machine was impeccable. He was in college, but the insurance people said if you were under twenty-three and on your parent's policy you could be treated in the children's ward. He looked like an old man now, hair fallen out and big eyebrows gone stark. An old man freakishly surrounded by walls painted primary colors and toys wiped down hourly with hand sanitizer. The weirdest thing about what chemo does is your eyelashes fall out. They never show that in movies. Cancer patients always look chic with turbans if they're women with artfully drawn on eyebrows if the producers are real authentic. But they never do the eyelashes. Maybe that's where actors draw the line. In real life, no eyelashes make you look like an alien and it probably hurts something fierce to pluck them all out for a movie role. On the other hand, now that Ezra was always either throwing up, sleeping, or hooked up to machines, sex was totally off the table. That was good, because pity sex was something I'd feel obligated to do.

Eight hours a day sitting in a too-sanitized chemo room was maddening. It only took me an hour at most to do online classes, and I'd used up all my work-study money during the academic year. It wasn't re-upped until September. So I started scholarship hunting.

God, there were so many. One of the many stipulations was having a tribal card—that's what separated us, the "real Indians," from the wannabes. Or that's what everyone thought. There were people, I'd met some, born on the reservation with skin the color of clay and black, black hair snaking down to their waist. If that wasn't enough to prove them NDN, it was in their birth names. Mankillers and Bear-songs. It was in their cheekbones, so much higher than mine. But I had the eyes, those too-green Cherokee eyes like grass.

I applied for them all, it didn't matter the amount. Five hundred dollars, ten thousand, it was all the same to me. The embarrassing part was getting recommendations. From the poetry teacher it wasn't so bad. I asked the director of my nonprofit, too, and she said "Sure—just write it yourself and I'll sign off." The third was from the director of the cancer ward. She saw me there every day.

I got every single scholarship I qualified for, nineteen to go into my junior year. Had I known this loophole, how to take advantage of white guilt, I wouldn't be already $50,000 in student loan debt and counting. For the first time, after two years of school, I'd start the fall term with no loans.

It felt weird, like I was getting away with something. Like it was a hack my white skin should have gotten me barred from.

I met Zadie at the airport with her parents and sister, holding a sign with her name and armed with a box of Voodoo doughnuts. She hugged me just as long as tight as she did her family. I noticed. And she'd thickened at the waist.

"Hey, Down Bitch," I whispered into her hair, and her shoulders shook with laughter.

"Are you going to go see your dad?" she asked me over kangaroo burgers at Fuddruckers. It was off the highway en route to Salem, where her family lived.

"I don't know. He wants me to. I can't afford it."

"Yes, you can," she said. I just chewed.

"When are you going to go see Matt?"

"Two weeks," she said.

"When does he come up here?"

"I don't know. We haven't talked about it. It's easier for

me to go to him, rather than him up here. Anyway, have you heard from Stephanie?"

"Not really, but I've heard about her. Apparently she's stripping at The Mermaid 2."

"Seriously? You know that for sure?"

I shrugged. "Steven from the fraternity saw her there. Some bachelor party night. Stephanie had the whole group kicked out. I guess you can do that when you're a stripper, just tell the bouncer and that's it."

"What does she need to strip for? Her family has money."

"I guess they got tired of funding her coke habit. But Steven said she looked like a pro."

It was August, summer term was closing down and Ezra's sickness seemed to plateau. He told me he ran into a guy he met during freshman year on campus. "The guy told me, 'You look like a cancer patient!' When I told him I was, he just kind of walked away."

"Well, that was awkward for him."

"Yeah. Probably won't say that again to anyone." Ezra had lost weight everywhere but his stomach. Not that he was ever fat, not like me, but he'd beefed up that little frame when we indulged one another. Now, his thighs were a quarter the size of mine. His arms were so sinewy they looked like Tyrannosaurus rex arms on his frame. But his belly stuck out like he'd just lost at beer pong. He disgusted me. And I resented his presence in my space. My home.

The landline shrilled like a colicky newborn from the living room, Ezra hobbling over to get it. "It's Kalin," he said.

"Julia? Julia, your dad wants to talk to you." She sounded resigned when I talked to her now. Like she'd made a big mistake running away from a decades-long marriage to be with some wild Indian who just up and got cancer on her, ruined her plans. All this, the cancer and chemo and Indian hospital, was from a prison tattoo and dirty needles. "It was the squirrel," my dad had told me a week after his diagnosis. "That's what we all narrowed it down to. That squirrel I had put on my arm in Texas all those years ago." Texas. He never said "prison," but we knew.

"Oh. Okay," I said, and I heard the phone passing hands.

"Julia?" It barely sounded like my father, the man who was supposed to be a Stoneclad. This was how he sounded when he was still mostly asleep, just a whisper of a voice to him. "How are you?"

"I'm—I'm fine. How are you?" When did we start getting so polite?

"Good. I'm good. Are you—are you coming?"

"I don't—we'll see. Maybe."

"Okay. Okay. I love you."

"Love you, too." And Kalin took the phone back.

Two weeks later I got the call. My dad had died in his sleep. It was quiet, the passing. Or at least that's what I was told.

"YOU DIDN'T GO to the funeral?" Amanda had spread since I'd seen her last, birthing hips stubbornly staying as wide and obnoxious as they'd been when they'd stretched open for her daughter. Now, Casey was two years old, still pulling at her mom's nipple. Had those nipples always been that big? That brown? I couldn't remember what they'd looked like when we were twelve, heads stuffed under her comforter while we took turns reading *Scary Stories to Tell in the Dark*. They were back, Amanda and her husband Chuck, him flush with severance packages. Poor Casey, she looked nothing like her beautiful mother, not a nugget of Hawaiian in her.

"No. I mean, it was so fast. You know? I couldn't, like, get everything together."

"Did you tell them?"

"Tell who? What?"

"Kalin, your family. About Ezra. His cancer . . .".

"No. I . . . I didn't want to make it all about me. You know? Like, 'Hey, your dad has cancer,' and then I'm like, 'So does my boyfriend!'"

"So how'd they take it?"

"They didn't. My cousin. Bret? I haven't seen him for years, but we're friends on MySpace. He told me I'm basically blackballed. Apparently Kalin announced at the 'celebration of life' that I'm an ungrateful, selfish bitch. I think, actually, that's the first time she met any of the Oklahoma family. A lot of them only speak Cherokee, so who knows how much they even understood."

Amanda just nodded. She felt things, like responsibility to family. To her obese, lumbering mother with hands like a boorish laborer. She wouldn't have missed a funeral. "Are you sure that's all?"

"What do you mean?"

"You just didn't want to go? There's nothing more to it?"

I didn't have an answer for that.

Ezra's chemotherapy sessions continued through the summers, and we had our schedule down tight. He'd throw up in the same rhododendron bushes when we arrived every day. I'd go to the cafeteria at ten when the egg sandwiches were the freshest. In some ungodly laughable job security move, there was a tanning salon one block away from the entrance to the hospital's dermatology clinic. They offered happy hour specials, targeting hospital visitors and patients who had nothing else to do on weekdays at one in the afternoon but roast color into their flesh. I bought a package and started going daily. Brown skin made you look slimmer, kept my oily face in check and covered up old blemish wounds while keeping new acne from sprouting. When I got back to the kid's chemo hall, Ezra made me sit as far away as possible. After this many weeks of pumping the chemicals through his veins, he couldn't stand the smell of cooking flesh. But I thought it made my extra, extra large and stretchy maxi skirt outfits look a little better.

And I started growing out my hair. I'd destroyed it the past year, going platinum blonde while dying the underbelly of it an almost black. The stock I'd created from freshman year at the salon had run dry, and I couldn't fathom actually paying twenty dollars for "hair mud" and other salon extravagances. Plus, long hair was for beautiful women. Right? And maybe it would make me look thinner.

"You don't, like, want me to shave my head, do you?" I asked Ezra. Some of his fraternity brothers had done so in a big show of camaraderie. But it wasn't a big deal for guys to shave their heads.

He smiled. "No, I think one of us looking like a monster is enough."

"Okay. I'm growing it out then."

"Alright."

My hair grew painfully slow, three inches at most per year. It had never made its way below my bra line. But it was an achievable goal, one that required no effort except to resist impromptu salon visits. I dyed my grown out, split-ended hair with a cheap drugstore box dye. Brunette again, I looked boring. Fat and boring.

When Zadie found an apartment near campus for her senior year, one year ahead of me thanks to her stint at her first university, we began plotting the coming year's events. Both free from the sorority, there were no arbitrary rules stopping us. She just took alumni status instead of a break when she went to Australia. No required, dry events were going to keep us out of bars on weekends. And Ezra, having no interest in bars or dancing even when he wasn't old-man sick, had already volunteered to be our DD.

"You sick of the hospital yet?" Zadie asked me, showing up at my apartment one of the few times Ezra was out, alone, playing D&D at a friend's house. She had a king-sized Reese's in hand, knowing I loved them.

"It's not so bad. I mean, I just do homework. Read. When school starts again, I'm writing grants for my work-study while telecommuting."

"Is there a gym there? At the hospital?" She was always working out. Hiking, running, weights, yoga, kayaking, whatever. Once, she'd dragged me to the campus gym, and after I'd figured out how to even get the elliptical machine moving, I couldn't fathom how anyone could do it more than twenty minutes.

"I don't know."

"Huh."

She and I spend day after day at The Slaughtered Goat, where the queens knew us and poked at my boobs while telling Zadie how beautiful she was. Zadie, she could bring home any gay man she wanted, making them instantly question their sexuality or veering far off the space on the spectrum they'd occupied for so many years. It was in her teeth, the way they slightly jutted out like everyone with a great orthodontist had. It was in the total lack of fat in her face, the freckles spraying across her nose. But she mooned over Matt, brushing off the men that clustered around her like flies searching for her sweetness.

"He's an ice skater," she shouted over the pumping music.

"What? Who?"

"Mike."

"He's a . . . figure skater?"

"No! Ice skater. There's a difference. I think."

"I'm pretty sure you could have found a figure skater right here!" She talked about Mike constantly, but it was nothing of any depth. I didn't really know what he did, what he studied beyond the broad description of "biology and something to do with sea turtles." I didn't know anything about his parents, if he had any siblings, or even a hint about his personality or interests. Besides, of course, the newly revealed skating. "So when are you going to see him again?"

"Next week. My classes aren't even taking roll this quarter, so I can do the work from wherever."

"Is he ever going to come up here?"

"Yeah, right before classes start for him in August."

"So we'll see if he really exists then."

"He's a real boy. I promise."

I spend all year dreading this. The doctor visits, but I felt compelled. There were no deductibles, no co-pays, no nothing at the campus health center. And it was pretty nice. Newly built with free condoms tucked into every possible space. I hadn't had my period in six months. At first, it freaked me the fuck out. *Pregnant, pregnant, pregnant,* my brain told me. I did not want this baby. I just knew it would be a boy, and be just as spindly short at Ezra. Even if it had his smarts, his mind, it wouldn't be enough.

But I wasn't pregnant. The first home test I took, no line showed up at all. The next five were all negative. Maybe it was a fluke. Stress, right? That's supposed to make you skip your period. Now that it had gone quiet on me, I missed it, those rocking waves so sharp.

My normal doctor was on vacation, so I got a middle-aged stout woman with a bad perm. "Hum," she began. She started every sentence with Hum, like she was announcing her debuting brilliance. "You're not pregnant."

"I know."

"Hum, we can do some tests. Maybe diabetes, I don't know."

"Diabetes?"

"Hum, yes, maybe. But at your weight, menses can just stop. Have you thought about losing weight?" At my weight? What weight was that? I hadn't looked—not this time.

"Uh, maybe."

"Hum. Maybe you should think harder. I'll order tests, but regardless of your menstrual cycle, it would be in your best interest to lost at least fifty pounds. Much more would be better."

Fifty pounds? Was I that fat?

I had no idea how many calories a person was "supposed" to have in a day. I didn't even have a ballpark idea of how many calories were in average foods. Calories were never talked about when I was growing up. Sure, my mom was always moaning about getting fat, how thin she used to be, how she only ate lettuce leaves dipped in mustard for three days at a time before she couldn't take it anymore and binged on a steak sandwich. "That was before you were born," she said. Like I'm the one who made her fat.

Dieting, from what I knew, was synonymous with starvation. You'd starve, starve, starve 'til you got to whatever number you wanted to see on the scale. When that didn't work, you got liposuction. Tummy tucks. I still remember my dad holding my mom up like he was her crutch as she hobbled in from liposuction, her midsection black and bright purple. It was the closest and longest I'd ever seen them touch. But I never did see any difference in her tub of a stomach.

That Friday, I went out again with Zadie. We traipsed from the Goat to the karaoke bar across the street, the seemingly straight one where lost gay men wandered when they didn't know the city. A middle-aged, partially Latino man named Daniel followed us. He was smitten with Zadie, sure, but he was more interested in getting a free tour of the city from someone who wouldn't try to take him home at the end of the night. He had a boyfriend back in San Francisco.

"I'm here to see about opening a new Sephora," he said. "I'm the manager of one in California, but they're talking about moving me up here to manage the opening of a new, bigger store."

"Do you get discounts?" Zadie asked.

"Only for women I adore, like you!" He said all the right things. He was comfortable. It's what I loved about the gay clubs. I didn't have to feel too bad about Zadie, Amanda or whoever I was with getting all the attention. Here, we were all told we were beautiful. All groped and grabbed without anything really sexual behind it. I could forget about Ezra and his bald head.

The night kept going, like it had something to prove. From the karaoke bar to a late night drag show to the dirtiest of gay male strip clubs. It was the first one Zadie and I had happened into years ago, one notorious for being shut down every other month. "We should leave," she'd said when we saw the cop in the corner. He wasn't doing anything, just surveying the crowd. Waiting.

"We're not doing anything," I'd told her.

"Still."

When the cop got on stage and began unbuttoning his blue pressed shirt, we knew we'd found home. That night, a taut stripper stuck himself into me, through his underwear and my slip of a thong. Could you get STDs from precum and through cotton? I didn't know, but I got a full panel screening at my next pap smear anyway.

That club is where we took Daniel. I bought rounds of drinks, because I liked acting like the man. Like I didn't need any of them. By now, Daniel was too drunk, slurring and counting on the gluey tables to hold him up. When Zadie went to the bathroom, the one with piss covering a quarter inch of the floor so we were trained to wear our cheap shoes and hold our hems up, Daniel leaned over and said, too loud, "You'd be really pretty . . . if you lost weight."

"Oh. Thank you?" Was that what I was supposed to say? Suddenly I felt stupid. Going to the Goat, you could wear anything and everyone loved it. I'd picked up ridiculous tutus in bright colors at thrift shops, paired them with six-inch stripper shoes and wore tank tops so low half my bra showed. Of course I had huge tits, why did I think it was so delicious when people pointed it out? I was fat.

"I'm just saying this to help," he said. "I . . . I used to be fat." Like I should compliment him. Use him as my inspiration.

"Okay."

Zadie came back to the table, and Daniel leaned back like he hadn't just shredded up my world with his mean little hands.

One month before school started, and I'd decided. I couldn't count calories. There were so many, and I would only be allowed a few. I'd found out 1,200 was the ideal number for women to lose weight, and something as mild as a peanut butter sandwich could easily be 600 calories depending on the jam, the peanut butter, the size of the bread. No. I couldn't live on two sandwiches per day. I'd go mad.

But Atkins, that I could do. I'd heard about Britney Spears being on it for a week before she said she went crazy and felt faint. But there were no real calorie limits, not really. I'd even skimmed over the official Atkins guidelines and knew which foods were good to go for the initial stage and for maintenance. But that first stage, I could do that forever. Lots of meats, cheeses, vegetables and there were even a ton of sugar-free candies with almost no carbs. They had a laxative effect, but that was even better.

"I'm going to do low carb for a year, and not weigh myself until then," I told Ezra.

"Sounds good." He wasn't listening, hunched over the coffee table mapping out his world for the next D&D gathering. He didn't say I wasn't fat.

So I decided, just like that. Just like I did most things. It didn't matter that I didn't know what I weighed, not just yet, because it was on the horrific doctor's chart. I'd start tomorrow, which meant it was my last day. I celebrated with a slice of pizza, chicken Caesar salad, and an entire package of marshmallow chocolate cookies.

It was scarily simplistic. Giving myself permission to eat as much as I wanted, but only of certain foods—foods that I actually liked—and I had no idea what Britney was talking about. One week after going off carbs, I doubt I lost much weight if any, but my period came back in full force. It happened the same day the doctors called me with my blood results. "Hum. You have prediabetes, 111 fasted level, but that's not high enough to stop a cycle. We can test you for some rare diseases that might cause it."

"I'm good, actually. It came back."

"Hum."

I wouldn't weigh myself, didn't even have a scale, but

you can't deny the shift in how clothes fit. By the time Zadie's Matt came into town, my size twenty jeans were already loose. But Zadie didn't do what I thought she would. She didn't schedule dinners to show him off, didn't bring him to The Slaughtered Goat, didn't even stay in Portland. Instead, she went quietly to Salem to stay with and introduce him to her family.

I just met him once, at a cinema gathering she pulled together half-heartedly. He looked better in pictures, but maybe it was how he carried himself. He was quiet, totally uninterested in any of us.

"What do you think?" Zadie whispered as we stood in line for investments in diet sodas.

"He seems . . . nice."

"You don't like him."

"I don't know him."

"Yeah," she said. "I know. Hey. Are you losing weight?"

10

I DELIGHTED IN the pounds seemingly sloughing off, a buffer of dead layers that I no longer needed to protect me. The real me, it emerged from within. I watched the pant sizes drop, 20 to 18 to 16. The shirt sizes shrunk from an XXL to an XL, and sometimes even an L if there were no buttons to strain at my chest. Magically, my bra size stayed the same, a 42DD. Beneath the strange layers of fat that clung only to my thighs, never creeping down to my calves, my mother's legs appeared as my own. But longer, leaner. I no longer looked like a popsicle perched on top of freakishly skinny calves. My butt was still flat, but that was the Indian. We all had it. I was starting to look normal.

My hair kept growing, the fake colors and old bleach from the past two years sickening me now as it inched toward my waist. Snip, snip every other month to keep trimming it away. And I kept tanning, willing my father's color to peek out from my pores. I'd heard that he was cremated and that Kalin kept the ashes with her. She should have let him be free.

"I think I'm pregnant. Again." Amanda's daughter was walking, talking, asking for her breast. "It was an accident. He raped me, when we were in Hawaii. It was in the ocean."

"How did he rape you in the ocean?"

"I don't know. He just did." Her husband was always raping her; the words had no weight at all. "I think I'll give this one a Hawaiian name about something to do with the ocean."

If Amanda hadn't gotten pregnant again, she'd have to go to work. Carefully on the brink between high school and what should have been college for her, she'd instead opted for a handful of community college classes and loosely declared herself an early education major. I think she'd taken maybe four classes total. I know because I'm the one who did all her creative writing assignments for her. Love poems, sweet anecdotes to the husband who kept on raping her.

She'd had a brief stint working at the childcare center for a VA hospital the year before I started college, and she'd found herself pregnant with Casey. Work didn't suit her. It hadn't suited her mother either. Maybe that's all genetic.

"Hoping for a boy, I'm assuming?"

"Yeah. Actually, just kind of hoping this starts keeping him home more."

Casey hadn't saved them the first time, just sent them sprinting to the courthouse so Amanda could get on good insurance before the hospital bills started mounting. A baby wasn't going to save whatever mess she was trying to contain now, either.

But I didn't really care. I was getting *thin*.

The weird thing about losing weight is you start learning the language everyone was speaking around you and to you during the Fat Years. It's different, probably, when you've been fat your whole life. At least that's what I'm guessing. But I wasn't always fat. I was Normal in my teen years. Maybe, yeah, I was a little chubby as a kid. But I was never The Fat Kid—that title belonged to a poor girl Brianna whose mother meanly cut her black hair like a boy's (as if she didn't have enough troubles). My thickness my mother wrote off as baby fat, and the other kids had easier targets when it came to Fat. For me, they focused on my quietness, my weirdness, my propensity for all As.

When you're fat your whole life, I guess you don't know any different. It's like not having a television. "I feel so bad for you!" kids would say when they realize you had no clue who *Ren & Stimpy* were. But you'd just cock your head with an, *I don't know any different* and go on your way. When you've always been fat, the looks, insults, and bullying are the norm.

That's not true when you weren't born fat. I was called a whore in high school because I loved my body. I adored the curves that came early, the brown thighs from the hours in a tanning bed. With a mother who demands nothing but perfection and, for all her bipolar shrillness *wills* you into being beautiful with all her words, you start to believe it. I thought I was beautiful.

And then there was Ben. The bad years. And college. Ben, he'd started off with saying how elegant Natalie Portman was. Audrey Hepburn. He adored the slightness of their bodies, their lack of breasts and boyishness. Their Hershey eyes and thick eyebrows. I had none of that, and at fifteen, I began wishing I was more like them. Maybe my curves weren't a good thing at all. Maybe that was the only reason why I was the high school slut before I'd even kissed a boy—it was the thigh highs and platform Mary Janes. The plastic, baby backpacks and too-small Superman baby tees. But that was my armor, flimsy as it may be. And I couldn't give it up.

Whore, slut, whatever they wanted to call me, but it was almost never Fat. That was a rarity, and not even Ben dared use that little big word.

But college? Things had changed, a new language was being spoken, and I didn't even hear it. I never learned it. Women began dumping the compliments on me like dirty water they were trying to unload. And I lapped it right up like a dehydrated dog. "Your breasts are amazing!" "You look so pretty!" "Oh, my god, I love your dress!" Thank you, thank you, thank you. I just didn't know. I didn't know women only complimented those they felt were safe. Gay men they'd never fuck. Little kids who needed them. Fat women who were no competition so they felt like they'd done a good deed by doling out compliments.

You can tell you're getting Normal and then Thin when women stop saying nice things to you. When gay men stop lathering on the compliments because they know exactly what it's like to need a pity party in need of some kind of consolation prize. The *real* way you can tell you're looking good is when straight men start looking while the women around you don't say a damn nice thing.

Zadie and I, we ran into Juan at the Goat. It was a rarity, his beauty was too much for those gummy walls. She'd disappeared, the neon bathrooms swallowing her up, and Juan pulled me close. "You've lost so much weight!" he said.

"Thanks!" I was fitting into some size fourteen jeans. That was the official starting point for plus-sized. I was almost, almost, not a plus anymore.

"No, I mean. Are you anorexic?"

"What?"

"Are you eating?"

The compliment I thought had been plastered, truly, onto me for once stiffened up and fell away. "No! I eat all the time. It's just—Atkins."

"Okay. Well, be careful."

Why can't you just tell me I look good? I look thin?

That was the same night Zadie got too drunk. It wasn't common for her. She didn't have blackouts. Brownouts. She remembered most everything. It was also the night I, no matter how many whiskeys I downed, couldn't get a buzz. Juan has sobered me up real good before he disappeared with another Mexican boy.

"Hey! You know my friend? Melissa from the math program?" Zadie said into my ear.

Yeah. I knew Melissa. Zadie talked about her, but I'd only met her once. She'd come to the Goat during happy hour along with a fistful of sorority sisters last year. She was quiet, but the kind of quiet that was born from contempt instead of missing confidence. I was indifferent to her but saw how she doted on Zadie. Worshiped her. Couldn't stack the compliments high enough. "I think she's in love with you," I'd told Zadie that night. I was serious, but thought she'd take it as a joke. "Yeah. I think so, too," was all she'd said.

"What about Melissa?" I asked.

"She told me—she told me after she met you . . . because I talk about you a lot to her, you know? She told me you were too ugly . . . I mean, you know, overweight . . . to be friends with me. Isn't that crazy?"

I know how it sounds, but it wasn't like that. Zadie, she'd never said a single thing about how I looked. Not when I met her and I was Normal. Not when I blew up like the blue ribbon judges were coming. Not now, until now. This was her drunken way of acknowledging the weight flown away, her way of telling me I looked good.

But all I could say was, "Oh."

I fucking hated Melissa.

"I think my grandfather's dying." Ezra said it like it was so simple. I felt like I should feel something. Empathy, sympathy, but what I wanted to say was, *Try having your dad die.* But I couldn't. I hadn't even cried when I'd gotten the call from Kalin.

"Really?"

"Yeah. He's been in the hospital the past couple of days. Fell down, but now they're keeping him for observation. He's pissed." He hadn't told me any of that.

"In Florida? Is your mom going?"

"She's already there, her and her brother. They're staying with my grandma." Ezra's grandfather was the one who got on that boat and came to America from Syria. His grandmother had Italian roots. His grandfather, a gruff looking and sounding man with mushy insides, still spoke Arabic, but only when he was so mad the English words couldn't come fast enough. I'd never heard it. But I remembered him, the warmth that radiated. We'd met when I was at my fattest, and he'd said, "I always knew Ezra'd find a beautiful one!" It wasn't forced; it was like he really meant it.

"What do you think is wrong with him?"

"I don't know. Probably cancer."

His grandfather died the week before classes started, but there would be no funeral. No celebration of life. Instead, his grandmother got on antidepressants before she even got his body ashed up in the crematorium. The story went that he died in the hospital spilling over with life. He was attached to machines, tubes spitting out of his arm like he was some kind of robot, and they'd put a catheter in him (I didn't know why) but he hated it. Seemed to think it made him like an animal, a child, and he refused to use it. When his bladder got so full he couldn't take it anymore, he came raging down the hospital hallways with his bare ass jiggling behind him in the open-backed hospital gown. He was screaming in Arabic, and it took four nurses to hold him down on a bed. He was a big man. Slowly, the English words appeared in his voice like a fortune in alphabet soup.

"The bathroom!" he'd yelled. "I want to use the bathroom like a *normal human being*!"

"You have a catheter," the nurses had told him, over and over again.

"No catheter! No catheter!"

"Sir, you can't use the bathroom for urination. You have to use the catheter."

"You people! You know what? You know what? Just so you know, *just so you know*. I'm going *right now*." Those were his last words, the last thing he said before making the nurses change the sheets one last time beneath him.

It was an unusually harsh fall day, but Ezra didn't care. I'd never seen him cry before, and he barely did now. Instead, when he got the call from his mom, he walked out of the apartment to a picnic bench huddled before the untrimmed trees, sat on the eating part where students normally left smelly takeout containers, and let out a few dribbles of tears. I followed but didn't know what to say besides, "I'm sorry." I don't know if that was enough.

What about me? Where were you when I got that call? But I knew where he was. Throwing up in our little bathroom while his body reeled from all the poison.

"I got approval to take that poetry class distance learning," I told Ezra the weekend before classes began. There weren't many poetry classes offered online, and he still had at least one more quarter of chemo. There was no way I could take real classes.

"From that professor you like?"

"Yeah. I don't know. She probably needed to make a certain quota to keep the class going."

I'd chosen a poetry class before because it was one of the few lower-level creative writing classes left. And it seemed effortless, even though I hated critiquing other people's stuff even more than I hated having them rip through mine. But something came alive inside me there, kicking and flailing in my gut. I wrote about all the shit I thought I'd forgotten. That embarrassment of an almost one night stand right after Ben and I broke, the one with the twenty-six-year-old banker who was well over six feet and seemed grown. About the two abortions, and Ben asking with hate in his voice when I pondered keeping it, "How do I even know it's mine?" I had it vacuumed out the next week. My god, it would be four years old now. About my dad dying, how he used to make me brown cows at midnight with milky streams licking down the glass, and how I miss what I wish he'd been. There were all these things up in me, all these hurts, and I didn't even know how bad they wanted to come out.

That wasn't all. The professor, Sarah, made us memorize a poem per week. It could be anything, from any published poet, of any length. It being long or hard or famous wasn't the point. "If you're ever in solitary confinement," she said, "you need beautiful words besides your own. To keep you company. Otherwise, you'll really go mad." I chose Kim Addonizio's "What Do Women Want?" after seeing her read on campus accompanied by a bass. It was for extra credit that I saw her, but I fell hard for her words. Maybe those beautiful words were all that were keeping me from going crazy now.

"Sounds like an easy quarter for you, then." Ezra had also been keeping up with online classes, inching his way closer to an engineering degree. Now those, a lot of those classes could be taken online. Engineers make a lot of money, that's what I'd heard. Poets, writers, they don't make shit.

"I don't know. This one's supposed to be for seniors," I told him. *My life isn't easy. Writing isn't easy.*

"Well, I suppose you have plenty of writing fodder this past year then. Am I going to get to be your muse?" I didn't totally know what a muse was, but I had an idea. I knew you couldn't claim that, couldn't push yourself onto becoming someone's star, even if in jest. Instead of answering, I poured a generous whiskey. I'd weaned myself off of using diet coke with it and had largely given up weed. Marijuana just made me want to eat, and even though I didn't count calories, it was pointless fat-mongering. Plus, I got super vegan when I was high. It's like I could taste the living animals inside what they became. Little cubes, flattened patties.

"I'm applying for a PhD program in Georgia," Zadie told me over Sunday's all-day happy hour at a bistro famous for martinis and fondue. The great thing about fondue is you can just ask for veggies instead of bread. Or get meat. It was a virtually carb-free bonanza.

"Seriously? Why Georgia?"

"It's got one of the best math ed programs in the country. There's not many of them."

"So this will be your last year here."

"Maybe. Hopefully. Will you come visit?"

"Of course. What does Matt think about all this?"

"I don't know. He's graduating this year too, but the programs he's interested in—marine biology and all—are in places like southern California, Hawaii, Florida. I don't think he really knows yet what he wants to do."

"So you think you'll stay together? Through a doctorate program and all?"

"That's the plan. Right now, we're actually applying for a joint summer internship together right after graduation. It's in the middle of California, tracking birds for twelve weeks. They give you a cabin and everything, and prefer couples. Since they need two people to do it, and it's a lot cheaper for them if it's a couple."

"So, what, you're going to just nest up in the middle of nowhere for three months writing down what birds are doing?"

"Yeah. It's romantic, don't you think?"

"I mean, I guess. If you're into that sort of thing." It was mean, of course Zadie was into that sort of thing. And who was I to judge? My boyfriend was shot through with cancer that had carved black half moons below his eyes, seemingly permanent. He disgusted me but (thank god) had zero sex drive. I was shrinking and didn't need him anymore—what I needed was my increasing addiction to sugar-free chocolates. They gave me incredible stomach cramps, but I could eat entire bags and have no guilt while the weight kept waddling away. Just a few more weeks until I could weigh in. See what miracle I'd conjured up.

Zadie, let her have the birds.

11

"THERE'S MY LITTLE GIRL." I don't know when my mom's voice started that old lady shake, but it was slipping into her voice more and more often. Those monthly phone calls, the ones that dragged me down with obligation, were showcasing an aging in her that I'd never thought would happen. She wasn't the same person who used to smack me on the back of the head just in case. The one who called me "you little shit" numerous times each day until I was well into my first year of college and told her to stop. Genuinely confused, she said, "I thought you liked it?"

"How are you?" Treat her like a stranger, and she was a little less inclined to snap.

"Oh, you know. Nothing new here. The grass needs to be mowed. I found some kind of granola bar wrapper on the desk. Is it yours? Do you remember seeing it when you were here?"

"It's not mine, and I haven't been there in almost a year."

"Just thought you might know. Oh. And the warshing machine isn't working." I hated the *r*'s she put at random in some words, the Arkansas that stubbornly stuck in her teeth.

"Did you send in that application for the hearing aids?"

"Yeah, yeah. Going to the hearing doctor next week." She wasn't even sixty, and already her ears had failed her. After my entire childhood spent being told to speak up, slow down, talk clearer, enunciate better, it took getting hit, slowly, by a car blaring their horn at her as she jaywalked to realize that maybe, actually, *she* was the one with the problem.

"So . . ."

"So, how's school?"

"I don't know. It's the first week."

"What classes are you taking?"

I balanced in between wanting to share and knowing she wouldn't understand. "Uh, Comparative Analyses of Foucault and—"

"Don't use that college speak with me. How's Ezra?"

"The same. He thinks some of his hair is coming back, but I don't know."

"He seems like a *good man*." She stressed the good man like it was some kind of endangered animal she watched on television.

"Sure. Hey, I have to go to class—"

"Okay, love you . . . say it."

"What?"

"*Say. It.*"

"Ok, love you, bye." God, I hated her.

Julia,

Happy fall term! Your Phi Z sisters understand the reasons why you took early alumni status, but we'd still love for you to be involved. As the new term and formal recruitment begins, we're looking for Panhellenic members to help during the process. Would you be interested?

It was signed by a name ending in a "y" that I didn't recognize. But what the hell.

"Did you get one of those sorority emails?" I asked Zadie as we tucked into roasted chicken at the McManning's Tavern on campus.

"I get all the sorority emails. Which one?"

"Asking to do the Panhellenic thing for rush."

"No, didn't get that one. I think they all still think I'm in Australia, and I'm not going to correct them."

"I'm thinking about doing it."

"*Why?*"

"I don't know. I'm bored. I'm only taking online classes, I'm at the hospital forty hours a week, and it might be kind of neat to see the whole other side of things. I mean, it's been two years since we were in recruitment."

"Yeah. I guess."

"How's Mike?"

"He's good. Just took the GRE and is applying for early acceptance schools now."

"When are you going down again?"

"Hopefully next month. Then we need to decide where we're going for Thanksgiving and Christmas."

"You think you're going to marry him?"

"I don't . . . I don't know."

The rooms seemed smaller. Dirtier. I could pick out every stain on the carpet and chip in the baseboards. I'd been here since my own sorority recruitment of course, including that time my sophomore year I was on the other side of the curtain. When I was the one picking out cheesy themes and refilling plastic cups with diet soda. But this was different. I felt like I should have a managerial badge.

"Jessica! So glad you could make it." Corinne appeared with thicker thighs and a puddle of weight at her waist.

"Julia," I told her.

"I know. What made you decide to come?"

"Well, I was invited, so . . .".

"Yeah. Here, let me show you what you'll be doing." Was she some kind of Panhellenic god? I didn't know, I didn't know the rules here. This seemed to be her territory. "It's just been so hectic, but that's good! A lot of ladies have signed up this year, so at nationals we're hoping to make quota."

"Oh! Are you . . . you work for nationals now?" It suddenly made a quivering spoonful of sense. This is why I got the special invitation. This is why Zadie had no idea what I was talking about.

"Oh, no. No, not yet. I meant 'we' as in the sorority. Here, right through here." She ushered me into the main room where eighteen-year-old girls would soon squirm and size each other up from eye corners. "Gina, I found—"

"I'll take it from here," said a woman with a short, severe haircut. "Julia? Phi Z?" she asked, glancing at the nametag I'd plastered across one breast.

"Yes, I—"

"Thanks, Cori," Gina said, nodding to Corinne and dismissing her in an instant. With her thin, dyed-red hair and beady rat eyes, Corinne slipped silent back into the hallway which was her apparent designation. "Now, you," Gina said. "We're going to have you taking the ladies from party to party."

"Okay."

"They're nervous, so. Some of them might need some reassurance." Wouldn't we all?

I shouldn't have done it, and I knew it immediately. Most of the sorority, *my* sorority, I didn't recognize anymore. Even the sisters, most of them looked so young. And the recruits, my god they were babies all wet, blinking eyes, and mouths agape. I could have walked right out of there, and nobody would miss me. Nobody would even know what name to ask about, and another anonymous Panhellenic whatever could have slid right into my place at the front of the duck line. My mouth got tired of forming the same words. "Enjoy, ladies! Please remember, no watches in the parties. Yes, for Saturday night you need to wear pantyhose and closed-toed shoes." Mind numbing. Did I really think time and these women, some of whom whispered behind my back about how fat I was, would have stayed still for me?

"You look so good! So good!" said Melanie. "How much

weight have you lost?"

"I, uh, I don't know. Actually. I'm not weighing myself until a year after I started low carbing, and that's not 'til November."

"Seriously? How can you go a year?" Her eyes were semi-clear for once, and some of that youthful dew had rolled off her cheeks. I could see Melanie as she'd be in ten years. A smudge of extra weight, her springy hair gone limp, and those crooked front teeth no longer endearing.

"I don't know. I just can." I was a size ten. Probably about the size I'd been when I started college.

She shook her head in wonder. "I couldn't do it. Low carb. You know? Especially with the munchies." Fucking Melanie, one of the blessed with those keep 'em skinny genes.

"How's recruitment?" Ezra asked when I got home. He could spread out, cover every surface with wires and toys and action figures. There was no point in having a coffee table, a bartop, even counters. He took over it all.

"Not worth anyone's time, but I can't just stop going now. It'll be over soon."

"Yeah, I heard from the fraternity that they're doing some new kind of rush this year. I think they're waiting until the sororities get the new girls, then throwing competing parties to try to win them over."

"You mean screw the new girls before they know any better."

"Well, yeah. And that."

It was weird, being a junior. An Upper Class Man. I could register for the 300, 400, even some 500 level classes without having to get special permission. Suddenly the literature classes had names that were a lot longer, sprinkled with apparently famous writer names I didn't recognize. Most of them encouraged meeting in person once, probably so professors and students could form snap judgments about the people we were about to volley words, essays, and mini dissertations back and forth with from the safety of our homes and hospitals. Sarah, the poetry professor, she didn't age. It was like she'd always be a fifty-year-old Jewish woman with bad shoes and a mouth that didn't close all the way. "Now, at the end of the term," she said, "I highly encourage all of you to enter the Mayer Awards Competition. It's usually for seniors, but there aren't any rules about that. It includes an award ceremony at the end of the year and $500. Most of the recipients go on to the MFA program at Iowa." Iowa, it was always Iowa. The Writer's Workshop there was the Harvard for poets and, as Sarah always managed to mention, it was her alma mater.

I thought about it, I really did. Applying to Iowa, even though that meant braving the GRE and standardized tests terrified me. Well, the writing and everything was okay, but it was the math. I just couldn't do it.

The Foucault professor looked like a fallen priest, a middle-aged man reminiscent of a young Quentin Tarantino. I imagined him with a vicar's collar tucked below his unironed button-ups. And he was tall, over six feet. He looked like a man and I wished, god I prayed, that I could have been with someone like that. But my thighs, they were still too thick to even flirt with the idea of fucking a professor. I wouldn't even know where to start. All the others, I forgot their faces, their voices, the moment I left their classes.

"I feel bad," Ezra said that night. Ezra rarely felt bad, beyond the physical pangs.

"About what?"

"You."

"Thanks."

"No, I mean. I feel bad you did all this. The online classes, me living here, the hospital all the time . . ."

"It's fine." It wasn't fine, but what was I supposed to say?

"I just want you to know, it's not all in vain."

"What's that supposed to mean?"

"I'm not just going to up and leave when all this is over."

"I didn't know that was your original plan." Was this it? I couldn't sniff out his next move. But, for all the loathing I had boiling beneath my skin for him, suddenly the thought of him leaving—of me having to start over, of me wasting the past two years of what should have been the most amazing years of my life—had me holding back a rage that had been gestating in my heart.

"It wasn't! I just mean . . . I wanted to tell you . . . I'm in it, you know. For the long haul."

"Oh." That was it, and I had no say. So I swallowed the rage ball like stale bubblegum I couldn't stick under the desk because a teacher was watching.

"Let's do something for Halloween," I said to Zadie over the phone.

"Like what? Punch?" Punch was the annual Halloween party from the wildest, oldest fraternity on campus. We'd gone once before, but that was during their one transitional year when they were remodeling the house and had to hold it in a hotel room.

"I don't know. I guess?"

"What about Ezra?" she asked.

"He's actually down to go this year. He's feeling up for it."

"So he'll be DD."

"Yeah. That's what I mean."

"Cool, okay. I'm actually not seeing Matt 'til Thanksgiving. I'm going down then, then he's coming here for Christmas. So I have nothing going on."

"Okay. We should do a themed thing. Biblical, maybe."

"I'll be the Virgin Mary."

"I'll give you fake blood tears." That damn Foucault professor was sticking in my head, his university photo popping up every time I logged into the system to upload papers or "participate" in the mandatory online discussions. If I was actually stuck with Ezra for good, the least I should get out of it was a little fantasy.

"I don't want to be a priest," Ezra said.

"Come on. Why not?"

"I was thinking . . . maybe I'd go in drag."

"You went in drag to the last costume party we went to."

"Yeah. People think it's funny." Maybe it was because he was the size of a woman. Or that it was so easy to just put on a wig. "Would you do my makeup?" he asked.

"What? Oh. Yeah, yeah, sure." I didn't tell him I'd already picked up a priest's outfit from the mall. Instead, I just shoved it to the back of the closet to lick up dust and cobwebs.

Myself, I spent almost $600 on a costume. Thigh-high leather boots, a black corset, leather booty shorts and black wings. With fake branches, I bound together a crown of thorns and hot glued nails into it. Some kind of Jesus-inspired, fallen angel freak of a show with makeup that took an hour to apply. But it took longer to put on Ezra's.

I hated seeing him as a half-woman. He didn't shave close enough, and the chemo had given him a beer swell like my father's. There was no beauty of a woman in him. No soft skin, full lips, rounded hips, or heavy breasts. It was an abomination of what a woman should be.

With Zadie, she never needed to show off, to show skin. Instead, she showed up to the apartment with a rented Virgin Mary robe that would keep her warm from the Portland nights. She was lovely, and added the four trails of red tears to her face juxtaposed her blessings with something terrible. "You look freaky," Ezra told her while he sat up straighter.

I'd gotten used to it. Right before his cancer diagnosis, I saw it. How he spoke different, sat straighter and walked taller when she was around. "You have a crush on Zadie, don't you?" I'd asked him when she left.

"Yeah," he said. Just like that. Like it wasn't something he should be embarrassed to admit.

"Oh."

"Everyone does," he said. Like that made it okay.

"Okay."

"Don't worry. I know I can't have her. That's—that's why I started dating you. You know? Because you were close with her."

"No, I—"

"That's not why *now*," he said. "But. You know. That's how it started." In less than a minute, he'd rewritten our history. And part of me hated Zadie for it.

Now that he was bald. Now that I was the one who took him day after day after day for the cancer, the crush had settled into something small and safe for him. Of course he was in love with Zadie. Everybody was. Still, I never told her.

The two of us, her and I, suckled from the same bottle of tequila starting at four in the afternoon. Neither of us liked the brand, but it was a hangover of a bottle from one of the parties we'd thrown post-Couch Guy and what seemed like years ago. One of those nights we decided to make fliers and invite everyone in the building. On credit, I bought a keg and spent an ungodly amount in the liquor store. It was rare, for a bottle of hard alcohol to appear unopened, sealed and abandoned in college, so it was kind of like a gift from the gods.

By six o'clock, I couldn't feel anything but elation anymore. "Someone put water in this bottle!" I said as I careened from the living room to the bedroom. Ezra had been gone what seemed a long time, and the blood tears had long dried and began to slightly crack under Zadie's eyes.

"What do you think?" asked Ezra as I walked in. He'd scrubbed his face, taken off the dress he'd found at Goodwill, and became a very fake-looking priest. He didn't look like my Foucault professor. He didn't look like a priest. He looked like a little kid playing dress up—but it was better than him miming a woman.

"You found it," I said.

"You're drunk." I shrugged. Of course I was drunk. But, as if he were a dog, I had to encourage his good behavior.

"That looks hot," I said. It was a job to get those three words out. And I had to say "that." That. Not "you."

At eight o'clock, I focused real hard on the clock hands to make sure I was getting the time right. They kept moving. Dodging. "Should we go?" I asked. Zadie had settled into that kind of mellow drunken state she always achieved effortlessly. Ezra kept pulling at the white collar and itching his legs through the polyester.

"It's early," they both said, but I didn't care.

Sometime, somewhere, somehow I was in the back seat of Ezra's Jeep. It was dark out, and my angel wings were broken on the floorboards. It took an hour, no, a minute to get to Punch. Parking was a bitch on the old west hills and there were already red Solo cups scattered across the lawn. Brownouts are a bitch, memories charging me in flashes. A right hook here, a jab there. I did a round inside and lost both Zadie and Ezra en route. There was the bathrooms, one of the bathrooms, where Melanie was holding Stephanie's head as she vomited into the sink because the toilet was too gross. Stephanie? She looked bloated and was so drunk-high I think we both forgot the fallout. Nobody else was familiar. Lots of slutty this and that, lots of rubber masks stained with jungle juice. Then I was trying so hard to eat Taco Bell back in the Jeep's backseat. We were moving again, and the depths of my brain were telling me to stop. *It's carbs, it's carbs*, but I needed the beans and tortillas. It was the only thing keeping me conscious, mopping up the alcohol like it was a tiny sponge while the pipes burst and the dam of liquids flooded forward. And in the front seat? My god. A priest drove around the Virgin Mary while their voices stirred together.

"Do you remember last night?"

"It was Halloween," I told Ezra. I should be more hungover than this. I was tired, sure. But the pains hadn't started yet.

"Do you remember anything at the party?"

"I remember going in. I think I saw Stephanie. I remember Taco Bell." I despised these tests, all designed for me to fail.

"Yeah. You went in for about five minutes, then passed out in the Jeep. I think you had alcohol poisoning."

"What time—what time did we leave?"

"I drove Zadie home at around two."

"Two? Then what—what time did we get to the party?"

"You wanted to leave early. I think we got there at nine?"

"So you . . . you left me passed out in the backseat for five hours?"

He lifted his shoulder in a *What can I do?* gesture. "You were sleeping."

"What if I was dying?"

"Well. You didn't."

12

NOVEMBER, and I'd collected a seasoning of extra scholar-ships. Now there were well over twenty. It was nothing. All I had to do was tell the truth. Cherokee, former homeless teen, dad in prison throughout my childhood, low-income, first generation college student, and the money just poured in. With every congratulatory letter, Ezra got quieter. "Af-firmative action at its finest," he would tell me. It wasn't my fault having a grandfather from Syria didn't count for anything.

He was feeling better. I could tell, even with the same amount of chemo getting threaded into him every day. Maybe you build up a tolerance to it just like with alcohol. A week before Thanksgiving, his oncologist called in the whole family from Mitchell for the Big Meeting that had been scheduled so many months ago. His mom looked the same, his little sisters both getting a little more slender in the right spots. "Ezra has been a model patient!" the oncol-ogist cooed. She couldn't help it—she was used to talking with six-year-olds all day.

"And?" his mom asked. She didn't drive all those hours, brave the Painted Hills as the first snow fell just to be cod-dled.

"And, well, I'm happy to report that during the last

round of tests, we found no signs of the cancer. As of today, Ezra is cancer-free."

"Oh, thank god," his mom said while his sisters clutched each other's hands. Child number two had battled and fought what I'd since learned was one of the easiest cancers to treat. I didn't know that at the time, not when the diagnoses were falling all around me like tornado dustings. All I'd known is that cancer killed my father, and it moved fast. Like once it had decided on a person, it went all in. Had I known, had I known.

"I'm still going to recommend some radiation therapy for the next three months," continued the oncologist. "But that's really just a safety measure. The radiation therapies today, they're not like what we grew up with," she said, looking pointedly at Ezra's mom. "They're much safer, and any immediate side effects are minimal. Some patients experience mild unpleasantries on them, but many don't."

"So when does the chemo stop?" his mom asked.

"We have one more session scheduled this week, and I think we should finish it out, and that's it. I have radiation scheduled to begin the first week in December. Don't worry, it's not like chemo," she said, suddenly shifting to me. "It only takes a few minutes twice per week."

So that was it. All this hand-wringing, headbanging, and it was done. Ezra got weak, got bald, but in the end, he was shooting straight back to normal. And me, in the midst of it all, I'd lost that normality I'd fought so hard for my first year.

I'd asked Ezra once, early in the treatment, what color he thought his spirit was. I guess some people might call it their aura. He was atheist and I likely was, too, but I just wanted to know. In case he died, how would I recognize him when I was gone, too? I figured he'd think it a stupid question, but instead he answered immediately. "Neon green," and I could see that. He was a neon green. It suited him, and yet I knew that wasn't the color I was meant to find. I had always seen a whitish, slightly warm tone to myself. It was a boring color, but those bright colors scared me, like the body had left a sludge in the spirit that it just couldn't shake.

The week Ezra began radiation, registration for winter classes began and Zadie went to Southern California. She still sometimes, for hours, would lock herself up in that apartment and attach her whole self to her phone. I'd gotten used to it. When Mike was home and bored, she was on call. When he was gone, counting sea lions or checking tortoise eggs, she would walk (sometimes barefoot) with me to the Goat to get fawned over by aging drag queens.

It was the first time I'd registered for "real" classes, and my nerves were getting to me. I'd put off the Big Weigh In for two more weeks because that was the soonest the campus doctor could see me. I didn't want to use another scale, and I needed the validation of seeing that old number in print first. I could almost, almost, comfortably get into size eights. Size tens were a little too loose. Was this fifty pounds? I had no context. I didn't know if I'd made it, or maybe I was just imagining the whole thing.

But Ezra's doctor was right, radiation really wasn't anything compared to chemo. It seemed to take minutes, and Ezra said it was nothing. I'd gone this far, though, and I would be at every goddamned radiation appointment no matter what. No matter if it meant I couldn't register for that one class I really wanted because it overlapped with his hospital times by ten minutes.

"Are you planning to come down any time soon?" my mother asked during our obligatory calls. I don't know how I'd never noticed before the passivity in every word she chose. Not, "When are you coming down?" or "I want you to come down," but "Are you?" Are you.

"I don't have any plans for it," I said. Silence. She knew it was almost Christmas break. "Did you want me to?"

Her sigh was filled with saliva. "It's up to *you*, Julia," she said. "Whatever you want. I know you're busy."

"Okay, okay. Ezra has a week off of radiation while the hospital is on holiday, and I think he's planning to go to Mitchell. I can come down then if you want. The week of Christmas." Otherwise known as The Week After the Weigh In.

"If that's what you want to do," she said.

The day before the weigh in, I ate as little as I could. Foods that I thought wouldn't weigh me down, like a big bowl of spinach and a handful of sugar-free chocolates. It worked, the sugar alcohols sending me racing to the bathroom just thirty minutes later with fake Butterfinger orange bits still in my teeth. In the toilet, almost whole, barely chewed spinach leaves floated. Good, nothing had stayed in me. Normally, I tried to drink a lot of water, about 100 ounces per day, in order to flush myself out and maybe eat a little less, but not today. I didn't want all that water playing with the scale. Instead, I let myself get real hungry and sucked on sugar-free mints to trick my tongue into thinking it was getting something more.

The appointment was scheduled at 8:30 in the morning, as early as possible so I wouldn't be tempted to eat or drink anything beforehand. I didn't even brush my teeth in case a touch of water made its way down my throat. Onto the scale.

Since it had been a year, things had changed. The staff had changed. I was seeing a new doctor, a thinnish woman in her thirties who didn't share any history with me. She didn't know about my period stopping, my size twenty and up jeans, and probably couldn't tell until she peeked under the robe that my tan was from long fluorescent bulbs and not my dad's Cherokee genes.

"Let's get your weight and height first," she said. This was a college doctor—they didn't have nurses to do the dirty work for them first. Kicking off my shoes and willing myself not to shiver in the Oregon winter (I'd worn the lightest-weight clothes I could find, which meant a flimsy button up and stretchy pants), I sucked in my breath and half-closed my eyes to blur the numbers on the scale in case they got too scary to watch. One hundred fifty two. That couldn't be right. That was almost my high school weight.

"One fifty two," the doctor murmured to herself as she jotted it down. Like she didn't even care. Like it wasn't a miracle.

In the exam room, she booted up the aching computer and pulled up my old chart for updates. Height, check. Address still correct? Check. Weight—"Hmm, this is . . . what's your middle name?" she asked.

"Colton." It was stupid, a part-boy, part-horsey name that came from my grandfather.

"Is this right? Your appointment last year, it says your weight was 267?" Fuck. I hadn't known it was that high.

"Uh, yeah. That's right." Like I didn't care. Like I hadn't just worked a miracle.

"What—what happened?"

"Just, you know. Diet and exercise."

"Well, good job!" she said.

And that was it. That was what I'd labored a full year for, and I was still short of winning. I remembered being 145 in high school, remembered that number on my mom's kitchen scale. I could get there again, couldn't I? Just keep eating how I was. I was almost never hungry and still didn't know calorie counts in anything. Or maybe it was exercise I needed. One more year, one more year. I'd do it again, no weight peeking, for one more year.

Somewhere along the line, maybe it was one of those long stretches in the hospital with Ezra or maybe it was while this new doctor pried open my labia with cool steel duck lips, I just knew. This wasn't a diet, it was for life. I couldn't go back, I knew what happened. You get fat, fat, fat all over again. When I'd decided this a year ago, I'd decided for life. How did it feel? I didn't know. I didn't know how I felt about never tasting bread again, no pasta, no bread crumbs or nonspecial desserts or anything that made me feel like I'd swallowed a dinner of cotton fluff instead of a dinner of bowling balls.

"Have a good Christmas," Ezra said as he kissed me goodbye. It was automatic, his too-wide nose always crushing mine. He was leaving the day before me, and I was taking a Greyhound to Central Point because my car likely wouldn't make it over the snow-packed hills of southern Oregon.

"You, too."

"Okay, love you," he said as he dragged the old, plastic creaking suitcase out of the apartment, banging its sides against the frame.

"Love you, too."

And I was free.

I don't remember exactly how it happened or when, but it must have been when my mom and I were first feeling one another out again. After I'd been living in a car, and I think after I got my high school diploma at sixteen, walking in that massive community college commencement ceremony like it mattered. As the bus rumbled from stop to stop, taking a half hour break at the McDonald's parking lot in Cottage Grove, I tried to remember. How can you go from not talking for years to smoking weed together? Drinking like we did every time we saw one another, even if it was just once a year? To test her, I would bring a pack of Ezra's cigarettes and light up in the bars. She never said anything except, "I used to smoke to try and stay thin. Can't do it anymore," as I blasted up my lungs in front of her. She used to tell me that when she was pregnant with me, she'd stand away from the microwave when she'd use it. Grew vegetables in the backyard and only ate the cleanest of foods. And for what? So I could kill my liver in front of her and line my lungs with soot? "It's your life," is all she ever said when I questioned her.

The bus had a gas stop in Central Point, but you weren't supposed to get off until the official stop in Medford. But my mom lived just one mile from the Central Point gas station, so I took only carry-on luggage and got off for good there. Apparently they don't do head counts on public buses.

Everyone thinks this, but I swear her house shrinks every time I visit. Like it got wet a long time ago, and now it's tightening up and redefining its borders. I came armed with DVDs that she might like, hell-bent on exposing her to new things. We ordered pizza, and I scraped off the toppings with a fork, leaving the carb-filled crust to toss in the street for the birds.

"You got so thin, Julia," she said. It wasn't worry. It was awe.

"Yeah. Not eating carbs."

"You look good."

She watched me scrape off the good stuff, the tomato sauce, cheese and linguisa. It was okay to her, because that was the expensive stuff. Had I ate the bread and not the meat and cheese, she'd have railed at me for being wasteful. Before I put in *Monster*, we smoked from the little blue pipe I'd bought freshman year, the one with gold veins and a touch of pink. And we talked about my father. When she started to get sad, the water filling up her eyes, I told her, "It's for the best. You know? That he died when he did. After he left and everything."

"Why?"

"Imagine if he'd died when you were still with him."

She nodded, like she'd never thought of it. Maybe she hadn't. "You're right. You're right," she said. And the stories started coming. She told me again how they'd met, one of the few stories I never tired of hearing. "I fell in love with his words," she said. He was in prison serving five years when she read one of his love letters to a girl she waitressed with. My dad was probably bored and writing to whichever woman he'd been messing around with before he was sentenced. He'd been in and out of jail his entire life, but this time he'd messed up in Texas. And they didn't take it easy

115

there on brown men. After getting drunk and into a bar fight, after wrapping a glass pepper shaker in a cloth napkin and beating a man nearly to death, the judge had had enough. Once, my mom had said the guy became a vegetable, my dad beat his brain to mush. Most times, she left that part out.

But my dad's words, even to another woman, hooked my mom hard. She began writing to him instead, the other waitress uninterested in a prison romance. They didn't meet until my dad ran away from a halfway house, hitchhiking from Texas to Oregon in semitrucks three years later. "They took my shoes, they took my shoes," he kept telling my mom when he'd called her from a payphone. That had been it for him. It wasn't enough to be out of prison, put up in a halfway house, and allowed to leave from dawn 'til dusk. They took his shoes when he returned to keep him from running, so that's all he could do.

We were high, so the "They took my shoes" mantra was incredibly funny. She laughed until happy tears stumbled down her cheeks.

We shouldn't have watched it. *Monster*. Somehow, as Charlize Theron fell in love with Christina Ricci and only got fake love back, the talk turned to Amanda as the weed began to settle in our bones.

"She's had another baby?" my mom asked.

"Yeah, just recently. A boy." Amanda had named him Taylor, what she thought would be a good rockstar name and the name of her childhood crush. Her husband didn't know that last part. The Hawaiian name she'd given him informally, "Moana." It was like a secret word whispered only to him, like Mormon men do when they rename their wives to the moniker they'd use in heaven.

My mom shook her head. "Two kids before she's even twenty-five." She'd always half-despised Amanda, ever since Amanda had taken the curling iron and given me a makeover in sixth grade. In thirty minutes, she'd stolen the quiet, subservient little girl away from my mother and made me look like everyone else. I was eternally grateful.

The marijuana flowing through my veins turned me protective. Amanda was the closest thing I'd ever had to a sister. "A lot of people do that," I said. She wasn't here to defend herself.

"*White trash* people," my mom said. Like she was better because she didn't have me 'til she was thirty-four.

"I'm not any better than her, you know." The rage bubbled in me fast, like it was lit by a gas stove.

"Of *course* you are! Of *course* you are!" my mom began to yell. "You're beautiful, and majestic, and brilliant and successful and—"

I hated it; I hated all of it. How did it take me so long to figure out? I'd soaked it up all my life, the over-bloated compliments and doting from her. It was hard when you had nothing to compare it to. No siblings to see how she treated them differently, no excessive time spent watching friends with their moms. But I got it now. She didn't see me. She didn't even know me. All she saw was a reflection, a do-over for herself. I was a decades-long project that still wasn't shaping up quite to her liking.

"I'm not," I said. "Just stop."

"You little shit," she said. "Unbelievable. I hope you end up with one *just like you*." She pouted, like a child. I could see her at four years old, an unexpected sliver in her parents' thumbs. She'd been wildly unplanned, a child of the depression with a sister fifteen years older. Her whole life, she wailed about how her mother was a saint her father had killed. None of it was true. Well, the saint part, I don't know, I don't remember Mamo. She died when I was too little, but it was from emphysema. My mom swore it was because Papo "made her" work in a mill with fumes floating like angels, not from smoking her entire life. The only stories I heard about Papo were how he always told Mamo she was getting fat. My mom that she was getting fat. I don't know if there was any more to him than that. And my mom hated her sister, Callie. Hated her for asking for a few minutes alone with Mamo when she was dying, like it was a request steeped in strangeness. My mom had told her no.

"You know what, I think it's best if I just leave," I said. She went into her bedroom without a word, slamming the door. The sound of daytime television blasted through the house, stabbing at my eardrums. She must have taken her hearing aids out.

A calmness pools around me when I'm angry-anxious and logistics kick in. Step by step, I map out what to do. I had no car. Get the phone book. Call a local taxi company. Thank god I had cash. Get to the Medford bus station. The office was closed since it was Christmas Eve, but the schedule showed the next bus to Portland would arrive in nine hours, just before midnight. Fine. I could sit and read that long.

My bag became a lumpy seat, the only buffer between my increasingly bony ass and the freezing cement floor. It wasn't raining, but the cold slapped through the little tunnel of a pergola something fierce. Nobody else was there, so I had no shame in piling layer after layer over me, using sweaters as blankets and snuggling in four T-shirts deep. I shook and it hurt to let my fingers peek out to turn the pages, but I'm sure people have been colder.

"Hey! Hey, you!" the homeless man with his long gray beard limped around the corner. "What are you doing?"

"Waiting for the bus." I mean, obviously. I was crouched in a bus station an arm's reach from their locked glass door.

"But what are you really doing?"

"Waiting. For a bus." God, go away. Normally I could veer away from the men and women in their torn up coats and dirty fingernails. But where could I go now? Everywhere was closed.

"Mmm, hmmm. I know you. I recognize you. There's a shelter nearby. Come with me."

"No, like I told you, I'm waiting for a bus."

"Ain't no buses here."

"Whatever." I dug in my pockets and, like a gift from

the heavens, found a few quarters. I'd call Ezra from the payphone nearby, an excuse to do something. But I had to walk by the man to get there.

"I'mma come back for you!" the homeless man said, as if the quarters held some kind of treasure he couldn't touch. He couldn't come near. "Make sure you're okay! I'll be here in a few hours, don't you worry!" and the cold swallowed him back up.

Ezra answered. "Where are you?" he asked. "How's your mom?"

"I'm in a bus stop. A closed one," I said. "We got into a fight and a—a homeless man? He's stalking me. Said he's gonna come back and check on me. He thinks I'm homeless. Do I look homeless?"

"When does the bus come?" he asked. He didn't answer my question.

"Midnight."

"Huh. Well, have a good ride. Call me if you need me."

I hung up without saying anything else.

My swift departure earned me a few days alone in the apartment. I cleaned, shoved Ezra's stuff into the hallway closet. Zadie, bored with Matt in Salem, came up for another try at integrating him into her life but he just didn't fit. He kept glancing around, looking for an escape route. Only once did he really look at me.

"What are you?" he asked, pulling the words from nowhere. I don't know what we were really talking about when it came bolting out his lips. Grad school, classes, how big the turtles were that he researched last.

"What?"

"I mean, you look something. Not all white. Hispanic?" Zadie's eyes were growing bigger and bigger beside him, but any words were lodged in her throat.

"Half Cherokee. Half white," I said.

"Oh. Real Cherokee? Money from the tribe and all that?"

"Real, uh, yeah. But Cherokee tribes don't give money

to their members."

"All tribes do," he said.

"Oh. Okay."

"I'm sorry about that," Zadie whispered when we went in tandem to the restroom.

"It's okay. I'm used to it," I said. I was. I'd been spoken to in Spanish at Mexican restaurants, called exotic when I was tan enough, and heard *mamichula* under hushed breaths as I passed groups of brown-skinned boys in the mall. It made sense—we lived along the I-5 corridor, a straight shot from Tijuana to Medford and Portland. I didn't mind; it made me feel closer to my father who would always point to himself and say, "Indiano," when Mexican waiters greeted him in Spanish. Him and his whitewashed daughter.

"It's not okay," she said. "Mike is being—different. I don't know. Maybe he's not. Maybe it's me, or Oregon, or something. It's better when I go down there."

"So what are you going to do? Spend your whole life only having a relationship in California?"

"I don't know. Maybe the summer will change things. We got it, by the way. The summer research project with the birds."

Amanda was drowning. She had a newborn, a not-so-newborn, and a husband who'd taken a job in Salem which meant at least a two hour commute each day. Saddled with milk-heavy breasts and a brand new mortgage with a balloon payment, Chuck had charmed her into letting him spend half his nights at a comanager's apartment in Salem, a place where he could play video games and escape screaming babies.

I don't know how he did it, even though I'd seen him work her. He had a high pitched voice, like a woman's. Amanda told me he hated going through drive-throughs because he'd always get, "Is that all, ma'am?" He constantly fidgeted, dropped things, and even though he was her type of good looking as a teenager, that had gone to fat and thinning hair and too-red cheeks now. But he still worked her, and he knew how.

"Want to stay over this weekend?" she asked. "Chuck has inventory at Best Buy so he's staying in Salem Saturday night."

"Sure," I said. It was an excuse to get away from Ezra, and the last weekend before classes started.

"We can watch horror movies, and Taylor's been sleeping better lately. Like the old days."

It wasn't like the old days. Amanda could be talking to me about how Chuck would sneak into their room when she was sleeping, hold her down, and tongue her clit even as she shrieked against him and their daughter banged on the door. I don't know how much of that was true, but she talked like the kids weren't right there, even as she picked up Taylor, pulled out a breast with a stretched out nipple and let him start sucking. Her daughter rushed over, trying to throw a blanket over Taylor's head.

"Stop it, Casey," Amanda said.

"But I—you—brother," she tried to explain.

"You think this is something Julia hasn't seen before? She saw you breastfeed."

"No," Casey said, like it was unfathomable.

"Uh, yeah," Amanda said, and Casey wandered away, confused that there was life before she could remember.

"So are you guys doing good then? The house looks good," I told her. It wasn't true. I mean, maybe it was a nice house for some people, but it looked clipped right out of an *Edward Scissorhands* neighborhood. The kitchen turned suddenly into the living room with no warning, and the carpet was stained with mysteries.

"Yeah. I guess. Chuck works a lot."

"And you?"

She cocked her head, like she'd never thought about it before. "I guess I got what I wanted."

13

IT'S A STRANGE THING, coming back. I didn't fit here anymore. I saw girls, young girls, roaming the halls in Phi Z
sweaters who I'd never met before and they didn't even
glance at me. Don't they remember? I was the one who
perched on the ritual table like a dirty, proud pigeon, saying
when they could speak or not. Maybe it was because I used
to be fat and I wasn't anymore—I couldn't change how I ate
if I tried now. One of Ezra's friends was moving to Nevada,
picked up a job working security at a casino, and was leaving
behind a real, grownup two-bedroom duplex almost in the
Laurelhurst district, but not quite. It was a serious place
with a full basement and washer-dryer hookups. The rent
was less than what we were paying for my hideaway tucked
into the trees.

"I think we should take it," Ezra said as we huddled in
the grassy courtyard below the apartment, him smoking
and me shaking. I was always cold now. His hair was starting
to come back, and it was like it had never left. The shadows
of his caterpillar eyebrows were beginning to shoot up from
his skin like a spring garden.

"I guess," I said. "It's not like we're on campus for anything besides classes now."

It was almost dark, but a big, fat blackbird pecked away

two strides from us, persistent at the frozen ground. A rustling in the trees above.

"What's the—" I began, but a flying, ungraceful beast stole my voice as he flew from the air. A raccoon tackled the poor thing, only allowing a sliver of a squeak before it was silenced.

"What the hell . . ." Ezra began. Of course there were raccoons on campus, with the sugary cocktail remnants and drunken junk food trimmings spilling out of the dumpsters. But I'd never seen anything like this. That bird was almost as big as the raccoon was. "Hey!" Ezra yelled to the raccoon, already tucked into its victory.

It looked up with eyes shining and foam framing its mouth. One staggering, stiff step, then another. The bolt of energy it had managed flying out of the tree was probably its last feat. It walked like Cujo. "It's rabid," I said, and we both ran back to the heavy wooden doors of the apartment with its scuffed up kickplates.

Yeah. Maybe it was time to move.

Moving, it made everything feel real. We were true adults, halfway through our junior year and plotting What to Do Next. I'd learned what graduate school meant, that it was more than the mysterious Oregon Institute of Graduate School sign that I constantly passed on the Sunset Highway. Apparently, it was like a super school within a school at a number of universities and colleges. Even at ours. And I wasn't ready to leave yet. To do what? What I was doing now at the nonprofit? That was fine and all, and my ego was stroked every time I secured a grant, but could I do that for life? I needed more time; I needed to buy more time. I'd been cheated out of the four years I was promised.

"What do you think about grad school?" I asked Ezra as we watched the movers push pile after pile of poorly taped boxes into the duplex. It was a single level with huge picture windows looking out onto a tree-lined street, but there were two small concrete stair flights they needed to take to the entrance. The brick was beautiful, the rose bushes big, but the doors were old with gold hardware. The wood-burning fireplace I already knew we'd never use.

"I don't know," he said. "It would be helpful as a software engineer I suppose, but I'm just kind of burned out of it." Cancer, it had eaten up the more aggressive dreams he'd had along with his small amount of muscle. The full ride he'd earned with valedictorian status, perfect GPAs and interview skills only took him through the first round of chemo before the give-ups kicked in.

"Where at?" I asked. "I mean, if you did."

"Don't know," he said.

"The university, it has a master's degree. In writing. There are a lot of technical courses, too . . . I'm thinking of applying."

"Yeah?"

"Yeah. A lot of the business side of things. Maybe you'd want to apply, too?"

"Maybe. I guess."

"I could write the essay part for you if you want." Bribery, begging, and I had no idea why I was dragging him along with all his heavy apathy with me.

"Okay, sure."

Early admission applications were due in the spring, and it gave me something to do. Gather recommendation letters, get sealed transcripts, write our essays and that was it. The program was relatively new and was hungry for applicants from backgrounds besides literature. I knew, with my endless scholarships and tribal enrollment card, that I would be set. Ezra, a left fielder, I didn't know. At the very least, he'd probably be the only engineer applying. The two sealed, addressed envelopes leaned against our new-old kitchen backsplash gathering oil splashes and food bits, anxious to get in the mailbox come spring.

Valentine's Day weekend, Mike made plans to go to

Tahoe with his dads, and it sent Zadie into a spin. I couldn't exactly ditch Ezra on that date as much as I wanted to. Instead, I helped Zadie find a bar offering specials and cheap decorations for those in relationships whose loves were far away. Most of them, they were military orphans with spouses and lovers overseas. Zadie was the only one there because her boyfriend chose a weekend of hiking with his parents instead of being with her. I convinced Ezra to spend the evening surprising our single friends with boxes of chocolates and flowers, showing up uninvited to confused faces, but it kept the romance out of us.

"Oh, you know us!" I'd tell friends we hadn't seen in person forever. "We've been together so long, we don't really need to do the whole dinner thing." I wanted the whole dinner thing with a desperate moan, but not with Ezra. Not with anyone I knew. But maybe that's how it is. You're with someone through cancer, through your dad dying, through your fattest years and they don't say a single mean thing to you, you stay. You stay.

The next morning, Zadie called. "I think I did something bad," she said.

"What?" She slept with someone. I knew it. A relief spread over me, an itch my scratch had been waiting for since the Australia letters. She was free from Mike.

"I . . . I'm not really sure? I don't remember much of what happened last night. But. This morning? There's shit everywhere."

"What? What do you mean?"

"There's shit. Everywhere. On the walls, the floor, all over the bathroom."

"Is it . . . is it yours?"

"Of course it's mine!"

"Well how am I supposed to know?"

"Oh. My god. I got drunk. *Real* drunk. I don't even know how many times I drunk dialed Mike, but there's no reception where he is, thank god. I don't think I left any voicemails. I just—I just have flashes. There were so many women.

125

I was just sad. You know? I missed him. And then . . . I don't know what happened?"

"I'll come over."

She wasn't exaggerating. The little apartment reeked of some kind of sick animal. How there was no vomit, I don't know, or maybe the rugs had already lapped it all up. "Oh, fuck." But Zadie, she seemed not embarrassed. Confused, yes. And with a raging hangover. But it was like having shit all over your apartment was something that happened to everyone.

I didn't know the best, safest way to clean up human poop, especially when it stank of well cocktails and seemed to be smeared by hand into the door frames. "What were you *doing*?" I asked her.

"I don't know. It looks like I was fingerpainting."

"With your whole hand."

"Yeah. It was hard to shower this morning with a couple of logs still in the bathtub floor."

Two hours and four bottles of bleach later, the apartment smelled like a serial killer had just completed a ceremony and we'd left white spots everywhere. On the dark, french oak floors, her good bedspread from Anthropologie, the curtains, and all the shoes she kept piled by the door. "Well. At least the landlord won't be able to say it's unsanitary when I move out."

"When do you move out?"

"Yeah, I—I'm moving out when we go for the bird research this summer."

"Where are you putting all your stuff? What about when you get back?" The room that was so disgusting just a few moments ago was suddenly a haven. It was her; it was Zadie. It's where we'd curl up the morning after drinking at the Goat with Burger King croissan'wiches, the ones I'd eat the middle out of in the past year while she downed the buttery rolls without gaining a pound.

"A lot I'm selling, the rest I'll keep at my parents'. I should start getting notices of where I got into grad school soon. If. This summer . . . I'll probably just spend a couple of weeks back here after the research."

"Oh. I'm applying to grad school here. With Ezra."

She was quiet, fingering the bottom button hole of her now bleach-splattered shirt. "Is that what you want?"

"I think I want Iowa. But I'm not going to apply."

"Why not?"

"There's no money in poetry. And I don't like the idea of critique classes, you know? Watching my baby get torn apart in every class." I wouldn't know what to do with a bleeding, screaming newborn anyway except cry with it and scream for help.

14

SOMETHING HAPPENS IN OREGON in the spring, like the rains water the bad with the good. My mom called, leaving voice-mails like nothing had ever happened. She never asked where I went, what I did that last time, so she never found out about the homeless man that blew into the bus station like a dirty Jesus looking to save. Instead, it was all, "Just calling to hear your voice. I love you," and I'd try. I'd try my best to forget about the messages, but I'd always call her back. I don't know why it felt like I needed her now, when I'd been so crazy to get away from her my whole life. After talking to her, I felt less like myself. She siphoned feelings like that.

Ezra almost looked normal again. The radiation treatments were coming to an end, and it was all very anticlimactic. They should throw parties when someone the nurses were probably gambling on went out the front set of doors instead of the back. But the radiation was in a totally different part of the hospital and we didn't know any of these scrubs-laden people. We didn't even park in the same lot anymore, so I never got to see if his favorite throw-up spot in the plush bushes ended up killing a part of it or not.

It was the classes that were really making me itch. One

poetry professor, not Sara but a young one tangibly trying to force her way into being serious, continued to promise to "take us outside" like she thought Portland rain would listen to her. I never got that, the desire for classes outside. Why would I want sticks to poke at my butt and bugs to needle under my calves when there were desks made for holding bodies and central air inside?

"Julia, can I talk to you a minute?" the young professor asked while everyone else wiped their notebooks with forced critiques into purses and messenger bags. We were almost seniors and nobody carried backpacks anymore.

"Sure," I said. If it was about last week's poem, the one that was supposed to be "inspired" by her favorite poet and not ours, I was ready to throw down. I knew it sucked, but how would she like being forced to grovel below a stranger she didn't believe in.

"I don't know if you got the letter yet. Or if they've even been sent out. But I was in a staff meeting yesterday? And your poem, the one about your father, was selected for the Mayer award."

"It—it was? No, I . . . I didn't get any letter."

"Yes, well. I wasn't asked to tell you, but. The awards are in the student union's assembly area in a month. It's during our class time, and I just wanted to let you know you're excused for that. If you want." There was no congratulations. Maybe this wasn't a big deal after all.

"Doesn't it—doesn't it normally go to seniors?"

"I don't know. I think so? Normally yes, but I don't think there are any rules about it. A first year student could have won it."

But they didn't.

I'd submitted a piece about my father. You could only choose one, one poem to stand for you. I'd written about the days leading up to his funeral as if I were going, but I didn't lie. I didn't say in the poem whether I went or not, but readers would probably assume I did. What daughter didn't go to her own father's funeral? In it, I imagined what

I thought he looked like in his dying days, his strong, thick teeth shaved down to fingernail-thin bits. About how he met my mother and they fell in love with each other's words. They'd both had beautiful handwriting. About all those times people thought he was Mexican because they didn't think a real, live Indian would be sitting in a button-up waiting for tableside guacamole. And about how, at midnight when I'd hear him rustling in the kitchen, eating entire jars of green olives before shooting the juice, when I was little I'd pad out to him. My mother never knew, never heard us. I'd prop myself on the kitchen counter ledge, and he'd make me brown cows, coke and ice cream, spooned together just right with the milky streams licking down the glass. We never talked about it—he just took out the beer mugs I loved so much and started scooping vanilla when he saw me.

I didn't know if I'd won because the famous judge felt sorry for me, because he'd probably watched someone slip away too, or because it was actually good, and I didn't care. I'd stand up in front of that room, read that poem with perfect Spanish in the parts that demanded it (*Indiano, Indiano*), and there was nothing they could do about it. Everyone who ever tucked this award into themselves before me had gone on to Iowa. But I just couldn't leave Ezra now.

"Hey, that's awesome," he said when I told him, but he didn't look up. In the basement, he'd dragged an old ping pong table, and as a surprise, I'd bought him a huge D&D map. It fit it almost perfectly, and he'd had a custom thick plastic made to keep it safe. Here, he hosted games every weekend that went on for hours. Stinky boys and men lumbered down the decrepit wooden stairs with their takeout and Mountain Dew. The first few times, I listened in as I passed, but it was always boring. They talked like there were real monsters to be fought. Like sitting there next to the old washer and dryer we got for seventy bucks on Craigslist would do any good even if there were. The game got rid of him for the whole weekend.

Until the fire.

It was a rarity that I would nap like this, in the middle of a Saturday, but I had just bought my first pair of size six pants and I could give myself a break. I'd been taking boxing classes at an old, seemingly authentic gym where all the heavy bags were held together with tape and the ring was barely keeping it together. Women weren't common there, but the men weren't bothered by it. "Women only" sessions were forced into being by a tiny blonde thing, not even one hundred pounds, who bobbed and weaved no matter what she was doing and had to fly sometimes hundreds of miles to fight someone in her weight category.

After my first session, I couldn't walk for three days. When I had to, I inched down stairs backwards. The warm up that day had been running three miles with a sprint in the last quarter mile to finish. One of the women threw up, kept on running straight to the big rusted garbage bin outside the gym. "That's how you know you did it right!" said the blonde. Throwing up was a good thing. It meant you probably wouldn't do it again that day and your stomach wouldn't mind the jabs and hooks.

It was a hell of a lot better than some cardio machine. I balanced it with good yoga, making a spreadsheet of all the free classes in the area and going studio to studio so I wouldn't have to pay. Yoga I'd tried once before, with Zadie in school. I didn't know anything about it then, and it was an elective at school, but it was held on the same wrestling mats where guys got hard-ons, and we just did one pose for two minutes that first day. It was partner yoga, and the teacher chose the partners. I was paired with a really fat girl, but on reflection, I was probably fatter than her. I hated feet, and we had to massage one another's toes the whole time. Then he told us we had to memorize these muscles and bones in the body I'd never heard of before, and I never went back for another class. This yoga was better. Sometimes it had me concentrating so hard I really did blank my mind out. It was so strange when the quiet took over. Afterward,

I felt different. Longer. Stretchier. Like I'd used my body as I should.

I don't know if it was the fighting or the peace-seeking that knocked me out, but I woke up when the smells began to reach for me under the bedroom door. God, it was hot. And it was just May, there shouldn't be this kind of warmth already. Grabbing a pair of old men's boxers in case one of the D&D guys was en route to or from the street with a cigarette, I lurched with sore legs and one eye open into the living room—and that's when I saw the flames.

They were crawling up the kitchen cabinets and tonguing at the ceiling. This place was old and the landlord didn't care, so there were no smoke alarms. On the stove was an abandoned pot of boiling oil with angry cubes of tofu in it. Tofu fries. One of Ezra's half-healthy favorites, but he was gone. What to dos ran through my head, and I knew water wasn't enough. I needed sand, but where the hell would I get it? We were too stupid to actually have a fire extinguisher, so I'd need to smother it. A stack of bath towels were crammed under the bathroom sink adjacent to the kitchen, and as I threw on the bathtub water to soak them before flopping them onto the pot, the stove and flames, I counted down the cost. These were the good kinds of towels, the thick kind from Macy's. Ten dollars, ten dollars, ten dollars more.

"Hey! Hey!" I yelled as the stack dwindled. Even now, even when the place was burning down, I couldn't say his name. I hated saying anyone's name, like I had a right to it. The muffled sounds, words like "dragon" and "quest" would sometimes leak up, but I never heard the stampeding feet I needed. Turns out, the flames were easier to simmer than I thought. We had three towels left over.

I assessed the damage before I showed him the fallout. For the most part, it was the wooden cabinets. The doors, really. Only a tiny part of the ceiling was black, and it didn't look chewed through. Maybe paint alone would fix it. Our grad school applications were somehow unsinged, still propped up solid next to the electric can opener.

"Hey!" I said, walking down the minimum four steps required and leaning down so I could see them all huddled around the ping pong table. We had all kinds of chairs down there, including two horrendous almost-matching beasts in neon-green vinyl that Ezra had found by the physics department dumpster.

"Hi," Ezra said, glancing up. He hated being bothered down here.

"Did you know you lit the kitchen on fire?"

"What?" That made him put those dumb multi-sided die down.

"The kitchen. It was on fire. I just put it out."

Eyes got big all around, and like obedient ducks they all finally waddled up the stairs.

"Holy shit," he said. "Why didn't you get me?"

"I tried. I used almost all the good towels."

I gave him a week, but all he did was call and admit it to the landlord. She said she was happy he was honest, and he said he'd take care of the repairs. That was all he ever did about it. The next weekend, when he was prepping to be the dungeon master and there was still soot and blackness all over the previously cream-colored kitchen, I knew. I'd be the one cleaning this up. And I planned it perfectly.

From Wal-Mart, I got bright white interior paint and a cheap flathead screwdriver. There was no saving the wooden doors, at least not for me. They needed cleaning and sanding, which I just couldn't do. Instead, I'd just take them off and call the kitchen French country without the glass panels. They had that on *Friends*, right? Maybe all over New York? Kitchen cabinets that were just open shelves so you could see what kind of cereal people liked, if their bowls matched and how neatly they stacked their plates.

The rest, the cabinet frames that were real bad I'd sand by hand and just cover up with paint. White, white, white, everywhere. I'd need to paint that whole kitchen, walls, ceiling and cabinetry in order to erase the tofu incident. When Ezra saw me turning my hands raw with the sandpaper, the stepladder and quarts of paint piled on the counter, he said, "You're going to do this all yourself?"

"Who else is going to do it?"

He pursed his lips before heading downstairs to wage war on imaginary dragons in his invisible wizard's robe.

It took eight hours, and the guys commented as they walked by. The one who was oldest and most often the dungeon master pointed out spots where the paint was running. Another said the color was too bright. Just one said Ezra should be helping. I smiled at them all and let their words wash over me. It didn't matter how dirty anything was, I could always just paint right over it.

In the end, I don't think it looked bad. In fact, all that white made the room look bigger. And the open shelves were trendy, but I had to rearrange the cabinets' guts and face all the canned foods outwards—arrange them by color instead of an order that made sense—because now all our guilt was on display. My area for Atkins bars took up three whole shelves. The white paint on my tan arms and thighs looked pretty, a dressing I didn't even know I wanted. In contrast, I looked like a real Indian and this was my war paint.

"I got in," Zadie said.

"What? Where?"

"Georgia, where I wanted. Uga."

"Huh?"

"UGA. They call it Uga. That's the name of the team's mascot, too. It's a bulldog. Do I have to be into football now?"

"I don't know. I don't think PhD students are expected to have a very big foam finger collection."

"Yeah. Mike's still waiting, but he's only really hopeful for Florida and Hawaii. Florida's not far from Georgia."

"So it's all official now."

"Yeah. I got on a list to get connected with other grad students looking for roommates. That might be a good idea, a way to meet people." I was jealous. What if Zadie liked her new roommates so much she forgot about me? They would probably be math people like her, and they could talk about the best ways to make kids not want to shoot themselves in the head when they were faced with story problems.

"Probably, yeah."

"It's going to be so weird," she said. "I've—you know, besides Australia, I've pretty much been in Oregon my whole life. This whole southern thing, I just don't know."

"It's only for a few years."

"It's for longer than undergrad." That was true. It was longer than we'd known each other. "What about you? Make any decisions yet?"

"I can send in the early application June first, and I may as well. It's the only place I'm applying, so I'm just letting the answer dictate what I do next. I don't know; it all went by so fast."

"What about Ezra?"

"He's doing it, too. We've just been sitting on the finished applications for weeks."

"Well. I hope it all works out."

"Yeah. Me, too."

The day of the Mayer awards, Ezra cut class to sit next to me, but I knew he didn't want to be there. I just didn't know why. If we couldn't at least pretend to soak up each other's happiness at this point, when we were still so young, then what was the point? Sarah sat in the same row but on the other side of the room, looking poignant with her big teeth forcing her lips ajar as always. First, they announced all the other awards. The little ones I hadn't qualified for or didn't bother to complete. My name was printed in the program, so that made it real. I'd keep it and put it in the hope chest Ben's parents had given me on my eighteenth birthday. It's what I'd wanted, but I had no clue why. It was a funny but kind of sad name for a container that looked like a short coffin.

Since it was the big award of the evening and most of the English department felt obligated to attend, there was a big lead-up to the announcement. The host went over who Mayer was (I forget), why the award is important (can't recall), and who the celebrity guest judge was this year (never heard of him). Finally, "This year's Mayer Awards goes, as a rarity, to a junior. Julia Tanner." I let the years of forced stage presence in all those plays, concerts, folk-telling festivals take over, and my slender legs carried me to the podium. I'd worn heels to find safety in the clouds, but didn't need them. The whole production seemed forced, and I couldn't help but glance at Sarah. She looked unhappy. This award should be en route to Iowa come September, and she knew it.

I'd prepared thank yous, even practiced reading the poem, but when I got up there they simply handed me a thick envelope with too-sharp edges, shook my hand, spun me around to smile for a photo, and encouraged the applause once more. That was it. I'd bared the ugliest part of my self and sold my dead dad out for this.

"Congratulations," Ezra whispered as I sat back down, but I felt like a sham.

"Thanks."

"Do you want to stick around after, for the appetizer reception thing?" I looked at the grim lineup of hard cheese gone soft, coffee, and tea. Student workers who got jobs in the school's catering department curdled together in stained aprons.

"Nah, let's just go." I'd rather celebrate, if that's what we were going to call it, over bunless burgers and salads at McManning's.

"It's early," he said. "I'm going to make the last part of my class then."

"Okay." I didn't go myself and hunker down over seasoned meat. Instead, I grabbed the gym bag out of the car and changed in the athletic department's cool, handicap bathroom. Down a long hall, I found the gym that hadn't been updated in years. A dark-skinned girl manned the desk and barely glanced at my student ID card. I could do this. I spent an hour straight on that elliptical machine, watching slim bodies all around me endlessly pound themselves into oblivion. I could become one of them.

15

AMANDA AND I were seeing each other more often. This happened when Chuck started disappearing—always had. "Ugh, I need a *break*," she said. "I'm with the kids *all the time*. It's exhausting. I love them and all, but . . ."

"You know what you should do? Get your mom to watch the kids. I'll take you out."

"I don't know. She doesn't like babysitting babies."

"They're her grandkids."

"Yeah. But she still hates Chuck."

"So she's making you suffer for that?"

"Kind of. I don't know. I'll ask her." I don't know what combination of words made her mom agree to it, but just like that Amanda was free, leaking breasts and all, on a Friday night. I didn't invite Zadie, because this was a redo. This is what should have been. When Amanda and I were teenagers, she was the one who flirted with going bad, hid bottles of vodka in the trunk of her first car even though she never had more than a sip. I don't know what she was hoarding them for, but her mom found them and went batshit insane. I'd heard that Amanda had held a few parties with some girl I barely knew when they were eighteen and on their own, but by then I was with Ben in Portland. By the time Amanda could really drink, she was pregnant and devoted to faking some kind of life she'd seen on television, one where swearing wasn't allowed and the wives always had makeup on.

"Where are we going?" she asked as I parked in Chinatown three blocks from The Slaughtered Goat.

"You'll see."

It always took Amanda hours to get ready. When we were younger, I thought it was because her thick black hair was so untameable, but now I knew better. She could spend forty minutes applying layer after layer of expensive creams and powders to her eyelids, gluing on one eyelash at a time to her Asian no-lash lids, then straightening, curling and straightening her hair again. Her outfits were designed to be tight at the chest, flow over her belly, and skim her thighs which she'd always hated. She had always been thick there, with big calves that couldn't be squeezed into any boot. Me, I'd decided that only fat girls wore cardigans and shrugs, useless attempts to hide their worst bits. I had taken to thin, tight T-shirts that went to the elbows to hide my upper arms and somehow danced over my stomach making it look flat. And jeans, because I knew that the tag inside said the right thing. Said what Julia Robert's character in *Pretty Woman* wore.

"Oh. My. God. What these girls are wearing . . ." she said. I'd never thought of it like that. They teetered on heels way too high and definitely when they sat on barstools their skirts were so short they must plaster their labias all over the vinyl. You could wear a G-string, a thong at most, in those skirts, and I wondered how many vagina juice marks I'd soaked into my own clothes and skin over the years.

You couldn't really tell the Goat was a gay bar from the outside, not if you'd never really been to a club. The rainbows woven into the Budweiser signs were discreet, and really there were rainbow flags all over the block anyway. I didn't even know if Amanda knew what that meant. As women, the cover was five dollars. It was free for men.

"Now this is the place to go to meet boys!" Amanda said

as I led her in. So many were lovely with the fresh lines in their hair, their shirts unbuttoned just so and their searching eyes that crawled over us and dismissed us all at once.

"Well . . ." I said, pointing to the men in nothing but tighty whities dancing on the bar in back. The screens all over the place showing hardcore gay porn instead of the football and soccer that you'd expect.

"Oh my god! What the—is this a . . . is this a gay bar?"

"Uhm, yeah," I said.

"You took me to a gay bar?"

"Yeah . . ."

"You should have warned me!" she said with a laugh, that same all-in, big open-mouthed laugh I'd fallen for over ten years ago. For a second, I glimpsed the Amanda I'd met, the one who didn't care if my mom hated her because she wasn't going to let me walk around middle school with poodle bangs anymore. The one whose style I loved so much I couldn't help but copy. If she pointed out a shirt she liked at the mall, I'd go right back the next day with my saved up bills in hand to buy it. I envied her little netting of stuffed animals in the corner of her bedroom, such a unique way to be girly. At her house, it was the first time I ever had a bagel. It sounds strange, but it's true. Bagels and cream cheese just weren't something my mom ate, so she never bought it and I never tried it. They were amazing.

In between waiting in line for the unisex bathroom and pawing through the free condoms while we held in our pee, the bright colored drinks and the letting men grope and grab us, I relished in what could have been. What could have happened if it weren't for Chuck and babies.

"You're *so* gorgeous!" said a tall blond man to Amanda, and she soaked up the compliments. Why her? Why was it always her? I was at least four sizes smaller than her now, truly a size six, but that didn't make me pretty. I didn't even want the blond man, wouldn't have if I were looking and he were straight. But I wanted the attention. "Can I kiss you?" he asked her, and she opened her eyes big at me.

Without waiting, he swooped in and swallowed her plump lips with his. It just lasted a second, and his boyfriend looked on in boredom. "Thanks, doll!" he said as he wandered away.

"Oh, shit! Oh, shit! Don't tell Chuck. Don't tell Chuck," she said.

"Tell him what? That some flaming gay man kissed you? I doubt he'd care."

"He'd care, okay? He'd flip shit."

"Okay, okay. It's not like I was going to tell him anyway." Chuck had always been the crazy kind of jealous, even as he crawled from one girl's bed to another in high school all while claiming Amanda was his soul mate. She was a flirt, sure, but he was the cheater. It's what had broken them up countless times. I think it's partially why she had that abortion at seventeen, but then let the next one take just three years later.

The rest of the night was eaten up with rehashing the kiss, the only one besides Chuck's Amanda had known in years. I didn't get the big deal. Ezra and I had an agreement. I could kiss all the girls I wanted because he was supposed to think it was hot. GOGA, girl on girl action. Really, I just don't think he cared. For me, women, men, girls, boys, it didn't matter. Sometimes I craved softness, other times the big roughness I knew other men offered, but if all I could officially get was softness that was fine with me. But I couldn't picture women when I was with Ezra, even for all his petiteness. So men it was. Faceless men crafted in my mind, and I always wanted to be on top so I could pretend Ezra was taller than he was.

That blond guy though, he ruined the night. Got Amanda all worked up with fodder for girl gossip for years to come. I shouldn't be mad at him, shouldn't let it get to me. I should feel bad, feel sorry for her that a brief kiss from a gay man was the highlight of her life. In that moment, she didn't have chafed and leaking nipples or a husband that came home just three or four nights a week. Why couldn't I just let her have that?

"You know, men love big boobs so this is totally your element," I told her. Big boobs. I used to be fat, I knew what that meant. It was the fat girl compliment. Unless they were fake, you couldn't have big boobs and be skinny. But you couldn't exactly get mad at someone for calling out your huge tits either, especially when you let them spill out like Amanda did. Her face didn't quite fall, but it changed.

"The incredible side effect of having kids," she said. *I'm not fat, I'm breastfeeding.*

"Yeah," I said. What was wrong with me?

I was boxing three times per week now and no longer got that kind of paralysis sore. I don't know if I was looking any stronger, any more toned, but I was lifting more. Hitting harder. They were letting me spar with the men, the ones who would be a little gentle and not let their testosterone take over when a woman hit them. I kept checking my arms and stomach in the mirror though, and they looked the same. What they don't tell you about losing weight is that it just doesn't disappear. You can't go back, and we all have different amounts of elasticity and collagen. But that disappears with time. I was left with fat pockets and loose skin that looked like crepe paper. Like an old woman with paper-thin skin that looked ready to tear.

I was still with the Atkins, had accepted some kind of truce with the elliptical machine, and could finally jump rope for more than two minutes without messing up. But I still didn't look like some of the girls my age. Like Stephanie had looked. My bellybutton still disappeared under skin rolls when I saw down, and my upper arms looked ready to take flight if I wore cap sleeves too short. My thighs, if you looked close, folded into each other near my groin. The fat that had filled everything out, made me look tight, wasn't there anymore. I was a deflated balloon and no amount of shadow boxing or sparring would fix it. It wasn't fair. I'd cut out so many foods, carved out so much time for sweating, lifting, panting, and it still wasn't enough.

And Ezra? He hadn't said anything about it—but he hadn't said anything when I'd gotten fat either. Maybe he didn't care, didn't notice, or both. Is that what love was supposed to be like? Did he not even realize that I was way too good for him now? The cancer had whimpered away from him, but he'd never be the same. It had taken some big pinches of what little muscle he had, and now it seemed he'd always have T-rex arms. It didn't help that he had a penchant for holding his forearm jutting out from his body, hands limply hanging at the end, like he was waiting for someone to slip a purse onto his skinny wrist. Once, when his half-sibling's father was in town and the whole bastardized family gathered for an awkward lunch, the gruff old man had mimed Ezra's effeminate way of standing. "Yeah, I tend to do that," Ezra said as he forced his arms down. I was embarrassed, but for me. Not him.

"I'm sending in our applications today," I told him.

"For what?"

"For grad school," I said, pointedly. He didn't care at all.

"Oh. Okay."

It was very anticlimactic, even though I drove to the post office just in case the mailman, perpetually drunk and singing as he slung envelopes into waiting slots and metal boxes, misplaced them. Once they were in the big, blue containers, it was done. Whatever was going to happen, I couldn't do much now. Except keep getting thinner. Stronger. I wanted the remaining traces of baby fat to slide off my cheeks like melting butter.

Not a lot of people apply to a nonterminal master's program at a state university, especially for early admission, so decisions were made fast. When the envelopes came, they were slender like just one piece of paper was inside. I knew what that meant from the movies. But I was wrong.

"We got in," I told Ezra as I tore them open. The congratulatory letters were identical, and they misspelled his last name. "Wow, cool," he said.

I didn't know what I was supposed to be feeling, but it was something like relief. Not because a big dream had come true, although it kind of had. Three years ago, I didn't even know what grad school was, and now I was going. Bachelor's degrees, I'd figured out they didn't mean anything. They were the high school diplomas of our era. But it was more like a relief when you finally throw up after having food poisoning. You feel better because the hard part's over, but the look of the sick in the toilet still makes your stomach turn. I'd done the math. I knew how much grad school would cost with living expenses and all. About thirty thousand per year for two years, and there was absolute no funding for English or writing programs. It would be all student loans all over again—sixty thousand more. And I knew how quick college years went by so I could just imagine grad school, but I didn't care. I'd sign up for it once more because I didn't know what else to do. Ezra, for him it wasn't a big deal. He didn't have any loans, so he was starting from scratch. Sixty thousand doesn't sound like much when you don't already have fifty thousand lurking in a far off lending bank.

To celebrate, we went to The Cheesecake Factory. It had opened just last year, and the lines had finally dwindled. But really, I liked it because they had a sugar-free low-carb cheesecake that I could eat with little guilt. I didn't even like cheesecake, but I got to feel normal. And I'd become used to it, asking for salads instead of fries. It didn't feel like a celebration though, even though both of us had made the calls to our moms that morning.

Now, my mom was used to it all. She expected it. She probably didn't understand why I wasn't starting med school. "My baby's going to grad school!" she cooed over the phone, and then I had to explain what grad school was.

"So it's like being a doctor?"

"No, that's a doctoral degree."

"Then what's a master's degree?"

"It's what comes after a bachelor's degree."

"And that's a four-year degree? The bachelor?"

"Yes, it's what I've been doing the past three years."

"So how is a master degree different if it's shorter?" It was pointless.

Ezra's mom knew what a master's program was, but he'd always been expected to shine. He was no longer the golden boy, the huge fish in that little Mitchell pond. He was the golden whale who had beat cancer. I thought he was joking when the port was removed from his chest during radiation treatment and he said, "I should get a big tattoo of 'Survivor' on my back." He didn't have a single piece of ink on him besides the little blue points from chemo so the doctors could keep track of what they'd done and where. All he had was keratosis, a condition where the skin looked perpetually like goose flesh. I was the one with an unfortunate sorority tattoo on my lower back, haloed by a pentacle tattoo above it. Both had partially keloided.

"Okay, Beyoncé," I'd told him, and that had been the last of it.

At least his mom reacted a little more normally, although she'd been expecting it. She didn't like that he was randomly getting a master's in writing, though, after years of him being all about engineering. "When he was five," she'd told me, "he would take apart clocks, toasters, anything, just to see how they worked and put them back together again."

"You let him do that? At five?"

She looked at me like *I* was the freak for questioning whether you should let a child who couldn't tie their shoes tear apart electronics. "He'd just do it anyway," she said.

Over cheesecake pregnant with Splenda and overpriced cocktails, I watched Ezra shove the good brown bread between his too-little teeth and felt the weight settle on me. Going to grad school together, that meant something. The cement stiffened around us.

16

THERE WERE NO big bangs when Zadie went, she left like she came (quietly). It was dinner at a chain restaurant with her family, me making Ezra stay home so I didn't have to watch him watch her. Her little sister, pudgy at eleven, saying she was hungry as she forked more noodles into her mouth. I'm good at walking away. At letting others. You just throw up the stoppers inside you and feel nothing. It's only later, with another round of hugs at the airport while we waved Zadie off to a remote research hub in the California woods to dive into make believe with Mike that I snuggled into nostalgia for comfort.

Soothing, for me, had always been in horror movies. The ones I grew up with. Every friendship, from those I made and lost in kindergarten to Amanda when we were eleven, was ritualized by my introducing them to dyed corn syrup blood and macabre aesthetics. My tastes lived squarely in the eighties like wide hips and heavy bones that wouldn't move. The night Zadie left, it was *The Howling 3*, the one that began with heartbreak. I didn't know 'til I was grown that this werewolf was real.

"That's Benjamin," I told Ezra as the thylacine paced back and forth on the screen.

"Who?"

"Benjamin. The last thylacine caught on camera. They're extinct now. This one, he died of loneliness in a British zoo. Just like Gregor."

"How much have you smoked?"

"Not that much."

"It's just a movie."

"No. This is real. This footage is real. They had a bounty on their heads, thylacines. They were hunted for money, but they only came out at night. They were so timid, sometimes when hunters spotted them the poor things would get paralyzed in fear."

"Why are you watching this?"

"I like it. I just found out it was real though. Some . . . I don't know, some online site about it."

"Why's it in the movie, then?"

"A lot of people think thylacines, Tasmanian tigers, are the basis for a lot of werewolf myths. Probably because they were so scared of people, they were rarely seen."

"Tasmanian devils?"

"No, tigers. These are different." Wasn't he listening? On the screen, Benjamin paced in his tiny confines, stretched his mouth in silence. There was no sound, the footage was too old. "He's so sad."

"Maybe he's chuffing, you don't know," said Ezra.

"Chuffing?"

"You know, it's the sound tigers make when they're communicating."

"I doubt it. He looks like he's screaming."

"Well. Maybe."

"Hey," I said. "There's a preserved one, in London. At the Natural History Museum. I want to see it someday."

"Only you would want to go halfway around the world to see a dead animal."

"He wasn't just an animal."

Last years were always easy in the hardest ways. The obligatory classes I had to take, no choices, were done so I packed the quarter full of upper division, obscure classes with long names. I would be two classes away from a second bachelor's degree in history if I wanted, but the requirement came with American history courses and I only had eyes for England. I loved the fairy tales from the hard years, reading about how fog was dragon's breath and King Arthur's mother was tricked into sex. They didn't call it rape back then. Now, I was normal sized, I guess, perpetually tan with only the inner creases of my hands giving away my whiteness.

The graduate program was letting us start classes the following summer, offering only a one-week interim of a break after commencement. The anticipation of a stress-fueled yet flawless segue was the catalyst for our last year. Come summer, Ezra and I would be in some classrooms together. It would choke my voice even more than what already happened in those brittle wooden seats. I had asked him so many times if he thought I was stupid because he was so smart. But now I'd have no choice but to show him.

"Hey! Julia!" Donna came bounding after me as I crossed the Park Blocks. She looked the same, her arms filled out a little more and her hair snipped to mid-back. "I haven't seen you in forever."

"Yeah, well. I took alum status early."

"I know. It's recruitment season," she said.

"I know."

"So we're—we're all supposed to ask alumni if they'd like to donate."

"Donate what?"

"For recruitment supplies. You know, twinkle lights, refreshments, that sort of stuff."

"I'm still in school. You guys know that, right? I'm living off student loans and work-study money." Okay, so the student loan thing was a lie thanks to the bundles of scholarships, but she didn't need to know that.

"I know. But we're not asking for that much—"

"I'm sorry, but when my dad died? And Ezra was in

chemo? The 'funds' that were put aside to help people in those kinds of situations were given to a girl to correct a bad haircut. I couldn't afford to fly to my dad's funeral. I had to take all online classes so I could take Ezra to the hospital every day. So, no, I'm not giving you any money."

"You don't have to be so selfish, you know. That's why nobody liked you." It was strange, to hear hate coming out of that freakishly squeaky mouth.

"I doubt that's the only reason why."

My summer classes had spread their legs and shown themselves, too tired to keep prim and clenched at this level of heat. Like the almost-500 level British medieval history class filled with history majors on the brink of graduation and I was besting them all. The professor would write the final grades of tests on the board, no names, and I was routinely the only one above 95 percent. Not from being smart. I recorded all the lectures, listened to them and wrote them down, then memorized them page by page by page. I could retain about fifteen pages, verbatim, but only for a few days and then they fizzled out like flat Coke. I simply spit back out on tests what the professor said. She thought I was brilliant because I regurgitated her own words. I guess that's how you make it in college. But I was falling in love. With the stories, with the history. For the rest of my life, I'd remember the year the Magna Carta was created. Some things, some dates, became imprinted onto my brain.

Seniors got perfunctory letters from the university early, already pitching us higher quality robes and add-ons to our commencement hats. The letters were signed Andrea Wochit, Commencement Coordinator. I'd forgotten all about her. I don't know if it was running into Donna or what, but I had to write to Mrs. Wochit, tell her that she could stop wondering if she'd made another mistake. She probably didn't remember me, and that was okay. I could still try to make her feel good, show myself I wasn't all selfish.

Mrs. Wochit, You probably don't remember me . . . What a

clichéd way to start. But it was true. *I came to your office three years ago when I was a freshman. I'd failed most of my classes during my first quarter, and you were kind enough to give me another chance. I promised you that you wouldn't regret it, and I just wanted to tell you that I'm graduating this year with a 3.45 gpa and am starting graduate school next summer pursuing a master's degree in writing. Thank you for taking a chance on me, I will be forever grateful.* There. Call me selfish now.

I didn't hear from Zadie until she'd flitted off to Georgia, but I hadn't expected to. There was no internet where the birds were, the nearest phone a ten-mile hike away. When she finally did call, that sweat-drenched Labor Day weekend from Georgia, there was a calm in her voice. A reserve. Something had died in there.

"We broke up," she said.

"What? Why? When?" This, I hadn't expected.

"Uhm, actually pretty much the day he picked me up at the airport."

"Three, two months ago?"

"Yeah . . ."

"Then where have you been?"

"Oh, I was there. We were there."

"What are you talking about?"

"Mike, he—when he picked me up? At the airport? He said it, we, this just wasn't working for him." She'd practiced this.

"So . . ."

"I don't . . . I asked him. You know? If we could just have the summer. I . . . I think I kinda begged him."

"You begged him. For a summer."

"Yeah. I know, I know." Like I knew I wasn't supposed to say anything about that.

"Are you okay? Are you in Georgia?"

"Yeah, I think so. And yeah, I just got here yesterday. I'm in a hotel right now, the stuff I shipped in June is all in storage." I could hear her deep breaths, could almost see the wells in her eyes. "I don't know what the hell I'm do-ing."

"At least I know how that is." Zadie just breathed, steady and deep, through the holiday. Yeah, some dates I'll re-member forever.

Like Halloween and Ezra in his pink prom dress. We counted that as our anniversary because we couldn't re-member the real date we went out. All we could remember was the night he was half-woman, I was Lara Croft, and I watched him get mauled by a fat black girl who had dropped out of school spring term of our freshman year.

I hated celebrating those anniversaries, counting them down. With each year, I felt accomplished though. Like I'd lasted. Already, we were talking about what to do this year. It would be three years, and on November 1 it would offi-cially be my longest relationship. Longer than Ben. That counted for something, right?

"What do you want to do for Halloween?" Ezra had asked me.

"I don't know. The usual, I guess. Dinner, whatever."

"No party?" he asked. I was partied out. Zadie was gone, and our circle had dwindled. A lot of our friends, even the ones filling out the outskirts of our lives, had graduated or otherwise moved on. It was just us, in our little duplex on the other side of the river. But his sisters were there, now. Both the younger ones had gone to the same university as us, following dutifully in his footsteps. It was Betty's first year, and she was in the real freshman dorms, in Ophelia. Ezra had tried to help her, I'd seen it. But in the third week, when he asked her if she needed help with anything or wanted to get lunch, she'd emailed him saying, *I'm a very busy person. You need to make an appointment if you want to see me.* I'd thought it was a joke, but it wasn't. Ann, she'd flown under the radar her first year on campus. This year, she'd told me she was rushing "my" sorority a year late, asking if it was a good way to meet people. I'd told her yes, because that's what she wanted to hear. It would seal all of us together a little closer, tighten those threads so it would be too hard to get untangled.

"No. No party."

"Can you believe it's been three years?" he asked. We were in our chosen spots in the living room. Me curled into the oversized red leather chair pushed against the windows, letting the light in for reading. He was hunkered on the couch, game control in his grips. It was the matching couch and chair set I'd bought right before he moved in with his chemo schedule. The legs on the couch had immediately broken, and for six months I used steel upside down bowls in their place, but I eventually I just gave up and let the couch rest right on the dusty floor. Japanese style.

"That's crazy," I said. I didn't know if that was a hint, but he never really talked about getting married. Shouldn't we? I mean, what else was there now? "How long do you think we'll, you know, date . . ." It was the closest I could come to asking.

"Before?" he asked, eyes stuck to the paused screen. Mario and Peach were eternally stuck on Rainbow Road, her pink dress flickering.

"You know. Something more."

"Oh. I don't know. Not . . . you know, I could never marry someone with credit card debt."

"You mean . . ." I had about three thousand dollars left to pay off. I should have done it with my loans or scholarships, my little paychecks or something, but I never did. They were from a defunct account Ben had set up in my name. All his clothes, colognes, and shoes were still following me around, just without him in them.

"It's just not very responsible," he said. So that was it. He had an excuse, one he'd tucked deep inside to pull out all these years later.

"I was sixteen," I said. It was true. The credit cards had come flying in when Ben applied with the right name, right social security number, wrong birth year. Nobody cared, but now it was too late. "You know after seven years in collections they fall off your credit score anyway."

"That's what you say."

"I'm not making it up."

"I wouldn't know," he said, pressing the start button as he lost himself in careening down a make-believe, floating raceway.

Amanda asked me to go with her for Thanksgiving break to southern Oregon, stay at her family's home if my mom's was too hostile, and for the sheer escape route, I agreed. Chuck, he said I was a bad influence. She'd told him about the kiss at the Goat after all, and he blamed me. Like I was the one in rehab. Like I was the one who flirted with their next door neighbor so hard there was a permanent desire path worn into the landscaping between their house and his. Chuck had to work, Black Friday and all, and Amanda was determined to give the kids the kind of winter holidays she thinks she had. The kind with big, juicy turkeys, falling asleep while football droned on, and good pictures.

It was about time for my obligatory showing up at my mom's anyway. And now I'd have a getaway plans if things went bad.

But they didn't. I think she was learning, my mom, that I was more like my dad than she thought. I had that wander in me, that's what he'd said. When I was about twelve, he was grilling burgers out near the barn. Past the swimming pool my mom had demanded be put in so she could sunbathe topless, hosing herself off every five minutes. The water went dry, the pool liner cracked, and the pony we had fell in four times. A Shetland pony, how stupid. My mom adored all animals that were a little off, stunted or squishy-faced. She said the pony was for me, for my fifth birthday, but everyone knew it was for her.

My dad, pressing the blood out of the patties and putting yellow cheese slices on half of them, looked at me—really looked at me—and didn't care if the meat burned. "You be careful," he'd said.

"What?" I wasn't doing anything. Wasn't even near the grill.

"You have that wander in you. Just like me. Be careful with that."

I didn't know what he meant then, but I got it now. It was easy for me to leave. To just turn around and go. I didn't think about the consequences and was too bullheaded to think I'd ever made a wrong turn. My mom, she liked to bluff, and I called them every time.

When Amanda dropped me off, my mom demanded a hug as always. I gave her the shortest kind I could. The kind where it's clear you don't want to touch the person.

"You lost more weight," she said. There was envy in her mucus voice.

"No, I don't think so," I said. I didn't really know, but I wore the same size.

"You did," she said.

"Amanda invited us to their place for Thanks—"

"Julia, I don't want to be around *those* people."

"What people?"

"You know what I mean." And the thing is, I did. I knew exactly. Normal people that required normal small talk and normal traditions.

"Okay, well—"

"We can just order a pizza. Or go to Food 4 Less. Whatever you want." Tacking "whatever you want" onto the end of a very short list of options is supposed to make you feel like you're spoiled. But I was too tired from the drive to fight it.

"Okay, okay." Thanksgiving was a stack of rentals from Blockbuster, takeout pizza where I systematically scraped all the toppings off, and Diet Rite. My mom refused to buy Diet Coke or Diet Pepsi. Diet Rite was cheaper, and she made me carry in eight 12-packs from the store.

"I can't carry them myself," she said. This is what our visits were becoming. Running errands for her, while she made me carry all the heavy things and then told me I was going to throw my back out. I wanted to tell her "I'm not weak like you," but I didn't. Maybe I was, I didn't know.

We'd never been big on Thanksgiving anyway. In the early days, when Papo and Mamo were alive, they'd come over and my dad would put the dining table in the living room, pull the leaf out of storage, and make the vinyl topped table stretch from the couch to the television. My mom always made the same thing, complete with cranberry sauce out of the can. I loved that sauce, the chemical goodness of it. When Mamo died, then Papo, all that stopped. Thanksgiving became the first of the season when my dad would disappear. It usually wasn't 'til closer to Christmas, but sometimes he'd start the binging early. For at least three days, somewhere between Thanksgiving and Christmas, he just wouldn't come home. Just show up days or even a week later smelling of piss and alcohol. I was supposed to pretend I hadn't noticed he'd been gone.

It was an uneventful visit this time, and that's the best I could hope for. When Amanda picked me up to drive back to Portland, my mom cried. I hated that, hated when anyone cried. It made me feel awkward, and I didn't know what to do with my hands.

"I'll miss you," she said, hugging me in the driveway. "Love you. Say it." She didn't even give me a chance had I wanted to.

"Yeah, love you too," I said, and Amanda rolled her eyes from behind the tinted windows.

17

I GOT A ROOMMATE! Zadie's email began. The subject was "Georgia." *I call her Fivehead because her forehead's so big. She's southern but from South Carolina, and blonde. She's single and has been living here since undergrad. She had a bedroom for rent in a house, but everyone has houses here so that's not really special or anything. Living with a stranger is odd, but at least she knows the area and where to go. We're going for a trivia night with some of her friends next week. Apparently that's a big thing here. Oh, yeah. And I signed up for online dating but I've only met two men. It's been interesting so far. (No winners.)*

I'd already promised. The week between graduation and grad school for me, I would go to Georgia. The little college town was two hours from Atlanta, and Zadie and I would squeeze in a night in the city. But I was nervous. She'd already told me about all the southern girls and I pictured them with their thin, lithe legs and little bodies. Their perfect hair and perfect makeup. "Southern girls don't sweat. They *glisten*," Zadie had told me. They had the ability to redefine their bodily functions.

Zadie had it all planned, her whole life, even after the Mike fallout. Not me, and I don't know why I did this. The scholarships I had were enough to cover tuition, books, rent, all the basics, but Ezra had thrown up a challenge with that whole credit card marriage equation. Quietly, without him knowing, I took out a few more thousand dollars in students loans—the maximum I could, given the school's supplied budget which outlined every student's need. And I paid off those credit cards. I didn't care that doing so would reboot the whole credit process, nudging them onto my credit report for several more years. All I cared about was proving him wrong, even as I felt myself dig a deeper hole with room for two. One I wasn't sure I wanted to be in.

Heading into January, the prize committees and all the random clubs and organizations I technically belonged to just because of my Indian blood (but never bothered with) began sending the invitations. The Native American student graduation ceremony where I would know nobody, but every participant got a queen-sized Pendleton blanket smudged by a medicine man. I knew these blankets cost hundreds of dollars, so I signed up. The diversity recognition ceremony where the university gathered the most unwhite looking students to showcase how diverse they were. Clearly, they didn't know what I looked like when they sent this invitation but must have salivated over my tribal enrollment status. There were English department ceremonies, a freckling of other minority-related invitations, the ceremony for women leaders, and one for students who wrote the best essays. I RSVP'd to all of them, collecting my certificates, plaques, and ribbons to stick in the hope chest.

Ezra went to all of them, too, but his excitement tangibly waned by the fourth. He didn't want to be there; it was obvious. He slumped next to me, a Nigerian student on the other side of him and women chattering in Spanish behind him. It was taking forever to begin, and little groups still scrounged around over the refreshment tables, looking for the freshest strawberries and thickest ham slices. "What's wrong?" I whispered to him, although I knew. His hands were clasped at his crotch. God, I hated his chewed-up fingernails. The smell his sweat leaked into all his clothes.

All the clothes I always washed.

"Nothing," he said, in that fake upward lilt that said, *We both know that's a lie. Ask me more.*

"Okay," I said. I wouldn't give him that, that probing he wanted. Instead, I stood up when my name was called and didn't care about the disapproving glances from all the other people with their matching ribbons who wondered where my color was.

But I got mad. Real mad, especially as I sat next to Ezra for an agonizing hour more. The chairs were little and crammed so close together some of their legs intertwined. I would not let my thigh touch his. I would not. It didn't matter that, to achieve this, I had to scoop my legs under the chair and my feet went numb from the cramming.

"Seriously, what's wrong?" I asked him as we filed out. I'd had an hour to marinate and the anger was starting to blister right below the surface. Hot and crimson like a real redskin.

"*Nothing,*" he said again. I knew this game. Once, in the early years, probably when I was just starting to go to fat, we were wandering around the mall when I realized I'd never seen him upset. Well, upset maybe, but not really, truly mad. So I asked him. I asked him to act like it as we rode down the escalators. And he did, so happily, refusing to speak and jerking his shoulders away from me. How easy it was for him, and he wouldn't break character. He made me beg him to. Not this time. There would be no pleases.

"You're jealous, aren't you?" I asked him. I was ready to battle.

"Yeah," he said. It was an honest answer and not what I was expecting.

"But . . . why?" I really didn't know.

"It's just . . . you're getting all these things. Going to all these award events. And what? Just because you're Indian? You don't even look it, and I worked so hard for so long. I had cancer and am still graduating on time. But because I'm a white male getting an engineering degree, that doesn't mean shit."

"You're mad at me because of that? *That's* not my fault."
I refused to yell or scream, almost never did. My rage was captured in a slow, steady rhythm that was nothing like my mothers. *Nothing.* And the swearing, whenever I could, I kept it out of my throat. I bristled when others threw about their *fucks* and *shits* in anger, so much like my mom. Uneducated, fearful, unimaginative—that's what I told people I thought of swearing. It put me instantly above them. But the reality was, it just reminded me of her.

"I didn't say it was your fault," he said. "It's just not fair, and I know how juvenile that sounds."

"Yeah, it does," I said. "Oh, by the way? I paid off the credit card debt."

"How?" he asked. As if he knew what I did with my money.

"Not really any of your business. Maybe the companies just forgave it when I told them how *white* I really look."

He had nothing to say to that.

I was given a choice, though likely from Nationals and not "my" local sorority. I could wear a Phi Z sash for graduation, complete with the white rose, the official flower. Maybe the offer letter was sent to all graduating seniors, whether they had alumni status or not. But the sash was only $60 and I'd earned it, hadn't I? Hadn't I don't enough to sling that yellow ribbon around my neck? And so I ordered it, but then I felt bad. Ezra and I would, of course, go to graduation together and celebrate with his family afterward. My mom, I told her not to bother coming. It was too many people, too long an event, and she didn't kick up a bit of fuss about it. Strange, that after a lifetime of being told I was going to college—no exceptions—and she didn't give a shit about attending. But Ezra, we'd be surrounded by his family, and I'd be decorated like a child was given free reign at the Christmas tree, and he would be all bare branches. So I ordered a sash for him, too, with his fraternity letters. It was designed by their national fraternity, and I had no say in this, but it was still so much plainer than mine. When they came, I pushed them to the corner of the closet shelf.

"I've been thinking," I told Ezra when he came home, that stupid little boy backpack slung over one shoulder. "What do you think of studying abroad? For the second part of grad school?"

"I don't know. I haven't thought about it at all," he said, dumping the backpack and his worn out shoes in front of the couch.

"Well, I have," I said. "I actually went to the study abroad office today? The one just off campus? They have a list of schools and organizations they work with overseas. I was thinking—I don't want to attend classes abroad, you know? But maybe do an internship abroad, once the core classes are done here?"

"Doesn't it cost a lot?" he asked.

"It costs a lot to go to school in other places, yeah," I said. "But they have a few paid internships. We could probably make enough for cost of living. Plus any financial aid from over here." We'd already had the financial aid talk. There was no funding for writing programs at a nonterminal degree granting school. Both of us would be on student loans for grad school, save for a smattering of little scholarships I could drum up that would be basically worthless.

"Well, I don't . . . where are you thinking?"

"London."

"Of course."

Yeah. Of course. There was no other option. I was smitten with *Beowulf* from my medieval lit class and didn't give a shit what Woody Allen had to say about it. Never trust a person who likes *Beowulf*, old man? How about never trust a person who fucks your adopted daughter. He didn't know what he was talking about. But it was Grendel I adored, not Beowulf. "He could not come near the gift-throne, the treasure, because of God. He knew not his love." Grendel was not the monster, but beautiful hero-monsters are so much harder to see than the ugly beasts who terrify us. I would see Beowulf, the real *Beowulf*. The original book was in the British Library, with a page turned each day. Not even a fire could silence it.

"So, what do you think?" I asked.

"Sure. Why not," he said. Maybe he didn't think I was serious, but did he really doubt my bullheaded follow through after all this time?

"I'm serious, you know," I said. And I was. That bitch at the study abroad office, probably the same age as me, had taken one look at me and my instant attraction to London and thought she had me pegged.

"You don't have to choose a country where English is spoken," she'd said. "There are *many* programs that are suitable for—"

"That's not why I'm looking at London," I'd told her, cutting her off.

"Of course not," she said. *Anglophile*, her eyes decided. "You know, these internships that you're looking at, there are very few that are paid. These are actually the only two in England, and should really be reserved for students who *truly*—"

"Are you saying I can't apply?" I asked her.

"No. I mean, I can't stop you."

"Who decides who gets the internships?" I'd asked.

"The organizations," she admitted. So she had nothing to do with it. The entire university here had nothing to do with it. Was it cheating, robbing some fictional student, out of a paid internship just by applying? I figured my Nativeness wouldn't count for much in England. They probably thought they'd slaughtered us all after Pocahontas anyway. It would be genuinely merit-based, my application. So how had she made me feel bad about taking the applications?

I didn't acknowledge her when I left.

Ezra and I, we didn't tell anyone about the applications. About getting our first passports ever, until we had to tell his mom. It was like having a Jewish baby—you didn't say a word until you were certain. Getting his passport was a nightmare. On his birth certificate, his mom had switched up his middle and last name, but on every other document it was the other way around. "We can't accept this," the post office worker told Ezra, studying his birth certificate.

"What else can I give you?" he asked. "This is my birth certificate."

"You need to get it corrected. Or get the other paperwork corrected. I don't really care which, but they need to match."

It took weeks of proving his mother's slip up was to blame, not that he was trying to trick the US government into giving him a fake passport. And his mom laughed at the whole thing. "I was high on birthing drugs, and your dad was pissing me off," she said. "I figured, I'll show him. I'll put his last name as the *middle* name. Sorry about that."

But when the passports finally arrived, they looked official, clean and empty. I hated how round my face looked, how the heavy eye makeup made me look like a middle-aged woman trying way too hard. Is that really how I looked? I tried going a day, out into the world, without full eyeshadow, liner, and mascara. Without making my eyes look more hooded by layering darker colors into the crease, without putting white highlighter on my eyebrow bone, but I looked naked and wrong. So I shaved my head instead.

Okay, it wasn't that simple. My hair stretched to the small of my back, or at least it did when I pulled it straight. And it was all virgin hair, the years of bleach and box colors finally grown out. I'd grown it so long, and now what? Get myself a cute little bob or cut it to my shoulder blades in layers? I was somewhat thinnish-normal-sized, and those were the kinds of women who could get away with a buzz cut, right? While Ezra was in class, I walked to the trendy barbershop down the street where they served you a cheap beer while other people's hair stuck to your pants.

"Just buzz it off," I told the guy.

"Uh, buzz it?" he asked.

"Yeah, you know. Like GI Jane."

He didn't believe me. Instead, he spent forty-five minutes giving me the shortest version of a pixie cut he could imagine, refusing to remove a few wisps along the forehead he probably thought was feminine, like the kiss curl of an Eton crop. "Do you like it? Do you like it?" he kept asking me, but what could I tell him? That I liked feeling my head get lighter as long locks cascaded down the chair? That it felt like he'd largely removed a suffocating rubber mask someone had glued onto my neck for years? I could tell he wouldn't go all the way, so I said yes and paid him thirty dollars for something I'd have to finish myself.

It's cold, when you have almost no hair. I don't know how men do it. I expected people to stare, to look or at least acknowledge as I walked the six blocks home, but nobody did. When I tripped over my reflection in store windows, though, I didn't look like a little elfish waif. I wasn't Audrey Hepburn. And, god, I really needed that makeup now.

It wasn't enough to sway me, though. At home, I dug Ezra's electric clippers out of the bathroom drawer, the one I'd gifted him one Christmas when he spent months saying he wanted one, but then never used. Setting the blades to military length, I finished up the job, scattering my own little hairs across the counter. There. At least my head didn't have any weird lumps or peaks. That would have been embarrassing.

But I probably shouldn't shock Ezra, not this bad, so I emailed him. *I did something*, I wrote.

What??

Shaved my head.

No, seriously.

Seriously.

He came home early. *That got your attention, huh?*

"It looks good," he said. Seriously? "I was expecting, you know, *bald* bald. Like just skin. You should have said a buzzcut."

"Sorry. I mean, I used your electric razor. So technically, it's shaved," I said.

"I guess so."

I emailed Zadie about it, and she demanded a photo. Most of the people I had classes with didn't say a word. Maybe they thought I was a cancer patient, taking early measures against hair loss so it wouldn't be such a shock. A few said they liked it. I became very adept at wearing earrings, lining my lips and trying to dress a little more feminine. I wouldn't have minded being mistaken for an androgynous little boy, but shaving my head made me realize I wasn't thin after all. I was just normal. And I didn't want anything thinking I was a normal, somewhat chunky guy with man boobs.

In February, we were both accepted to our respective internships in London—starting January of the following year. That would give us two quarters of core classes here, and we'd have to double up. Our program was actually a year-long master's degree but a lot of people stretched it out for two years. Or so we heard. If we doubled up classes for two quarters, we'd be insanely in debt all at once, but also in the clear to go to London and do nothing but pick up elective internship credits.

My internship was at a prestigious, international fellowship organization. The kind everyone knew the name of. Ezra's was at an independent publishing house where he'd be doing formatting and editing. Now, now we could tell people.

"Are you serious?" Amanda asked. "Are you gonna go to Paris?" I hadn't thought about it, but why the hell not? It was an hour's flight from London and cheap. Amanda idolized Paris, thought it was so romantic, and even though I had no interest in France and thought their food was too salty and their cheeses too boring, I *would* go to Paris. If only to showboat to her. And I'd send her something, like a magnet with the Eiffel Tower, to seal it all up neatly.

"We're going to try to find a flat before we go," I told her. Flat. I loved that word; it was so much fancier—no, *posher*—than an apartment. "Or at least I am. The equivalent of Craigslist there is Gumtree and I've already started looking."

She shook her head, "This is all crazy," she said. But she couldn't tip out all the jealousy; it clung to her thick hair like head lice. I could see it, smell it, and I couldn't help it. I lusted for it.

"You should come visit!" I said. Because that's what you're supposed to say.

"Yeah. Maybe," she said. We both knew she wouldn't.

"So, are you guys going to get married? Isn't that what you, like, do with college boyfriends?" she asked. The realness in her voice made me feel ashamed.

"I, uhm, I don't know. We haven't really talked about it," I said.

"Maybe you should. I mean, what else are you doing all this for, then?"

18

IT WASN'T SUPPOSED to happen like this. I knew better, and I thought he did, too. But that's how it goes, isn't it? Being blindsided. It was a Thursday in late February. It was that anomaly of a sunny Portland pre-spring day when everyone got too excited and pulled on their shorts too soon so their legs get goosey. Ezra was in some engineering class, one of those lectures that goes on and on for hours and me, I had forgotten—stupid—to print out an assignment for a Faith and Reason class. They couldn't quite call it a theology class, they'd tried, because it turned off all the liberals.

I had just enough time between my Arthurian literature class and Faith and Reason to speed home, just twenty minutes away, a quick mount over the Burnside Bridge, print it out and make it back to class. Besides the angry clock that stared me down from the dashboard, I was actually elated. It gave me something to do, a mission, besides killing an hour's time on campus.

I have a tendency to break things. Heavy hands or something, always have. That's why my mom was so reluctant to buy the saxophone in fifth grade instead of renting one. It took me just three months to destroy it completely. At home, I booted up the laptop, and nothing. It hummed like a swaying drunk and showed me a strange, old-fashioned looking screen instead of the old Phi Z wallpaper I'd chosen. The one where I was in the back row so I didn't look too fat. Fuck.

The sent folder, god I was stupid. I'd sent it to myself last week just in case something like this happened, but I'd gotten too excited at the excuse to drive to remember. I could have done this from the campus library. Ezra's spare laptop winked at me from the dining room table, the one I just had to have from the discount place that was a dark wood veneer and showed off every scratch and fleck of dust. I only had five minutes. Any longer and I'd be late for sure, especially with the hell of downtown parking. His booted up immediately, obediently, like it knew it belonged to an engineer.

And I didn't even think. Isn't that always how it begins? I went straight to the email folder, the same site everyone uses, and the email was empty. Totally empty. There wasn't a single item in the inbox. What the fuck, don't worry about that now. The sent folder, and there it was.

Of course I wouldn't be logged into my email on his computer. Of course not. He would be. But this email address, it wasn't one I recognized. J33pGuyPDX, who the hell was that? He'd been halfway good about the cleanup, just like all men. Just like my dad had been when Ben and I had found his secret online account. Ezra had cleaned up all the inboxed items, even deleted them permanently from the trash bin. But he hadn't deleted the sent emails.

Maybe he had before but had forgotten this last batch because it was relatively new and sparse. Christmas break, the time Amanda had driven me to my mom's and we'd managed to not tear each other apart for once. At first, Ezra had said he was going to Mitchell but changed plans when his mom decided to book tickets to see a friend in Costa Rica. I'd imagined he'd spent the time bent over Dungeons and Dragons books, making up monster names and sucking Mountain Dew through his gapped teeth. Not this.

What do you have in mind? he'd written the day I left. It

was to a Craigslist casual encounters ad, and (thank you, Craigslist), when you sent a reply to the anonymous address it automatically put a link to the original ad in your email. It was still valid. *Dom female seeks occasional sub for pegging. Discrete and professional.* It was obviously a hooker, or a pro dom or something. It was something you'd pay for. I don't know if she ever replied, or if he replied more and managed to delete those sent emails. I just didn't know. But the next one was stranger.

How about these? he'd asked, and linked to patent leather thigh-high boots with a vinyl skirt. But what I couldn't get over was who he'd sent it to—himself. The shoes weren't just a link, but a link to a shopping cart he had on a fetish site. They were his size.

It had been ten minutes, fuck the class. My head was cold, the adrenaline pumping the hot blood too quickly around my body to keep me warm. The fuck, the fuck, the fuck.

You there? I texted him.
Sup?
You need to come home. Now.
??
I know.
Know what?
J33Pguypdx
Don't freak out

I knew exactly how long it would take him. He'd take the same bridge as me, the homeless in their torn up blankets standing on the precipice of the Willamette River like they were about to take flight. He'd make the same turn at the eco-friendly drycleaner that I'd only used once. When they called me about the white linen pants I'd dropped off and whispered, like *they* were the ones who should be ashamed, "There was a little, uhm, *pee*, on them, dear. Would you like us to use a special stain remover on that?" I'd never returned. I didn't even pick the pants back up with the expensive stain removal magic done. He'd drive up our street like always, park in the spot nobody took because the birds loved shitting on it so much. Just like so many times before.

For those twenty minutes, I went back and forth between fetal position and strange animal mewlings on the couch to pacing the circle of living room-hallway-kitchen-dining room over and over like a dog with worms. I didn't know if I was in mourning, a rage, or just completely stunned.

And when he arrived, all calm with just his eyes a little wider than normal, I felt my mom's type of anger kicking at my throat. *Go away, go away, go away.*

"So?" That's the opening line I'd come up with when I had twenty minutes to prepare.

"It's not what you think."

"Don't fucking lie to me. Don't fucking lie to me! I read all the fucking emails—or at least all the ones you forgot to delete."

"What did you read?"

"I'm not giving you the information you need to figure out your lies. So, what? That's what you do when I leave? Are you gay? A cross dresser? Trans? What?" Suddenly, that time a year ago in the elevator showed back up in my brain. We'd run into one of his old fraternity brothers Caleb, one who had come and gone, disappearing like so many do. He'd been kind of quiet but nice. The three of us made pleasantries in the elevator. He got off before us, and Ezra immediately whispered, "Did you see his shoes?"

"His shoes?"

"*Look.*" Right as the elevator closed, I scanned Caleb's retreating back from his cheap flannel shirt to his jeans the wrong wash to the sparkling stiletto heels he was wearing. It was strange and shocking, and Ezra and I laughed about it. But now, maybe that hadn't been surprise in his voice when he pointed out the shoes. Maybe it was awe. Jealousy.

"No," Ezra said now. "I—I didn't go through with any of it." His voice was calm. He'd rehearsed this, sounding calm.

I could see him driving home, fast, his lips moving silently as he tried to guess my attack.

"Why? Because the prostitute never wrote you back?"

"She wasn't a—no! I just, I was just seeing, you know? I was bored."

"And the shoes?"

"The shoes?" he looked genuinely perplexed.

"The thigh-high boots and the 'What about *these*?' you wrote to yourself? Forget already?"

Remembering sunk into his face. Maybe he'd thought, for certain for certain, that he'd deleted any trace of those.

"That was just—that was for Halloween. I was just shopping."

"Fucking bullshit. And who the *fuck* talks to themselves in second person like that? What about these?"

"So what?" he asked. "That doesn't mean anything."

"It does. You fucking know it does." It was true, and I knew it. I just didn't know what it meant.

An hour went by. I'd once read that, no matter how bad the argument, two parties have said all they can say in twenty minutes. What is it about twenty minutes? After twenty minutes, the psychologist—I'm guessing it was a psychologist or someone like that—said that you just keep repeating the same things. Sometimes in different ways, sometimes exactly the same. There's no point in continuing a fight after twenty minutes.

I locked myself in the bathroom, balled up against the wall farthest away from the door where the coolness of the toilet brushed against my bare knees.

"Julia. Julia," Ezra said from the other side of the door. "Come on, don't be like that."

And I cried, god I cried those nasty kind of gasping tears we so rarely do. The kind I should have had for my father, or when the first better part of me was vacuumed out at eighteen just because of Ben's "How do I even know it's mine?" I cried them all, so hard my nose got plugged up and I wretched for breath. It was exhausting, exhilarating, and it made me feel so light. When I got all dried up, I was tired. Just tired. I wished I could still let the waters out, but there was nothing in me left to give.

Ezra had stopped scratching at the door a while ago. He probably hadn't left, unless he'd taken special measures to sneak out quietly. But no, he was sitting on the couch, eyes searching the computer screen when I finally crawled out of the dirty room where we took turns defecating and scrubbing our groins.

"Hey," he said. I waited to see if he'd flip the laptop closed, like my dad would always turn off the desktop's monitor when someone would walk by. I hadn't noticed that until Ben pointed it out. Had Ezra been nosing around Craigslist now? *Right* now? But no, he kept it open, the bright lights shining on his face. Somehow, it had gotten dark outside.

I didn't reply, but somewhere in my face he must have sensed defeat. How stupid I was. It was the oldest, easiest tactic. We do it to our tantruming children—just let them tire themselves out.

"What are we going to do?" I asked him. I was too weak to even do it myself. I had the perfect excuse to walk away, walk away right now with the whole history of us, the sheer length and the cancer be damned, and I couldn't do it. Nobody would have blamed me. Nobody.

"What do you want to do?" he asked.

"I don't know." The angry words, the ones I thought were my mom's, their little arms with the little claws had fallen asleep long ago. I just wanted everything to be okay. Not necessarily with Ezra, but just in general. God, I didn't want to deal with moving because I'd make damned sure I'd be the one to go. I didn't want to worry about grad school with him in my classes, or what if he went ahead and went to London anyway? Fuck, London. London. Everything was already all set, wasn't it? I couldn't let Benjamin or the monster go.

"It's—it's okay," he said. "I fucked up. Okay? Bad, but . .

171

. I don't know. You're the one who's always talking about how not everybody is totally straight, always having *Queer as Folk* on and—"

"You're blaming *me*? You're blaming me for being gay?" *Please be gay, please be gay.*

"I'm not gay," he said. "It was a woman, you know. In the ad."

"Yeah, who wanted to give it to guys up the ass. And get paid for it."

"I was just curious," he said.

"And the boots? Just be honest, because I already know. I just want you to say it."

"I—"

"Just fucking say it for once."

"I don't know! I don't—it's not like I dress as a woman for fun. In secret or anything. It's just, I don't know. Maybe I am a little bit of a, you know. But I'm not gay." I could tell, I had pushed him. I'd pushed him as far as he'd go. There was so much in him, all paddling in little circles deep down inside. No wonder. You can't love someone you don't even know.

"Okay. Okay," I said. "Here's the deal. I'm just tired, okay? I'm so fucking tired. And I just—I'll never mention this again. To you, to anyone. If we can just start again, right now. But I fucking catch you doing this shit again . . . I mean, I won't. You'll be smarter next time. Now you know. Now you know what to do. I'm going to—I'm going to regret this. So bad, so bad." And he smiled. He'd worn me down to dust and had barely done a thing to make it happen.

"Thank you," he said. And because he said it so rarely, I lapped it up, thirsty from all those tears.

It was an easy promise to keep. It's not like you want to go talking to everyone about how your boyfriend of three and a half years creeps on Craigslist for dom hookers and shops for fuck-me boots on the side. It was easy to keep from talking to Ezra about it, too. We both just wanted to forget. That was easy, too. We just put all our sights on grad school and London. At least when he tried to initiate sex now, all I had to do was give him a look and he backed off. Once, just a few days after everything crumbled around us, he'd backed off in a huff and shut the bedroom door briskly behind him. A streetlight lit up most of the opposite wall, and immediately a centipede—at least a foot long—scrambled from its hiding place in the corner across the wall, under the bedroom door and disappeared with its quivering legs. Scurried with its grotesque belly slithering across the filth of the floor, the damned little familiar he deserved. It terrified me, and I refused to close my eyes for more than a blink until the streetlights switched off and the pink began to spread across the wall instead.

And we still had one more quarter to go. It was only the end of the winter quarter with spring break in clear sight.

"I'm coming for break!" Zadie said over the phone. Already, in just a few months, a touch of southern drawl had made its way into her voice.

"Staying with your mom?" I asked.

"Yeah, except for a night or two in Portland. Can I stay with you?"

"Of course. We'll get stupid drunk and make Ezra be DD."

"Poor guy," she said, without anything genuine in her voice. "Dragging him away from Dragons and Doom to shuttle us around."

"*Dungeons and Dragons*," I said. Why the hell did I care?

"Why do you care?" she asked.

"I don't. So how's Georgia?"

"It's good. It's okay. Fivehead and I, we don't get along."

"Why not?" I was good at keeping secret elation out of my voice. I'd learned it young, used it when I knew my mom was so desperate to see that she could make me happy so I gave her none of it. It didn't matter how fabulous the birthday cake, how many presents she scrounged from garage sales to wrap up for Christmas (the most was thirty-two in one year), or if she pulled me out of school telling the principal I had a dentist appointment and took me to get a new pair of shoes from this place in the mall I adored where everything had at least a two-inch platform. Why was I so hateful? But after so long of acting apathetic, you can't do it any other way.

"Oh, lord," Zadie said. "I don't know, she's—she's pretty conservative. You know? And we've just been butting heads. She wins, hers is bigger. I had a couple of people over for wine one Friday evening, she was trying to study, ended up flipping out at them, and I was too drunk to do anything but laugh . . . it's just not good. And, well, I brought a guy over. I needed to get laid! They ran into each other in the morning. I think she was embarrassed because she was wearing a see-through shirt and no bra. Or makeup."

"That sucks," I said.

"Yeah, I'm moving out. Or, well, I just moved out."

"You moved out? Where are you living?"

"I got this place—it was pure luck, actually. It's like a little guest house behind this other house, but both are rentals. It's above a detached garage, just a little one bedroom thing. But, *lord*, it feels good to be living alone!"

"When?"

"Just this past weekend, actually. The move out was really bad."

"Why?"

"Well, five head, I think she didn't want to end on bad terms. So when I was moving my stuff out, she was moving her own stuff around at the same time. Into the garage for storage. And—I don't know why she did this. She has this box of seashells that she's been collecting since she was, like, a toddler. She gets one every time she goes to a new beach, or a special occasion at her family's beach house. She has a sand dollar she found the last time she saw her grandmother, all this stuff."

"Oh, god, Zadie . . ."

"It wasn't my fault! She—I seriously don't know why she

did this! But she left the whole box of seashells right behind my car. I didn't see them, and—"

"Jesus."

"I heard them. I heard something break, I thought I'd run over a squirrel or something and crushed all its bones! So I stopped, and I, I stopped with the tire right on top of them."

"What did she do?"

"She must have seen from the porch or something, but she came running out and she was trying not to cry. I kept telling her I was sorry, I mean I didn't know what else to say. 'Just go.' She kept telling me just to go. So . . . I did."

19

I HAVE TO ADMIT, Ezra's family took great efforts in including me with the whole graduation thing. His eldest sister living in Tennessee flew in, and they all stayed at a rented house just minutes from the massive coliseum. The biggest university in Oregon had no choice but to prod the thousands of graduates through the rows of the same structure that housed an NBA team. We looked like cattle in an abattoir, our long black robes seasoned with white masking tape spelling out the cleverest things we could imagine on our caps. Mine said *PhD or Bust*. Ezra's said nothing. Some people *mooed* in boredom.

It took hours, seriously hours. And it didn't help that the English department was far from the list of colleges to go first at commencement—not that it would matter. We weren't allowed to leave until all of us walked. It also didn't help that my last name began with a *T*. Ezra's, which began with a *B*, was at least one selling point for marrying him, right?

Everyone around me had phones. Everyone. Stubbornly, I was sticking to my no cell phone way of life, and I had Hollywood backing now. *Sex and the City's* Carrie Bradshaw notoriously didn't have a phone, and it was by choice. It made her seem unique and quirky in a good way, so maybe that's how people saw me. I didn't know where Ezra was, but we'd picked out an agreed meeting spot with his family already. It was under the tree that propped up the circus protest sign two blocks over. Once we'd all found our way to the photo of the tiger with its teeth cut out and the sad-looking lion, we were all going to the German *haus* across town to dip stale bread in fondue and drink beer that was too heavy.

"Julia," the woman said, appearing by my side like I should know her.

"Uh, yes?" Did I do something wrong?

"It's me, Andrea Wochit."

"Oh. Oh! Hi." How had she found me in this sea of black? Assigned seats, of course. Of course. Well, this was awkward.

"I just . . ." she began, and then her eyes began to water. Oh, shit. She was going to cry, right here. I glanced around, but nobody was paying attention to us. "I just really want to thank you. For that letter. It meant, it means a great deal."

"You're welcome," I said, standing up. At least I had an aisle seat. "Thank you. For what you did."

"Can I—can I give you a hug?" she asked.

"Okay." It felt strange, having this little birdlike woman wrap her skinny arms around me. I'd never have recognized her. Couldn't even drum up a picture of what I thought she'd looked like in the recesses of my memory.

"I framed it," she said shyly. "It's in my office now. I don't work in admissions anymore, but still."

"I'm just glad you got to know," I said. "So you don't have to wonder if you should have regretted it."

"I don't worry about regrets anymore," she said. I wondered what that would be like.

When it was finally my turn and the people in bright orange caps, so we'd know they were in charge, shuffled me forward, I wanted the announcer to flub my name. Call me Judy like some people do, or pronounce my last name

Tay-ner, but he didn't. What a hard job that must be, especially with the scores of Nguyens and other hard names at this so-called multicultural, diverse school. I'd been watching everyone else take their stiff folders and shake the stiff hand of the school president for ninety minutes, but it was all a show. When I got up there, I found out his hand was surprisingly cold, and I couldn't even begin to imagine everything it held from all those shakes—snot, feces, and probably a fair amount of semen. But what was really shocking was that the inside of the fancy folder was empty. All it had was a note: *Dear student, congratulations! The university is processing final grades now and, if you indeed qualify for a degree, your diploma will be mailed to you in August at the address we have on file.*

What a letdown.

The German food wasn't that bad, though. It could have been worse. I ordered a separate plate of just veggies so I could eat without thinking about getting bigger. I was sometimes in a size six, and if I tucked my chin just right in photos is almost looked slender. Underneath the graduation robe, I had on spindly heels and my most flattering jeans. This must be how women feel under *abayas*, able to fold secrets below the surface and feel as sexy as they want. It's just that nobody but them knew about it.

"Hey! Julia!," Anna said from across the table, her lips speckled with fondue cheese. She was getting too fat, you could tell. I wanted to tell her to rein it in now, before it was too late. Before she was also hiding a crepe-paper stomach and heavy wings on her arms underneath carefully picked clothes. "What's the internship thing Ezra was saying you're doing?"

"Oh, yeah. It's this paid internship with the state. I'm going to be working at the Division of Land Governance, the DLG, down in Salem for the summer."

"Doing what?" she asked, spearing another cube of cheese-covered white bread into her round face.

"I'm not really sure. It's an internship for 'diverse students' and pays really well, so that's really why I'm doing it. Plus it looks good on résumés probably."

"Yeah. Probably. It's in Salem?"

"Yeah."

"That drive's going to be a bitch."

"I know, but it's just for ten weeks." God, it would be a bitch. At least ninety minutes each way. But that meant I'd be gone five days per week at long, leisurely stretches. Ezra was letting me take his Jeep instead of my trembling car. He even said he'd take the hardtop off for the summer. At least I could keep my face and arms tan without carving out time for tanning sessions every other day.

"When does it start?"

"When I get back from Georgia, but orientation is actually on Monday. Right before my flight."

"But aren't you starting your master's during summer session?"

"Yeah, but I'm working the schedule around it. Taking the earliest morning classes, then driving straight to Salem. I'll have to work late, but at least I'll hopefully miss rush hour."

"I dunno. That seems kinda stupid," she said. I didn't really have a good reply to that.

I had a gift for it, piling as much on top of myself as I could to see what addition would make me break. I'd planned it perfectly, the Monday orientation in Salem followed by a quick drop-off at the airport. The day before I left, I thought about it. Checked it. Grabbed Ezra's spare laptop when he was being noisy in the basement to see what J33PGuyPDX was up to, but he hadn't stayed logged in. Whatever. If he was going to be pitching himself on Craigslist or ordering vinyl hot pants while I was gone, he was going to do it. I didn't care, and, in an awakening of a moment, I realized I really didn't.

There were three options for orientation times, and I'd signed up for the eight o'clock in the morning slot. An unpopular time, especially since most of the students were living in either Portland or near Eugene, and we all battled the morning rush together. I'd planned my outfit to look like I knew what I was doing, overcompensating because I knew I'd be the most white looking person there—and I didn't disappoint. In my group, there were two black students, one Japanese, two Latinos, and a token Pakistani. We were gathering outside with bagged breakfasts, which were usually easier for me to eat in public. It was usually eggs and meat, so I could pick around any carbs without people noticing. You couldn't really do that with sandwiches. People always looked at you weird when you peeled off the bread and pinched the innards with your fingers (or a fork if you got lucky).

I was the only one in the group who would be at the DLG. Actually, it turned out I was the only person in the whole program who was placed there, period. After thirty minutes of cheesy ice breakers and talking about how prestigious the program was (please, I would be in London in a few months at truly one of the snobbiest of organizations), we were assigned our very own guide and were led to our future work sites. My guide was a Mexican sophomore student at the local private university. I could see the youth in his face. Did we all look like that not so long ago? He looked at me with the same flattened eyes I imagined he gave middle-aged women who rang up his groceries and deposited his student loan checks.

"This is Marty," he said as we approached a frail man in his sixties who was waiting outside the DLG main entrance. "He'll be your supervisor and point of contact for the program." In the time it took me to shake Marty's hand, the boy-guide disappeared.

"Hello, hello," Marty said. He seemed unsure of himself. "Thank you for coming, thank you for coming on this, uh, Monday. It's Monday." How the hell did he become a manager?

He hadn't. As he led me through the building, pointing

out the espresso stand and the bathrooms, I found out his deal. Getting a government job, it was relatively easy at the entry level. Marty should know—he started here forty years ago. Then just never left. Over time, if you fly quietly and far enough under the radar, you'd just keep getting promoted. Or that's how it seemed. Now eking into retirement season, Marty held some kind of long, complicated title that had "VI" at the end, but I had no idea what he was the sixth of or if it even mattered. I also figured out the whole pension thing. Spend a long enough time working for the government and you were guaranteed the same income you had at retirement all the way until you died. That seemed like a pretty sweet deal, but the musk and sadness of the whole building made me feel like I'd never make it forty years. Maybe Marty wasn't like this when he'd started, but the dying building sucked all the life out of him to maintain its flaking walls.

"And here," he said grandly, taking me to the farthest back corner cubicle that faced two gray walls, "is your desk." It couldn't have possibly been any farther away from the rest of the cubicles.

"Oh. Thank you! It's nice," I said. God, it was hot. I'd been placed in the only government building in the whole city without air conditioning, I just had to be. Even at my super fattest, I would rarely sweat. That was sheer luck, or a lack of sweat glands or something. But here, in the cloying heat of a freakishly hot June, I could feel the dampness start to spread like a starburst in my armpits. The maxi skirt was a bad idea. It trapped the heat from my thighs, my groin, like a blanket. Sweat began to bubble and spread from between my toes to every surface and nook of my discount rubber shoes. The cap sleeved tee did nothing to ward off the heat, it just let my arm fat flap slowly whenever I stretched or moved.

"Do you, uh. Do you want to familiarize yourself? Spend a little, uh, a little time here? At your desk?" Marty asked, and he was looking at me so earnestly, willing me to say yes.

"Sure. Yeah, okay," I said.

"Great, great," he said, and wandered away. I lost his slim, hunched back immediately in the maze. What was I supposed to do now? I'd been introduced to a smattering of women, all women, as he wound his way through the cubes to get to this back corner, but I'd already forgotten their names. And now what? I didn't start until next week and wasn't even given a hint of what I would or should be doing. But there was a username and password on a sticky note on the keyboard, so at least I could log in.

This is what I figured out, all the good sites were blocked, and the homepage was always, always the DLG site. It looked like it needed a major update, complete with flash animation on the page where you could search your name for property nobody had claimed. I figured out the department was in charge of the land (obviously), property people forgot about, checks where the owner couldn't be found, and license plates of all things. Apparently the whole state license plate deal was huge, especially the salmon. Was I put in this department because it said "Native" on my application? Was this some kind of "sorry!" for taking all that Indian land, or did it seem like I belonged here because I was supposed to like salmon? There was nothing at all on the desktop except for the icons for Microsoft Office, a calculator, and a broken file with a weird name that wouldn't open. I checked my name for unclaimed property, then Ezra's, Amanda's, and Zadie's. When I started to search for anyone's name I could think of, I heard the breathing behind me.

"You doin' alright?" a woman's gruff voice asked. Shit. They'd at least been smart when putting together this makeshift of a cubicle. The monitor was heavy and placed smack in the middle of the desk facing the wall. Anyone could sneak up behind me and get a clear shot of what I was doing. Or not doing. Thank god all the good websites were blocked.

The woman, she looked like a caricature. Obese with wiggly arms and what looked like a Hawaiian bedsheet wrapped around her broad chest. I willed her to have blue eyeshadow on because it would be so fitting, but she just didn't. She didn't play along.

"Oh! Uh, yeah. Thanks," I said. I knew better than to come up with an excuse.

"Mmm-hmm," she said, eyes crawling from my shoes to my hair. I should have done my hair better, but it was hard when it was this short. "You remember my name?" she asked. It was a challenge and, even though I didn't look away from the huffing beast, I also had nothing to ward it off.

"Uh, no," I said. "I'm sorry—"

"Mmm-hmm," she said again as she wandered away. I hadn't even remembered meeting the Hawaiian hog.

Clock hands moved slower here. I'd stay 'til 9:30, then I had no choice but to go. To make it to the airport in time. I was already going to be here thirty minutes longer than what I'd been told. It was taking forever, watching the little white clock numbers on the computer screen. Finally, the two gave way to a three. Just seven more minutes.

"Uh, uh, Julia?" Marty asked from behind me. Thankfully, at that moment, I'd been flipping through the files in the cabinet to see if they were for me. They weren't, but he probably didn't know that. They had dates from four years ago on them and generous puffs of dust exploded with every flick.

"Yes?" I asked. I'd learned to say "yes" instead of "yeah" when I was pretending to be respectful. People liked that, and it made me seem older.

"I need to, uh, talk to you?" he said-asked.

"Okay."

"You need to, uh. Huh. How do I saw this. You need to uh, wear? More suitable clothes? From now on?"

"Okay . . ." My skirt went to the floor. The tee was a good one, brand new and made to go under blazers. Was I supposed to wear a blazer? A Hawaiian shirt? What the fuck.

"What I mean to say is, uh, some of the women here?

I'm sure you noticed it's all women. Except me. Some of the women here? Your, uh, dress? It makes them uncomfortable."

"How . . . how . . ." Fucking Kahlua Pork.

"If you could just cover your, uh, this area," he said, motioning over his own chest, "a little better?" Screw this.

"My chest? This shirt goes up to my neck. It's not a tank top." All of that was true and, really, at this point, I didn't know what the hell he was getting at.

"I know. I know it does. I'm just, I'm just the messenger here, okay? And, uh, if you could maybe just wear long sleeves? To work? I think that might make everyone a little more comfortable."

"You want me to wear long sleeves. And long pants or a skirt. To work in an office with no air conditioning." I couldn't quite get the words to swing up at the end to make them a question.

"Great! You understand! Thank you!" he said, and scampered away. I felt kind of bad, all that embarrassment coating him.

It was 9:35. I couldn't avoid the Hawaiian woman on my way out because I forgot where her desk was, but her eyes snared mine as I went by her own cubicle. It was bright and garish like her, and her eyes crinkled in amusement as she offered a tight-lipped grimace of a smile. I forgot to pretend to smile back.

20

AMANDA DROVE ME to the airport, not Ezra. Her hugs were different than Zadie's—perfunctory. Probably like mine. When I landed in Atlanta, Zadie was waiting at the gates, and she hugged me tight, like she meant it, with pure joy. My mom hugged tight too, but like I was the last buoy in her vision.

"Oh my god, your hair," she said, staring at what could now officially be called a pixie cut. My hair was naturally, randomly curly, which means cowlicks galore.

"Yeah," I said, automatically reaching up for it. I'd gotten used to it, to the reflections. And to the cold neck. "It's growing out now."

"It's not as short as I thought it'd be. How was the flight?" Zadie asked as I followed her to the waiting, ancient sedan with an UGA sticker plastered on the back window. She looked a little different, the new southern lilt more prominent in person. The Georgia sun had bronzed her, too, made her freckles multiply and stand out more.

"Good," I said. "The girl sitting next to me watched me pick the bread off the sandwiches and asked if I was on Atkins. She is too. It was nice not having to hide eating in front of people."

Zadie just rolled her eyes. "You're thin enough," she said.

"No," I said. "My mom used to say you can never be too rich or too thin."

"Uh, I'm pretty sure you can be too thin," she said. "Besides, you're normal. Just be okay with it."

Who wants to be just normal? It's the same as average.

Zadie had described her new apartment perfectly and, like always, there was something about her effortless style I could never match. Or maybe it was just because she had really expensive taste, and her belongings, no matter how slim, always cost a lot. The restored wicker chair with the plush muted cushion in the little hallway, the painting of the white chaise lounge above it. The velvet green couch with the real wooden legs. And her bed, piled high with thread counts in the thousands and hand-quilted blankets.

"This is it!" she said, heading to the kitchen and pulling down two wine glasses. It was barely two, but who cared?

"So," I said. "Tell me about the boys."

"Oh, lord," she began as she began ticking them off. I loved this, living through her. I tried to tell myself it was good I tied myself to Ezra almost immediately after starting college. Who knows what kind of stupid things I would have done otherwise, how many people I would have slept with. Zadie swears she doesn't know how she escaped all those STDs because so many times she had drank so much she didn't even ask about condoms. "This one guy, Amir? He was Indian. He asked to meet me at a grocery store for our first date, which was weird. Then we went shopping for groceries to make a picnic, and he took me to a park. Isn't that the strangest thing ever?" I thought it was sweet but didn't want to say so. "There was Xavier, a black guy—"

"Is this affirmative action or dating?" I asked her. God, I was jealous.

"I'm just seeing!" she said. "I'm open, you know."

"Yeah, I can see that."

"*Anyway*. Besides, this might be my last chance, this whole dating frenzy, to see what it's like with different kinds of people. And doesn't everyone want to have sex with a black man?"

Well. She had me there. "Maybe," I said.

"So, he was nice, I guess. We just went for drinks. And then there was Cheese."

"Cheese?" If a guy mattered, we never called him by name. Only the clear throwaways were allowed their birth names.

"Yeah. Because he really likes cheese."

"Original."

"I tried. He used to be fat, he told me that on the first date. But Used to Be Fat Guy is too long to say. Anyway, he was nice. Cute. He's a financial analyst in Atlanta and lives in Peachtree, so he had money. I dunno, I thought since he used to be fat he'd have some humility or something."

"Where'd you go on your dates?"

"Just restaurants. He met some of my cohort people for trivia night once." That meant something. Zadie didn't prance around men unless she thought they had sticking ability, and this one had come from Atlanta for her.

"So where's the wedge now?"

"Well . . . I don't know. The first time we had sex, I think we were both pretty drunk. It was fine. I'm guessing, I couldn't really feel much. But then the next time? He was like, 'What are *those*?' Pointing at the stretch marks on my thighs and boobs. And I was like, 'They're *stretch marks*. You have them, too.' And he said, 'No, I don't! No, I don't!' like I'd just called him fat or something. And even if I had, he did it to me first! I mean, what kind of guy has never seen stretch marks before?" I'd never noticed any stretch marks on Zadie, at least not like mine. Mine, from the going to fat to normal again so fast, were thick and nasty and purple. Hers were probably like most women's, fine little white lines that whispered about the time when they burst into sexuality like trees going to fruit.

"And you still slept with him again?" It's all I could think of to say.

"Well, we were already naked! But then it got worse.

He's like really into eating women out. Like, really."

"How's that worse?"

"Well . . . he, like . . . this is embarrassing. He wanted me to ride him? His face?"

"Okay . . ."

"But then, like, look into his eyes the whole time. Stare. I felt like I wasn't allowed to look away! I think he thought it was hot or something, but all I could see were his little eyes poking out between my legs and I couldn't help it, I just started laughing. I mean, he looked so serious and intent, but all I could see were those bugged out eyes staring up at me."

"Oh my god. He was probably going at it like he thought it was some rare brie or something!"

"I know! And then, I think I offended him. We didn't finish, and he drove me home . . . all the way out here! Most awkward car ride ever. Haven't heard from him since. Thankfully."

I longed for those kinds of stories, but my own, and I felt like I had shown up to a dinner party empty-handed—not even flowers or wine to show my graciousness. Zadie brought all the stories, and the only one I had, the good one, I'd sworn to keep locked up. It wasn't fair.

Zadie's friends, or "cohort people," were a neutral mix of bland. Most were from the South and their voices reminded me of my dad. They were nice enough I suppose, but I saw how the men's eyes glanced over me before dismissing me as uninteresting. The women, they were all above me. Most were, so that was nothing new. But these were a different breed, and even though Zadie was never attracted to the kinds of women who would contour their cheeks and constantly spread gloss on their lips like they were jellying up toast, there was an air about them. I guess maybe it was confidence. They either took pity on me and went overboard to bring me falsely into their circle, or they dismissed me like men do. This group, on a Tuesday trivia night, were an equal mix.

I had nothing to contribute. All they talked about was people I didn't know, math things I didn't know, and classes I'd never been to. I think Zadie felt a little bad until her fourth glass of Hefe. "Since when do you drink beer?" I asked her. It had always been cocktails or wine.

"Since here, I guess," she said. "It's what everyone drinks." It was true, but I hadn't paid any attention. Everyone had a coppery beer in hand, orange wedge straddling the rim. I was the only one with whiskey. I drank it straight now, on the rocks when it was hot out.

Even when the trivia came, I didn't speak up—even when I could. The only answers I knew, besides a random question about medieval England where I could show off for two seconds, was about pop culture. Nobody at the table answered those because how lowbrow were they, anyway? They were proud not to know that gossip piece about Beyoncé, so I played alone. Even though I wanted to tell them all they were stupid, were they incapable of reading celebrity magazine headlines when they waited in line to buy their overpriced beer?

"What'd you think?" Zadie asked me as we left, and I lied because she wanted me to.

"It was fun," I said.

"I checked, but there's no home practice game this Saturday," she said. "I wanted you to get the whole southern football experience."

"It's okay," I said. Thank god. I hated football, and thought Zadie did, too. I couldn't have stood being surrounded by those little tight bodies and men with their broad shoulders and designer beards again.

Instead, we did what we'd planned—we went to Atlanta. I booked a hotel room, and Zadie got the gas. It was just one night, a Friday night, and we'd make the most of it. It was hard to tell online exactly how good a gay club was, but The Tropics sounded big. But first, a country bar because it was the South and that's what you do. It took four hours with Friday afternoon rush hour to get there, and by the time we'd checked in and primped, it was almost nine already.

"Country bar?" Zadie asked as she called the taxi company.

"Yeah, let's see how it is."

Boots was about as country as a fraternity Cowboys and Angels mixer. It was one of those massive, warehouse-style clubs that was so huge it couldn't contain any intimacy or real theme. They didn't even have a mechanical bull or glass boot mugs, just country music and a mass of what seemed like teenagers feeling each other up. It was an excuse for the girls to wear white tank tops knotted above their belly buttons and comfortable shoes for once.

"Your tits are great," a little boy said to me.

"What?" I'd heard him.

"Your tits are great!" he screamed in my face. The whiskey had started to settle near my heart.

"You want to touch them?" I asked, and Zadie laughed.

"Yeah!" he said, like he'd just found something wonderful. It was a poke and it was on top of my shirt, but I felt like I'd gifted him something.

"Let's go," I told Zadie after an hour. This wasn't country. There were no redheaded sluts here, but they had tequila. We had two shots each as we waited for the taxi to call Zadie's phone and let us know he was out front.

"Where to?" he asked. The driver was southern black with that kind of roughness to him that had rubbed so long it had turned parts of him soft.

"The Tropics," I said.

"The Tropics? That's uh . . . you girls sure about that? That's a rough part of town."

"We're sure," Zadie said.

"You're the boss," he said, pulling away from the pool of girls who were already vomiting in the bushes outside Boots.

It took twenty minutes to get there, and I could tell Zadie had noticed the same thing as me. We hadn't seen anyone but black people for the last ten minutes. But it was Atlanta, not Portland. That was normal right?

"Here you go," said the driver, pulling up to a dark building with no lines. No thumping music. No queens prancing around the corner.

"Uh, thanks," Zadie said, thrusting a handful of bills through the bulletproof glass door that separated us.

The Tropics was a sprawling basement setup, one of those places we realized was perpetually dead before midnight. But they were open, the queen of a waitress in her purple leopard print bra hanging out of her satin dress prancing right over to us.

"Can I get you ladies a drink?" she asked, the matching purple glitter on her eyelids flashing.

"Whiskey on the rocks," I said.

"Same. With Coke," Zadie said. "Hey," she whisper-yelled to me when the waitress went for the drinks. The music was careening loudly around the room even though there were only two other bartops full of people. "Remember what we said last time I was in Portland? That in Atlanta, maybe we'd—"

"The ecstasy?" I asked her. "Yeah. But, I mean, where are you gonna get it?"

"I'm going to ask her!" Zadie said, pointing to the waitress.

I'd never done ecstasy before. Hadn't done anything besides pot, and Zadie had only done shrooms that one time years ago. It had freaked her out so bad I thought she was kidding when we first started talking about the ecstasy.

"Excuse me?" she asked the waitress when she arrived back with sweaty drinks. "Do you have any E?"

"You two cops?" the queen asked, her demeanor changing. No more smiles.

"What? No," Zadie said, looking at me confused.

"I need to hear you both say it," the waitress said, looking at me.

"No . . ." I thought that was an urban legend, that cops didn't *really* have to fess up when asked.

"Okay, then. Twenty each," she said, pulling a little packet out of her bra, the kind jewelry came in. Zadie handed over the cash. "Let's go," she said, motioning to the unisex bathroom and sliding a napkin over her drink. It was shockingly white and bright behind the double rainbow doors with a ten-foot trough of a urinal. Nobody was in there, and in my palm, the blue pill looked innocent. Like a sleeping pill.

"I don't know. Do you think—" I began, but she'd already swallowed hers. *Stop thinking*, I told myself, and followed suit.

"I don't feel anything," she said. That was the last thing I really remembered.

That's not totally true. There were flashes, but worse than brownouts. Suddenly we were back at the bartop and surrounded by six black men. They looked hard but had voices like little girls. Like Donna. Then we were in the lobby of The Tropics, and I think we were waiting for a ride. They were taking us somewhere.

Then they were gone, and we were in another kind of basement but this one was itty bitty. There was a bar there, though, so it had to be a club, right? Not someone's home. It reminded me of Steven's house from freshman year, but darker. For some reason, Zadie and I were talking to each other in British accents. I don't know why. I lost her, looked everywhere for her, but it was hard when you were only really aware every thirty minutes or so. Then I found her, huddled in a doorframe. She felt sick, or I felt sick, or something but I needed to get real air. Right now.

She was doubled up, almost unable to talk, and that made me the one in charge. The protector, the caregiver. I don't know how, but I found the stairs, and they were sticky. It had to have been a club, right? I vaguely remembered talking to people. A lot of people. But now there were just seven people at the most, and none were standing. This is when my memory started to really come back.

Zadie was behind me, following my footsteps up the clanging staircase and then we were outside. It was morning. Fuck. What the fuck time was it? A bank across the street flashed its helpful light. Date, temperature, time. It was 6:03 in the morning. We'd lost nearly seven hours.

"Hey," I said, nudging her. "Hey, where's your phone? Do you have your phone?" I don't know how she did it, but it was there, squeezed into her pocket. "Give it to me."

At least I had enough sense to just call the last number, the 24/7 cab company. Another miracle, we were on a street corner, the cross streets clear but sounding foreign in my mouth when I told the taxi company where we were. Someone new came, a kind of white-looking man with a warbled, thick accent. "Address?" he asked, and for my final incredible feat, I rattled off the hotel's address and knew it was right. Maybe I'd known; maybe I'd anticipated this all along. As I emptied my pockets and dug through Zadie's to pay him, pregnant and gray clouds tumbled across the sky.

I pulled the blackout sheets closed, the best thing about this hotel, while Zadie collapsed on her bed. We'd sleep 'til checkout, at least give ourselves that before the drive back. Only I didn't sleep. I think I got in an hour, and then the light in the room was so blinding it shook me up through the alcohol and E. *That couldn't have been E, that was speed or meth or something . . .* my brain tried to tell me, but right now it didn't matter.

A glowing sphere was floating above Zadie's head in the next bed over, hanging there like a Christmas orb. Instinct shoved my head under the covers, and I willed it to go. *That's your dad*, my brain tried to say. *No*, I told it. I'd always imagine he'd be a kind of simmering electric blue. Not this. And even through the impenetrable polyester blanket, I could tell. I could tell when it was gone.

I didn't say anything to Zadie about it, just shook her awake and carried both our bags to the car when it was checkout time. "Water," she kept saying. "I need water," and I took all five bottles from the mini fridge not caring if they cost six dollars each. I drove us home, stopping every thirty minutes so she could vomit on the side of the road.

"What the hell did we do?" she whispered at the halfway point, three bottles of water already down and back up.

"I don't know," I told her. It was the most honest I'd been the whole trip. The most honest in a long time.

It wasn't until I was back in Portland, let the memory of the poltergeist simmer in my memory for a few weeks, that I couldn't take it anymore. Ball of light, light ball, something rudimentary I typed into Google and there it was. It wasn't a sign from the heavens after all. It wasn't my dad. It was ball lightning, that was all.

"You thought there was a ghost, and you didn't *wake me up*?" Zadie said when I called to tell her.

"I know. I'm sorry." And I was. I'd left her on that polyester sheet to die.

21

GRAD SCHOOL WAS just like undergrad, only the classes were a bit smaller and the extra, added inflation of self-importance helped fuel me through the days. Those summer classes, probably because of the internship, Ezra and I didn't have a single one together. So I could pretend I was a full-fledged, smart, capable, and determined adult who wasn't carrying around an extra, sleeping limb. Monday through Friday, it was always the same—one or two morning classes, if I was lucky just a one hour drive to Salem, usually taking care of any homework while hidden away in the corner where nobody could see my sweat stains, then two hours driving back. The sluggishness of the summer made everybody work late, tricked by the delayed sunsets into thinking it was just five when it was really eight.

My first job at the internship was inputting data from surveys about what people thought of the custom license plates. How did they feel when they saw the Oregon salmon plates? Most of the answers were what you'd expect. *Like I should get outdoors more. Proud to live in such a beautiful state. Indifferent.* I lived for the moments when someone would write, *Ready for dinner!* or *Yum!* That's what constituted a highlight.

And the classes themselves? It's like we'd proven ourselves as undergrads, capable of banal reading assignments and surprise quizzes, so now they were giving us a vacation. Was I getting tricked? Were they really looking for something beyond putting together a fake pitch to a publisher or marketing strategy? But, no, it didn't seem like it. Grad school was apparently time to coast.

Was this it?

For the first few weeks in Salem, I constantly strained my neck craning it around to see if Marty or the Big Kahuna was sneaking up on me, but they never did. Marty, for the first couple of days, would come by once or twice, but I could recognize his shuffle from six cubicles down. After that, he just kind of gave up, satisfied that whenever I was supposed to be hunched over my desk I would be. Slowly, the sleeves of my shirts inched back upwards. They never dared flirt above my elbow, but Jesus. The heat tumbled into the decrepit building and seemed to pool in the corners. My corners. I'd never sweated so much in my life.

"How's the internship?" Ezra would sometimes ask when I crawled back home as the sun went down. I knew he didn't really care, so sometimes I said, "Fine." Sometimes I just grunted. Sometimes I said something totally nonsensical, especially if he was clearly not listening, but it couldn't be too long. Any more than about six words, and he automatically tuned in just in case it was important. I never asked how his days were.

The only time he really seemed to care was during that downpour of a summer storm, the kind they have in exotic places. The hardtop for the Jeep was safe in our garage when the waters began at noon. Ezra emailed me immediately, *Is it raining there?*

I don't know. There aren't any windows here. It's like Vegas. It's raining.

Well, that was just perfect. *Okay . . .*

It's fine I guess. The Jeep will be okay, just try to get home fast.

Of course. It was about the Jeep.

But as his birthday passed and mine slipped by with a perfunctory trip to a low-carb friendly restaurant, and he believed me that I didn't want any gifts, I began to suffocate. Wasn't it time to *do* something?

"I was thinking," I told him over a Saturday dinner of low-carb chili (black soy beans are the secret) and special, expensive "bread" that student loans were quick to pick up, "maybe we should think about getting married."

"Huh," he said, and I could feel it. He was tired of these sad attempts of mine. "Maybe."

"How much longer is it going to be?" I asked finally, shoving the bowl away and looking at him. I had just turned twenty-six and I'd known, I'd just *known*, my whole life that twenty-seven was my marrying age. And here he was fucking the whole thing up.

"I don't know," he said. "I mean, maybe. What else do you want me to say?"

"I want you to say that it's been four years and tell me whether I'm wasting my time or not."

"No," he said. "You're not wasting your time." And just like that, the upper hand changed. I'd had something over him since the Craigslist incident. He'd been kinder to me, the one in charge of winning me back. But now I'd changed it all by bringing this up, and he was the grand prize again. How did that happen?

It was too late, so I might as well go all in. "I think maybe we should go look at rings this weekend. Just to see," I said. I knew it was stupid, caring about rings at all but especially about making them a priority.

"Okay," he said.

On the other side of town, snuggled into the suburbs, Amanda's life was falling apart. "Hey," she said, her voice steady over the phone. "Can I ask you something? A favor?"

"Sure," I said. Ezra and I weren't going downtown for ring shopping for another couple of hours, and the basement had swallowed him up already.

"Chuck, he—he hasn't been home."

"What do you mean? I thought he stayed down in Salem sometimes."

"Yeah, but, this is different," she said. "I mean, I haven't seen him or heard from him at all."

"In how long?"

"Uh, nine—ten days."

"What the hell, Amanda? And you're just now doing something?" I knew; we both knew.

"I thought he'd come back!" she said. "Look, can you just—I can't do this. The kids keep asking where he is, and when I called his credit card company, they said they couldn't tell me anything . . . can you just help me?"

"Yeah. Yeah, of course. What do you want me to do?"

"He's not at his friends' place. I've driven by the past four nights, and his car's not there. He hasn't been at work, and I don't want to start asking people he works with in case—oh, fuck. Can you help me call hotel rooms around there? Or—"

"Yeah, I'll call them. Give me his credit card information, too." Amanda was always too forthcoming, too giving with information. She didn't know how to get people over the phone to do what she wanted. In person, with men, she could pull her shirt down too far and get them to buy her drinks, that was her gift. Mine was bred from the teenage years with Ben and taught me to game the system.

If you sound desperate enough, but reasonable and calm, you can pretty much get anyone to tell you stuff they shouldn't. Like when you pretend to be Chuck, who lost his credit card and needs to cancel it but wants to verify it hasn't been stolen by checking the last few purchases. It was too easy. All I needed was the credit card information, his birth date, social security number and mother's maiden name. Amanda knew all that. Oh, and the kind of convincing tone that wouldn't allow anyone to question why "Chuck" sounded like a woman even though I used my best low voice.

Figuring out he'd been charged six hundred dollars at a one-star motel in Aurora was a lot easier than calling one motel after another.

"I knew it, I fucking knew it," Amanda said when I told her.

"Are you—are you going down there?" I asked. The adrenaline was beginning to flow heavy through my body.

"Yeah, no. I mean, the kids—"

"Give them to your mom," I said.

"He emptied out our bank accounts," she said.

"What?"

"All the money, it's—it's gone." All the money? They'd never had that much, but I knew Chuck's grandmother regularly siphoned her miserly funds to them. They'd had enough to buy that brand new house. That almost brand new SUV. To keep Amanda in MAC and Nordstrom clothes.

"Do you think . . ."

"He's using again," she said.

"Are you sure? Cocaine again, or—"

"Cocaine for sure," she said. "That's his MO. But before he disappeared, he was acting weird. Like he did when we met and he'd slip. So I started checking for track marks about a month ago. You know? There were some. And he's losing weight. He didn't use to shoot up, but now . . . fuck, I think it's meth. Too." Her voice never shook, and she didn't sound scared. Or particularly pissed off. Just determined and needing, desperately, some proof.

"Do you want me to come?"

"No," she said. "I need, I'm gonna do this alone. And not 'til tonight anyway. My mom won't be able to take the kids until then, and I need some time to get ready."

"Well, good—I mean, call me if you need me."

"You ready?" Ezra asked as I hung up. He'd put on a belt and his best shoes, so that was something.

We went straight to the Northwest alphabet district, the fancy area where there were boutiques and the consignment shops were considered trendy instead of sad. It was one of the first places Ben had taken me when we'd finally made it up to Portland, where the trees lining the sidewalks were alight with Christmas lights year-round, not just in December. It's like Ezra and I knew where we were going.

We only went to one shop, a place we'd never been before. Probably because I liked the name of it, Gilded, and probably partially because we got parking right in front of it. But mostly it just felt wrong being in there, looking at engagement rings. It wouldn't have, I don't think, had I been with someone else. But I felt like I should apologize to the middle-aged women who ignored us, tell them *I know, I know. I should have held out for someone better.*

The costs were phenomenal. Three thousand dollars for something less than half a carat? And used? I knew about the whole clarity, cut, all those c-words, and it was really obvious when something was going to cost more than a new car, but anything between a thousand and ten thousand dollars looked pretty much the same. Was this seriously it? In my head, I'd always imagined some kind of better compensation prize. At least a big, fancy ring. Even Corinne had got that, but hers was a hand me down. I didn't have a rich grandma to pin me down with heavy jewelry, and neither did Ezra.

But there was one. "This one's nice," I whispered to him. It kind of was, and it took me by surprise. It had a yellow-gold band, which I never thought I'd like, but the claws that held the diamond were white gold. It made the diamond look bigger. Just a solitaire, just under half a carat, but it was shinier than some others. "Do you want to see it?" he whispered back. We were the only two people in there, and the clerks hadn't said a word to us in the ten minutes we'd been there, just scanned us when we walked in to let us know they were watching.

"This one," the clerk said as she made a big show about unlocking the case, like it was a big favor, "is from the 1960s. It was from a jewelry shop that shut down and had put some of the remaining inventory in storage, so it's technically new. But I should tell you, I forget the actual size of this one, women's fingers then were much more slender—"

"It's fine," I told her, slipping it easily onto my ring finger. I'd always had skinny fingers, even when I was fat. Spider Fingers, Amanda had always called them because they were so long and thin. My mom had called them Piano Fingers and that had led to eight painful, hate-filled years of piano lessons as a child. Me, I wanted to play the violin, but my mom said those kinds of fancy instruments sounded like dying cats and she wouldn't have it.

"Oh, wow!" the woman said. "I'm surprised. It's—" she began, squinting onto the placard tucked where the ring was, "a size four and a half. The average size these days starts at a six." Great, at least people would think my hands were skinny if nothing else.

Ezra tried to be discreet about flipping the little tag to check the price, but it was obvious what he was doing. It was $975, and suddenly that seemed very cheap and very expensive all at once. The weight of the diamond kept making the ring fall between my knuckles it wanted to curl up in my palm to die.

"Well, thank you," he said, and that was my cue. Give the ring back.

It had felt strange, that little touch of extra weight on that finger, and as we walked out the door I was furious. Well, thanks? That's what he had to say. We both knew I'd put the "just to see" addendum on my excuse to go shopping as a security blanket. He was supposed to offer to buy it, right then, and I'd at least have some kind of grip in all of this. I was twenty-six, twenty-six, twenty-six.

"How'd it go?" I asked Amanda. I couldn't wait any longer. It was almost midnight, but I never had homework and tomorrow was Sunday. Ezra had been consumed by a video game for the last four hours, wearing his big headphones that ensured I was far, far away. I knew Amanda would be up.

"He was there," she said. Simple, like she'd met her husband at a work conference on the other side of town.

"Did you—did you see him?"

"Kind of. Not really. His car was there, but I called the hotel and asked for him instead. They said they didn't have anyone of that name there, so I—I told them what was going on. Described him. He had . . . he had checked in with a girl. It was in her name, even though he used our credit card."

"Oh, shit."

"I don't know her," Amanda said, knowing what I was going to ask. "I only got her first name, but I don't know her. But they connected me to their room. I don't think they knew I was right outside."

"Did he answer?"

"Kind of. He was strung out, fucking high as hell. Obviously. I don't think he really knew where he was, and he was trying to act normal with me. I mean, his phone's been shut off for like two weeks, and he was trying to tell me he was at work. Doing inventory all night. Like I hadn't just called the motel room."

"So, what—what are you going to do?"

"I don't know," she said. "I don't know. I slashed his tires. All four of them. Scratched it up with the knife my mom makes me keep in the trunk, but I didn't have anything to smash in the windows. Would have made too much noise anyway." A year ago, Chuck had bought a little, thousand dollar piece of crap car just for driving back and forth to work. I knew Amanda had to be adding up whatever valuables they had left to sell, and it must have not made the cut.

"Do you need me to do anything?" I asked.

"Not right now. Right now, god. My mom is keeping the kids for a few days. They think it's, like, a vacation or something. I'm having the locks changed on the house at seven in the morning. I can't afford to pay for middle of the night emergency locksmiths. Just—packing up his shit. He doesn't have much that I can sell so I'm just going to leave it on the porch. I don't want it here anymore; I don't want to see it."

I could see Amanda, in my head. Resolutely and neatly taking Chuck's things, checking their value, then cramming them into neat little boxes. Like she was preparing for a move.

"I don't have any milk," she said. Like that should matter.

"What? Okay, so . . ."

"I'm serious," she said. "I don't even have milk or the money to buy it to give to my kids. He took it all, all the money." When she'd said he'd cleared out the bank accounts, I didn't think she meant literally.

"What are you going to do?" I asked again. It was all I could say.

"I don't want to move in with my mom," she said. "I can't, I can't. God. What are you—what did you do today?" At the least, I could distract her.

"Went shopping for engagement rings," I said. Anyone else, I'd feel like I was throwing it in their face, but not her.

"Oh, fuck," she said. "Don't get married. Dumbest thing anyone can do."

22

I PICKED THAT FIGHT because I was bored, picked at it 'til it bled. Even in the moment, I didn't know how I was so good at it.

"You let me paint that whole kitchen myself!" I said to Ezra. The landlord had been creeping around the windows, mad that the kitchen cabinets were gone and the shiny white paint was standing in for the beige she'd chosen in 1974. Not that she could do much when she found out we did have the doors, just removed them, but still. I had done a sloppy job. You could see the drips pushing their way down the walls.

"You acted like you wanted to," he said.

"Like I wanted to? Like I was just super happy to clean up your mess? And the worst part is, it wasn't even an accident. You were just so obsessed with getting back down and playing that *stupid* game you let it happen."

"I did not make the fire on purpose," he said.

It went on like this for an hour. Unlike the Craigslist night, I knew I wasn't poking around looking for an exit. I was just bored and wanted the upper hand back. Outside, the sun rained down.

"You know what? This is ridiculous. I'm sick of waiting around for you to be ready. Like you want me to tick all these tasks off before, you know."

Ezra was rarely silent entirely. But now, he pushed himself off the couch and lumbered down to the basement. Seriously? It's like he belonged there, in the underbelly of some old duplex that was a breeding ground for centipedes.

But he came back, still silent, and put a ring box in on the kitchen counter in front of me. "I was waiting for a better time, but you made me do this," he said. I think, I hope, there was a sliver of excitement within the simple Knowing. I watched myself, like I was watching a movie, open the box to reveal the ring I'd liked. It looked smaller now, outside the boutique. "The world's smallest handcuffs," Chuck had always joked to Amanda, and I could see it now. He was right. Was this what I'd have to wear now for the rest of my life.

Ezra dropped to one knee. I could hear his bones crack against the linoleum. I didn't want this.

"So, will you marry me?" he asked. This was it. *Run, run, run*, was stampeding through my head.

"Yeah. Okay," I said, and it was done. Weren't you supposed to feel something right now? I think you're supposed to feel something.

We told everyone he actually proposed near the rose garden, below a fountain I loved that sounded like I imagined cathedral bells did when the droplets sprayed across it. It sounded a lot better than we were fighting and he proposed in the kitchen he tried to burn down and I half-ass cleaned up.

"Are you happy?" Zadie asked when I told her over the phone.

"Yeah, yeah. I mean, it's about time, right?" She would never call me out, no matter what. She was just checking, to see if she was supposed to follow along or not.

"Okay," she said. "But it's not about time. It's not like you're getting a watch because you're retiring or anything. Anyway," she said, "when's the wedding?"

"Right after grad school for sure," I said. "After London. We're thinking of doing a destination thing in Hawaii since we won't really have a home or place or anything here anymore."

That was true. Already, we were planning an autumn garage sale to make as much extra cash as possible. The pound to dollar ratio was so bad, the cost of just about everything would feel double to us in London. But one good thing had happened, I'd already secured a flat. Okay, it was a flatshare. It was in a little house in Brixton where a Frenchman was looking to let out his spare bedroom and he was accepting couples. The rent was what we were paying now, but all we were getting was a little room with a barred window overlooking what shouldn't even be called a garden. I could tell from the two photos. But it was walkable to the tube station (I'd checked on maps) and we could afford it. What we couldn't afford was a hotel or even a hostel for two people while looking for a place to stay. I was just sad it wasn't our own flat.

The garage sale didn't go as planned, though. I thought I knew what I was doing. All those weekends racing from one sale to another with my dad, all so he could turn around and resell it at the flea market the next day, and I didn't soak up any of the good details. I was supposed to leave prices off and haggle with customers, I knew that, but I hated it. Instead, we put reasonable prices on everything, and I practiced letting things I loved go. We sold all of my DVD collection, all 248 discs, for sixty dollars. One of Ezra's D&D friends bought the couch, and at the end of the day, we made just under five hundred dollars. I thought my life would have been worth more.

Well, that was fucking stupid. People don't go to garage sales in the rain or cold, so we did it in late September which stuck us with three months of living like monks. To save even more, we covered all the windows in saran wrap to trap the heat. We closed off the spare bedroom, got intense about tucking wet towels under the doors to lower the bills even more. I think it worked. Ezra preferred to call the living austere, and Amanda said it looked like we'd been robbed. Not that she was one to talk.

"I can't sell *everything*," she said. "I'm trying to make all this as normal as possible for the kids."

"Does Casey get what's going on?" I asked her as we huddled on her now ottoman-less couch drinking out of plastic princess mugs.

"Kind of. She still asks where dad is, like, every other day even though I've told her he has his own place now. I think she's just confused."

"Well, yeah." It turns out, the bank won't just kick you out because you stop making your mortgage payment. It's a long, slow process. Amanda's lawyer, the one her mom retained for her, estimated that she'd get to stay in the house for about eighteen months before actually getting evicted. It helped that it seemed the housing market was starting to get shaky, so Amanda was far from the only person not making her payments.

"It's so weird to see that on you," she said, gesturing to the ring. "Do you like it?"

"The ring?"

"Yeah."

"Yeah, I mean. I kind of picked it out."

"Did you know it was coming? The proposal?"

"Sort of. We've been together forever and now, with London and all, it's probably about time."

"I guess," she said. "At least Ezra would always drive us around. I like that about him. And he seems normal. Stable. At least he's not a drug addict!" she laughed. When she smiled like that, with her eyes crinkling, she looked like she did when we were eleven and I asked her to sell Girl Scout cookies with me. Those were my first words to her. It was the first day of middle school, and all of us were lost. She was so beautiful, this black-haired girl with maroon culottes, and I wanted her to like me so bad. It's all I could think of to say, because, "You wanna come over?" to a stranger seemed way too forward even for a kid. How we'd gone from cookies to this, I don't know.

Grad school stayed laughably easy. It was just A, A, A all the way to a perfect GPA for both of us. I guess they really don't want you to flunk out of grad school because it looks bad. Undergrad is one thing, where all the blame can easily be hoisted onto the students, but with grad school they *really* chose you. The classes are small, the cohorts are selective, and the school wants to make damn sure it looks like they have only the most brilliant, driven, successful students on board. If I'd known it would be like this, I would have chosen a longer program.

Ezra and I had both doubled up our credits to get coursework out of the way early. We could have taken electives, but since we both had full-time internships waiting for us, the school was letting us ride out our credits on experience. All we had to do was send in monthly reports about what we were doing and how it complemented the program. I didn't make a single new friend in classes. And I realized, now that we didn't have a bed frame, the spiders and centipedes could crawl all over us.

"You wouldn't even notice if they did," Ezra said.

"I want Eden to sleep in the bedroom," I said. I didn't know if she'd scare any of them away, if they could smell her, but it couldn't hurt.

"She's fine in the basement," he said. "She likes the dark. Speaking of, though, what are you going to do with her?"

"I don't know. Haven't thought about it." Of course I'd thought about it. None of my friends could or would take her, and I certainly wasn't going to put up a post so a stranger could have her. Letting her go, that's what was really going to break me. She didn't escape anymore, we'd put an end to that with trial and error and just the right kind of tape for the top of her terrarium.

I didn't deserve her, anyway. I never skipped her meals,

not once, and even though ball pythons can go months without eating, she got a feeder mouse every week. Never frozen. She only bit me once, but it was my mistake. You're supposed to take snakes out of their terrarium to an established feeding area so they know when it's time to eat. They're smart. But I didn't, reached my hand in there when she still had that hunting look in her eyes, and she snapped out her fangs and sunk them into the flesh between my thumb and forefinger. I thought it would hurt more, but it was just a pinch like a piercing. You can't move when this happens. Snakes, their fangs retract and they can't just let go. Their jaws lock, like a bulldog, so you have to wait while they work their way out of your skin. I still had the little scars like a galaxy blooming in my hand.

But this autumn, it was bad. She was sluggish, and I swear her eyes had lost that clarity they always had. The dark chocolate brown was shifting to something more muddled, but it was happening so slow maybe I was wrong. "Maybe she's dying," Ezra had said. "She's old."

"No," was my only response. It went on for a month and even though she was still eating, it wasn't like before.

Yeah. It took me that long to research what could be wrong. She wasn't getting enough moisture, needed constant wet paper towels in her terrarium to help her shed. She was temporarily blind. And probably hungry. And confused. It just took one week to fix her, but still.

I knew where she'd go, but I hadn't asked yet. The manager of the pet store where I got her feeder mice had nearly twenty snakes at home but loved ball pythons the most. She would love her like I'd promised I would. I was sure of it.

The countdown was on, just three more weeks of sleeping on the floor. There was something about that too-low height that brought on the nightmares, but not tonight. This was real. It was two in the morning and I just knew. That mole on my stomach, my arm, all over, that was cancer. It was cancer I'd been baking into my skin all these years.

When I wasn't tan, I was incredibly fair. Whiter than my mom. She used to say all the Indian came out in my moles and my flat butt, but now I had more moles than ever. There were hundreds if not thousands of them. Ezra breathed deeply beside me.

It's easy to find images of melanoma online, and some of it was so monstrous I couldn't believe these people were just now seeing doctors. But some of the moles weren't much bigger than mine. Some were even smaller, less oddly shaped, and some people had skin cancer without it appearing first in a mole at all. I looked at those photos 'til morning, comparing the evenness of my edges to the pictures online. The symmetry of the browns and tried to remember if any had changed a lot lately.

"I think I have skin cancer," I told Ezra as he walked, yawning, into the living room where I was curled up against the brick fireplace we never used.

"What?" he said, and then immediately passed out.

People really do kind of pass out like they do in movies. It's almost in slow motion, and they crumple instead of falling straight like a board onto the floor. I guess that's probably to protect ourselves from smashing our skulls open.

He was only out for a few seconds, but we went to the hospital anyway. His cancer was back, that had to be it, right? But, no. It took awhile and some frantic research on his mom's end in Mitchell, but it was carbon monoxide poisoning. The windows we'd wrapped in saran wrap to keep our bills down did such a good job that the furnace had backdrafted the poison right into the house with no way to get out. The amount was so minimal, said the electric company, it would have probably been fine. Well, fine if we hadn't plastered the windows like leftovers and Ezra hadn't passed out.

I didn't want to go home yet when he was released, even though the electrical person had opened all the windows and said it was safe. There wasn't any carbon monoxide showing up on tests anymore.

"That was scary, huh?" Ezra asked on the way home.

"You faint like a woman," I told him. It was mean, but he'd stolen my big reveal.

"Sorry. Can't really control it," he said.

"And I wasn't lying, you know," I said. Had he even heard me before he passed out?

"About?"

"The whole skin cancer thing."

He sighed, like I was trying to bribe my way into some secret club only he and his sister belonged in. "I doubt it," he said.

"Why? I tanned almost every day for the majority of my life."

"I just—what do you want to do then? See someone in the hospital?"

"No," I said, dragging out the word. "I want to go to a dermatologist."

"Then go to a dermatologist."

"I was going to until you swooned."

Seeing a dermatologist is a lot easier than seeing other kinds of doctors. I guess they're not very popular. "You sure have a lot of moles!" the doctor said with glee. He looked like a shorter Clark Kent, but I don't think he'd be any more attractive if he took off his glasses.

"Yeah. A lot of tanning," I said.

He tsked but didn't seem that concerned. "Not good, not good," he said. "But a lot of people do it. Are there any you're particularly concerned with?"

I pointed out a few, but he circled even more with a fine-tipped purple Sharpie. "Just in case," he said.

"Is there—how does this work? I'm moving to London at the end of the month for a year and just really want to get this all done here."

"I'm doing the biopsies today, just a punch biopsy," he said, like I knew what that meant. "Then it should take, oh, up to a week for the results. It's the end of the year so a lot of people are trying to take advantage of their health insurance before it re-ups in January, so the lab is a little overworked. If there are any that are positive for skin cancer or are precancerous, we'd need to remove about one square inch of skin to make sure we get it all. I'm sure we can schedule that before you go if necessary."

"Okay," I said. "So no, no more in-depth treatment, or . . .".

"Very unlikely," said Ugly Superman.

It didn't take a week to get the results. It just took three days. Melanoma was found in three of the eight biopsies, but it wasn't advanced enough to warrant anything more than the bigger removal the doctor had talked about. The nurse made sure to say that over and over when she called. It's funny how the word "cancer" is rarely said by medical people, but you know it's bad by the "oma" at the end of whatever you had. I felt nothing. Because I'd already known.

When Ezra found out that all I needed was a very minor surgery and a lifetime of monitoring, he seemed relieved. I didn't know if it was because I was basically okay, because he wouldn't have to deal with my vomit and chemo and radiation, or because I still wasn't getting into that club of his.

And this is just how stupid I am. I wanted to look good in London. My hair was growing out fast with the biotin I'd added to my schedule, and I didn't want to look fat. They already thought Americans were so fat. So the day before I had a total of three square inches cut off of me, I made one last trip to the tanning salon and roasted that sickness deeper into me for forty-five straight minutes.

23

IT WAS THE LONGEST I'd ever flown, the stitches in my stomach pricking me every time I found a slice of comfortable window to lean against. It wouldn't be real, not really, until I felt the wheels touch down at Heathrow. But going to London via Chicago in between Christmas and New Year's was something both Ezra and I were dumb about. A blizzard grounded all planes at O'Hare and instead of the relaxed, noonish weekend arrival we'd planned, we spent two nights quarantined in the airport, not allowed to leave. "It should pass any time," was all they could tell us, and they didn't want a plane full of passengers—most not American citizens—let loose on the streets. Each of us was given a cot to sleep on at night and a thin blanket that did nothing to stop the shivers. I barely fit on it as is and couldn't imagine the shame had I still had all the fat clinging to me. I couldn't sleep, and thought about Eden and how she would be curled up below her heat lamp at the pet store manager's home, eyeing other ball pythons in terrariums across the room. Maybe it was the first time she realized there were others like her.

"I hope this isn't an indicator of things to come," Ezra said, and I didn't answer.

When we finally did take off from Chicago, even the

most comprehensive of baby wipe showers did nothing to get rid of the smell. My hair was greasy, but at least it was in that short, flippy stage where I could just pile more product into it. We landed at Heathrow at midnight.

I'd done the calculations, knew it would cost nearly two hundred US dollars to take a cab from the airport to Brixton. Instead, we took the train and then a series of buses, wheeling our pregnant luggage around cobblestone streets. "Pardon me, could you spare some change?" rang after us as we hauled our life down the unfamiliar blocks. At first, it was strange, hearing such proper British English pouring from the mouths of men with long, dirty gray beards. After the fourth time, we shook them off just like we did back at home. By the time we reached our actual stop, we were the only people on the bus and it was two o'clock on Monday morning. I had to be at work, two zones away, in six hours.

On black, empty streets, you don't know your environment. It's all the same. Manu, the guy who was letting us the bedroom, knew we were arriving late and left a key above the doorframe. It wasn't there, and there was no doorbell. Our knocks went unanswered. "Shit," I repeated over and over as Ezra explored the windows, tapping on each. Finally, a beautiful man with shoulder length black hair and a gauntness reserved for models with colt legs answered the door in a sleep stupor, pointed to the bedroom, and disappeared back down the hall. The bed was smaller than I'd thought, some weird size they didn't make in America, but it didn't matter. It was better than a cot.

In the morning, people—men and women—were passing through the house but didn't seem to live there. There were French accents, British, and some I didn't recognize at all. We exchanged nothing but glances and nods. The adapters I'd bought didn't work, so my hair dryer was useless and I left for the tube station with wet hair. It would take me an hour to get to the offices.

On the streets, even in the early hour, I was the only white-looking person. Jamaican accents rang out, sunrise fish vendors screaming their prices. Where the fuck had I put us?

Ezra didn't start work until Thursday, so he could figure it out himself. This wasn't London. This couldn't be London.

Thankfully, the tube was easy to figure out, but it was standing room only. I could feel my ankles and knees starting to puff up. What an idiot to wear three-inch heels, but they were all the power I had. On Doughty Street in Zone 1, it was all different. This was, kind of, what I imagined. Little boutiques and cafés lining the streets. Men and women in business suits, chins buried in their pea coats to protect against the English cold. It wasn't that big of a deal to me—the same kind of chill as Oregon.

"Julia?" said a too-thin guy not much older than me when I rang the bell. His accent was off, not quite like anything. "I'm Nicholas," he said. "The supervisor for the program."

Gay or British. Gay or British. It was a game Ezra and I had made up as we waited for our luggage at Heathrow. You just couldn't tell.

There were two other interns, both female and both beautiful. Miranda was from the east coast with brown hair to her waist, a flat face, and blue eyes that would probably turn milky in old age. Katie was from Florida, a real professional ballerina with puppy eyes and blonde hair. They'd been here two weeks longer than me, and I could see some kind of bond already cemented between them. I didn't belong, my whacked off hair and too-big body. On the ground floor, it was just the three of us plus the director, Harry, who apparently always came late and left early. It seemed his average work day was four hours, max. Like Nicholas, his accent was also somehow not quite right.

"We need to take one of the students for his visa at one," said Harry after he clipped into the office just after ten. He was tallish, middle-aged, with teeth in desperate need of orthodontics. "Then, to celebrate Julia's arrival, how about we head straight to the pub?" Nobody argued or thought it was strange.

"How long will the visa thing take?" I whispered to Miranda, the less intimidating of the two.

"Oh, maybe one hour at the most," she said. "We have to wait outside the Embassy, only the student can go in for their interview. But we still have to wait, just in case."

"So we'll be done at two?" I asked. Was this normal? And drinking, at two?

"Yeah, probably," she said. "Harry loves any excuse for a pub. Oh, and I'm supposed to give you this," she said, handing me a burner phone. "You didn't bring a cell phone, right? They want you to have one here." My first, and even I knew it was old school. A simple push-button, flat phone with just texting, calling, and two games. All my years of wanton demands that I would never have a cell phone fell apart in an instant.

She was right, although huddling together in the cold for an hour waiting for the near-certain visa approval of someone I hadn't met made my toes go numb. But the pub, it was exactly as I imagined. That's one thing movies got right about England. At The Apple Peddler, the dark wood paneling and horseshoe bar was straight out of a film producer's dream. Miranda and Katie drank wine, Harry a pint, but Nicholas had whiskey with me. By four, we were all tipsy and lurched down the street in all directions heading for our respective tube stops. By the time the train rolled into Brixton, I had partially forgotten that I didn't really live in London. Not truly.

Ezra wasn't home yet. Manu wasn't there, either. Instead, the door was unlocked and four Jamaican men were huddled in the living room smoking something that didn't smell like cigarettes or marijuana. They looked up in tandem as I passed by, just in time for me to see one hand another a fat fold of bills while taking a little baggie of whiteness. Oh, my god. I was living in a crack house.

For ten minutes, I waited behind the locked bedroom door, listening for footsteps in the hallway that never came. I must have looked blasé enough for them to assume I just didn't give a fuck. *Thank you, three glasses of whiskey.*

When Ezra finally got home, he had to say something before I'd unlock the door. "Is anyone out there?" I asked him.

"No," he said, giving me that look that made me feel paranoid.

"Listen, we're living in a crack house," I said.

"What?"

"When I got home? Manu wasn't here, just a bunch of Jamaican guys. They were smoking . . . something . . . in the living room and dealing in something that wasn't pot."

"Are you sure?"

"What do you mean *am I sure*?"

He sat down on the bed that creaked and sank so low it almost put his ass on the floor.

"We need to go," I said.

"I know," he said. "Okay."

I didn't think it would be that easy, or maybe that coating of anxiety was on him, too, and I just hadn't seen it. Did Manu even really live here? We didn't know—but we packed fast, cramming everything back into suitcases. "The rent, the rent," I said to Ezra, so concerned to be screwing someone over and then come after us. But we'd just stayed a night, so we shoved some cash under the door Manu had gone into last night and ran outside before anyone else might come in.

"This way," Ezra said, pulling me in the opposite direction of the tube station. Three blocks away, near a park and away from the vendors, was a phone booth. I should have been excited, my first time in one of those classic, big red booths, but my heart was raging against my rib cage. I let Ezra take care of all of it, calling the black cab and hiding the suitcases behind a bush so we didn't look so much like scared, sitting prey.

"Cabs are expensive," I said as it pulled up. It should have been another great first, crawling into this beetle-looking machine, but exhaustion and fear were overriding everything else.

"I don't care," he said.

"Address?" the drive asked.

"Can you take us to a hostel in Zone 1?" Ezra said.

"Any particular one?"

"No, just—whatever you recommend," Ezra said. As it turned out, the hostel was on Portland Street. It had to be more than a coincidence. More like a grand slap in the face. We'd come all the way from Oregon to end up right back where we started.

The one sprinkling of good luck? The cost of a "double room" was almost the same as a bigger, mixed room, so we splurged and got one to ourselves. We didn't care that we slept on a bunk bed.

"We need to find a place immediately, before we run out of money," Ezra said.

"I know, but I can't . . . I can't take off work for that," I said. "What were you doing today, anyway?"

"Figuring out just what kind of ghetto you got us in," he said. We were in the cafeteria, surrounded by people clearly younger than us. Dinner that night was baked beans I couldn't eat and a dried up piece of meat. It was the best thing I'd tasted in a long time. "It's okay," he said. "I'll do it. I'll find something this week, before I start work."

And he did. When he needed to, he came through. I toyed with the foreign ring in bed that night, listening to his body shift in the bunk above mine. Around and around and around, the weight grinding me.

Ezra had found us a flat, if you can call it that, in South Kensington just one block from the tube station. It was one of the richest areas in town, and we were told that Hugh Grant lived next door. Or one of his many flats was there, or something. But we never saw him. Our place was in the basement of some historic building, half the size of our old bedroom. It barely squeezed in a twin-sized futon to share, a one-foot long kitchen counter with mini fridge and microwave, and a standing shower. The toilet we had to share with the other four flats in the basement including the landlord's, and the high, narrow window in it was perpetually stuck open letting in the cold, rain, snow and whatever else found its way into the dredges. It was a paradise.

When you only have a closet to live in, it doesn't take you long to spread out. Suitcases became end tables and moveable mini closets. I figured out it now only took me thirty minutes to get to work, and Miranda was starting to seem receptive enough. Clearly, she preferred Katie and Nicholas to me, but oh, well.

And I figured out the whole accent thing. Nicholas and Harry were both Americans but had both been in England for years. Both had married a Brit, Nicholas a guy he met at university named Scott and Harry a woman named Anna, although now they were divorced. Like everyone else in the office, I went to the little French bistro one block away for lunch, but we'd all get it to go and hurry back to the office to fill out the daily paper's games page together.

"We simply have to stop meeting like this," Nicholas would say when we'd pass each other on our way for rich soups and fresh salads. "Or people will start to talk. And you know what they'll say?"

"What?" I would always ask, though I knew the answer.

"They'll say, 'Doesn't that woman know she's with a *fantastically* gay man?'" And, oh god, he was. With his perfectly pressed pastel shirts and expensive ties.

That first full weekend, once Ezra had settled into his own work at the publishing house and we'd finally figured out how to unlock the gate to the big, fake-looking shared garden with the pebbled walking path, I made Ezra explore.

"Where do you want to go first?" he asked.

"The British Library." *Beowulf* was waiting, and I'd be

damned if that whole Brixton, crack dealing episode was going to destroy what I'd been fantasizing about for so long.

It was anticlimactic and no photos were allowed. I expected something grander, an armed guard perhaps, but no. The thick book was just another display item, protected behind a thick plastic box. But you could see the ink, how the writer had pressed heavier in some places and had their own kind of ways of making "y's" and "e's." It was unbelievable in its simplicity. That something could last so long, through a fire and countless hands.

"He didn't know god's love," I said to Ezra as I read the entire two open pages, slowly, savoring it like it was meant to be.

"What are you talking about?"

"I don't know."

England has some incredible cheeses. At Sainsbury's, the big local chain supermarket just three blocks from our flat, you could buy a little bundle of sample cheeses that came with six different varieties. I fell hard for the Red Leicester, a kind of sharp British cheddar that ended on your tongue with an unexpected kick. The cranberry-infused white cheese was Ezra's favorite. We were there daily, doing like the Europeans do and getting new groceries after work. Sometimes we'd see ethereal looking ebony women who were at least six feet two gliding down the aisles, nothing but wine bottles in their little carts. Surely they were models or actresses or someone famous, but we didn't recognize any of them.

Sainsbury's was also right beside the closest Laundromat, a place we had no choice but to frequent every weekend. I got used to it, hauling the bag down the street, even though I felt like a pauper compared to all the slick cars driving by. In a city where you rarely saw anything but black cabs, our street was often host to Ferraris and Lamborghinis.

Early one Saturday morning, as we dragged the bags through the downpour to get laundry done early so we could head to the Natural History Museum to finally see the thylacine, I knew something was missing. I felt more exposed than normal. It wasn't until the laundry had made it through the washer, through the dryer, and was nightly piled on the futon in our room as we put the clothes away that I realized the ring had been in a jacket I'd washed.

"Shit, shit, shit," I kept murmuring as Ezra and I both tore through the pile, still warm, for the gray jacket. The ring was in there, but the diamond was not. The jog back to the Laundromat had never felt so long, but it was so early both the washer and dryer we'd used were vacant. Still, no diamond. The clerk seem unimpressed with our story, like it happened all the time. Maybe it did.

"It'll be alright," Ezra kept saying to me, over and over on the way home. I now had nothing for my naked finger except a thin band with dangerous prongs poking out of it. But somewhere, maybe deep in those machines or maybe dropped on the sidewalk, was a little piece of carbon that had mattered so much for some reason. Now, I couldn't remember why. Or why I was so upset.

"Do you still want to go to the museum?" Ezra asked.

"Yeah, yes," I said. "This wasn't Benjamin's fault."

24

"AFTERNOON," said the admissions attendant. "Student tickets?"

"Yes," I said, desperate to save any money we could. Her tight smile melted into just a thin, flat line. That happened, I'd noticed. In England, we looked like we could belong, but the minute anyone heard that American accent, any trimmings of kindness slinked away.

"I'm going to need to see some IDs," she said. As if we were lying, but we dutifully pulled our university cards out of our wallets.

"I don't recognize these universities," she said.

"They're in America," Ezra said.

"If I can't verify it, I'm going to have to charge full admission price."

"Well, you *can* verify it," Ezra said. "Just look up—"

"It's fine, it's fine," I interrupted, reaching for my thorny ring with the wicked prongs to twist in comfort. "Full price is fine." I think she felt like she won because that little curl of a smile returned. "Where's the thylacine?" I asked her.

"The what?"

"The thylacine."

"I don't know what that is."

"Nevermind," Ezra said, pulling me through the front

doors. Since it was a weekend, it was probably fuller than normal, but the soaring ceilings with the dinosaur bones pieced back together like a puzzle made it seem huge. I had no interest in anything else, this is what I'd come for.

"Come on," I told him, dragging him away from the feet of the T-rex. I couldn't stand it, both of them standing there with their short little arms at half-mast.

I knew it wasn't Benjamin, not really. Or maybe it was, who knows what they'd done with the body. But I expected something more when we tracked him down, hunted him like the Aussies did for so many years. Except *we* paid for *him*, not the other way around. Of course, in the empty, small hallway, a bored and fat guard was parked almost directly in front of him. I hated asking people to move, so I just inched awkwardly closer to him hoping he'd take the hint. Slowly, he kind of did, sighing heavy and shifting his big belly a little farther away.

"He's smaller than I thought," I told Ezra. Really, the taxidermist had done a shit job. Benjamin's eyes looked bugged and his coat looked like he'd been electrocuted.

"Maybe this one wasn't fully mature," said Ezra.

"I don't know. He looks so little," I said.

"It's a she," the guard said suddenly, as if it were obvious.

"Oh," I said. Wait. Maybe he knew something about them. You can't spend most of your waking days in a museum and not let a few facts soak into you. "Hey, actually, can I ask you something? Do you know . . . would thylacines, would they start chuffing? When they were communicating?"

"Sorry?" he said, his eyes widening while he grabbed instinctively for his little baton.

"Uh, did they, you know. Chuff."

"I'm afraid I'm going to have to ask you to leave," he said, moving his hand away from the baton and to his walkie talkie.

"Wh—" I began, but Ezra was tugging at my sleeve.

"Let's go," he said.

"But I want a picture—"

"Now," he said, like I was a child about to throw a tantrum over a dropped lollipop. The guard had the black box to his lips, thick thumb stretching for the big button.

"What the hell was that about?" I asked Ezra as we walk-ran through the doors.

"I don't know," he said. "But that guy was serious. About something."

Okay, so Ezra was right—chuffing is what some big cats do when they're talking to others and sometimes humans. It's also another way to say *fuck* in England. That's what Google says, at least. Still, we never did go back there, and I never got my photo. It was for the best. The Benjamin I knew, the one in the video, he wasn't there anyway. He was in sepia tone with a long split of a mouth and celestial lightness to his steps. Any part of him that might remain on this earth, it wasn't in that cold museum.

Weekly, I got emails from Zadie. Fewer from Amanda. From both, the focus was about men, for better or worse. With Zadie it was updates on the latest, YTG or your type of guy, because she thought I'd like him so much. After four weeks, she finally admitted the disaster of their first date. She was nervous, got there five minutes late, and after saying hello immediately went to the bar for a drink. He thought she was rude, but hot, it turns out, so he stayed anyway. YTG had followed his ex-fiancée to Georgia so she could go to the same university as Zadie. Promptly three months later, the fiancée dumped him after having sex with the same guy in her program three times in a row. Apparently that was the magic number to transition from one relationship to another. *I still look up Mike online, she wrote to me. I know it's bad. I think he's dating someone, but I'm not sure.*

The emails from Amanda were largely to the point and seemingly calm, except for the excessive use of exclamation points. Except they were juxtaposed, like a Salvador Dali painting. They started off normal, and she seemed to matter of fact about the most bizarre of things. *Omg Chuck disappeared again and I found him with his motorcycle crashed in a bush.* I didn't even know he had a motorcycle. Must have been something he'd bought with the emptied-out bank accounts. The way she said it, it sounded like he crashed into a bush on the highway and just decided to live there. I imagined she found him happily munching on Cheetos, leaning against the broken blue bike frame. For some reason, in my head the bike was blue. Apparently he wasn't hurt though because there was no mention of a hospital or anything.

So, Chuck's in the hospital, her email three days later began. Oh, here we go. *He had the kids and the place he's staying is on the ground floor. Someone walked by and saw him passed out with the baby crawling around, so they called 911. The police said he OD'd and there were syringes on the floor. Fucking asshole!!! He's in a psych ward now. WTF!! I had to go see him and get buzzed in past these bullet proof doors.*

As Ezra and I booked our flight to Paris for the first long weekend, a holiday I'd never heard of, I promised myself I wouldn't forget to get something for Amanda there.

It was supposed to be beautiful, Paris in the spring. There are songs or poems or something about that, right? The flight was $99 for each seat on Ryanair and just under an hour away. Ezra and I had spent the first few months surprisingly being okay in our tiny quarters, signing up for every possible weekend tourist attraction we could find. We went to the Roman baths where you could buy a shot glass full of the special water that some people said was the real fountain of youth for just five pounds. It tasted off, too salty, but as I opened my throat. I willed it to work. Maybe if you believed, it would come true. Like Santa. We did the Canterbury Cathedral, took the bus all the way to Stonehenge, and had real Christmas pudding that burned like cheap liquor all the way down. The pubs were nearly giving it away for all of January.

Stonehenge wasn't what I expected, not really. It felt unreal standing there, on the outskirts of this phenomenon that had been standing over five thousand years. Those rocks had to be tired. "Once a year, on summer solstice, the guardrails are removed and you can touch the stones," said the guide. Really? You tell us this now? We walked across Tower Bridge, ran into a random jousting competition, and saw the crows at the Tower of London. We even did the whole audience participation thing at a *Rocky Horror Picture Show* midnight showing, but it was the first time I'd watched Dr. Frank-N-Furter since the Craigslist night. Now, it felt embarrassing yelling out, "Bitch!" and "Arsehole!" on cue with Ezra so close and the good doctor's latex so familiar. Still, I kept the "arsehole" card because it had the "r" in it.

Paris, that had to be something different. But the Charles de Gaulle airport was monotone and kind of dirty. I'd practiced the most basic of French phrases, adamant that I'd at least try. "Des billets pour Louvre," I said to the man at the train station. Over and over. "Quelle? Quelle? Quelle?" he kept replying.

"Louvre! Louvre musée!"

Finally, I just wrote it down for him.

"Ah, *Louvre*," he said, shaking his head. "Fucking idiot Americans," might as well have followed.

We'd booked a cheap motel walking distance to the museum, one with an English name so they were used to people like us. The room smelled of smoke and the thick, dark bed frame overpowered everything. We had a view of a brick wall.

Okay, so I didn't really know what the Louvre looked like on the outside. All I knew is the *Mona Lisa* was there, and I think a famous sculpture. I didn't realize, when the glass triangles came into sight, that we were there. But the Mona Lisa, that wasn't hard to find. Just go to where the biggest crowd is salivating like hungry flies.

"It's small," I told Ezra as we both craned our cameras

above heads to take the exact same photo as everyone else. If I was supposed to feel something here, I didn't. It looked like it did in all the movies and books and everything. Or at least I thought it did. The thick rope was placed so widely around it, even if we'd waited to get to the front of the crowd you couldn't see it right.

At the Eiffel Tower, it was at least the right size. You could see it from almost everywhere in the city's speeding heart. But it was cold in the spring. Cold, gray and the streets were littered with graffiti spelling out words I didn't know. At least the clerk at the tower spoke some kind of English. "You want lift to the second floor?" he asked.

"Uh, how much?" I asked.

"Is fourteen euros more," he said. Fuck, who would spend fourteen euros to take the elevator to the second floor unless they were in a wheelchair or crutches?

"No, no thanks," I said.

"Enjoy," he said.

Turns out, the second floor is the top. The top of the huge, looming tower. I don't know how many flights of stairs we climbed, but it felt like winter all over again by the third set. "It's so cold," I kept saying to Ezra, as if he didn't know. About halfway up, there was a landing where you could break for the gift shop. Here, I bought a heavy Christmas ornament of a smiling bear climbing the tower and a chocolate bar with "Paris!" and a picture of the tower on the wrapper for Amanda. It cost, amusingly enough, fourteen euros.

By the time we reached the top, it was almost dusk. "Maybe if we stay up here awhile longer, the lights will come on," I said. Ezra shook in his too-thin coat. Leaning against the chain-link fencing, which reached all the way up so you couldn't jump, I tried to look for happiness. There was none. I was freezing, I think Amanda's chocolate was crumbling inside my pocket and pressed so close to my chest. My shoes had finally worn deep enough into my heel that blood was pooling inside them.

"Think they'll let us take the elevator down?" Ezra asked, and I knew right then we wouldn't be waiting for the lights to come on.

"I don't know," I said.

They didn't. Tickets for the lift weren't sold up top, but at least the walk down was easier. At the halfway point, the shop was closing, and the rains began to fall.

The next morning, there were no croissants on sidewalk cafés or brunches of local wine and cheese. We just walked around streets that looked the same, too intimidated to go into any shops where everyone would pretend they couldn't understand my bad French, and eventually found a restaurant with menus we could understand. I had a chef's salad. In Paris. It was the only thing I ate the whole time there—no escargot or tomatoes with foie gras. Ezra had a turkey sandwich.

"You want to just go back to the airport? See if we can get an earlier flight?" he asked.

Outside, the rain raged against the windows. We hadn't brought an umbrella, hadn't found one for sale, and our hoodies were soaked through. Paris was miserable. "Yeah, okay," I said. I didn't know what I was doing here anyway. Paris was a place you came with someone you loved, or at least were wild about. And when it saw us for what we were, it raged.

At work, I got moved up front to man the front office with Katie. Every day, she shoved a space heater under her desk and rolled her ballet leg warmers up her arms all the way to her shoulders. "It's so cold," she would say as she bit violently on her nails. Almost nobody came, and when they did, it was for an appointment with someone on another floor. Stuck so close together, we began to talk.

"I thought you hated me," she said. I'd heard that my whole life.

"No," I said. "I didn't know you." It was funny, they never

knew I just couldn't speak in front of them. The beautiful ones, the thin ones, the ones who got things just because they looked like they deserved it. Once, an old man came in, asking about some kind of paperwork, and he headed straight for Katie. That was fine with me. Right then, Miranda slipped in alongside Charmaine, an Irish woman who worked in the office once per week processing visa paperwork before sending it to the Embassy.

"Oh, my!" the old man exclaimed, like he was right out of a play. "So many lovely ladies with such lovely frames. You," he said, gesturing to Katie, "and you, and you," he said nodding to Miranda and Charmaine, "your figures are just beautiful. Such beautiful ladies." Then he looked at me, with my hair now to my chin and my heavy arms. "Well, good afternoon," he said, dropping eye contact and heading back outside.

"What a lecherous old man," Charmaine giggled as Katie and Miranda chimed in. Really, I don't think they noticed. I don't think they ever do, the lovely ones. They're just so used to all the compliments washing over them like a warm golden shower they pretend not to care for, but really do.

That night, Nicholas took Miranda, Katie, and me to one of his favorite gay bars. But Miranda disappeared in just an hour with a boy from Sweden she'd met in her first month. Sometimes, in the office, she told us the hateful things he said to her. How her American accent made her sound uneducated and she was getting too soft in the middle. Katie suckled on a gin and tonic, and, as I was talking to her, her eyes rolled back as she slumped to the floor. She fainted a lot more beautifully than Ezra. Nicholas helped me prop her up and force water down her when she opened her eyes. "That's embarrassing," she said, "I'm sorry. It happens sometimes. I didn't have much to eat today."

"You know she's anorexic," Nicholas whispered to me when Katie took herself to the bathroom. "Or bulimic," he said, eyeing her thin back with the bone knots that ran up it.

I didn't know. I didn't know those kind of people existed in real life. "How do you know?" I asked.

"Well, *look* at her," he said. "Besides the fact that she just passed out from not eating."

"How can you dance and be anorexic?" I asked him.

"I don't know. But you never noticed her hands?" he asked.

"Her nails? Yeah, she chews them."

"She chews them because it hurts something awful to stick your fingers down your throat with fingernails. And her knuckles are always scratched up. That's from her knocking them against her teeth when she gags."

"How do you know all this?"

"I just do." Nicholas. He was so skinny, too.

But I didn't care, not really, and two hours later we were all shitfaced and dancing madly to Hanson's "MMMBop." It was a do-over, just like I'd wanted. Me, in a London club, dancing with beautiful people to a song everyone made fun of that plastered such sad lyrics into such a happy rhythm.

"Hey!" I yelled to Katie as she jumped up and down. Drunk Julia had no boundaries, and I had to know. "Do you make yourself throw up?"

Katie was drunk, an easy drunk, and her eyes brightened like I'd randomly guessed the secret knock to her secret world. "Sometimes!" she said.

"That's what—" I began, but no. I couldn't bring Nicholas into it. What if she remembered in the morning and got mad? "That's what I thought," I said.

"It helps," she said. "If you want me to show you how."

Katie, I'd tried. I'd tried it before, but I couldn't make it happen no matter how badly I wanted it. Even when I was truly sick, even when I needed to throw up to get poisoned food out. It wasn't going to happen for me. "Nah, it's okay," I said, and she just shrugged and took another long draw from her straw, her wispy blonde hair bouncing in the rainbow lights.

25

IT ALL UNRAVELS even when you watch real close. I swore to everyone, to Zadie in my emails and Amanda on those rare calls, what I was looking forward to most was Christmas in London. I wanted the little traditional villages, the paper crowns from the crackers as we all sat around a pub table. Mulled wine and Latin mass at the Church of England. Some of it I got because it came tumbling down early. Like the real, aged eggnog and the coworkers who held hands, crossed, over The Apple Peddler's longest table as we counted down the time to pull the crackers apart.

Nicholas and Harry had planned it good, a surprise full Friday off and drinking that began at ten in the morning. As soon as Harry clipped through that office door, the whole lot of us were off—twelve in total once you gathered the plump women from upstairs who did important things with A4 papers that were too long and skinny to seem like real documents. We ordered bottles, rich roasted duck, and it was expected that we were sloppy before noon. It was six days 'til Christmas, just four working days, and everybody knew Ezra and I had tickets to Venice in hand. I wanted the water streets and the pickpockets at the Vatican.

Katie and I sat next to each other, bonded together with invisible thumbtacks after the past few months alone in the front office. The paper crowns exploded out of the crackers just like I'd imagined, complete with confetti and little plastic toys. We all sang Christmas carols, and if I'd known for sure of a British movie or television show around this time of year, I'd have felt like I landed right between its plump thighs. The one with Scrooge, maybe, but I'd never really seen that movie and couldn't decipher if it had British accents or not.

I kissed Katie, or she kissed me, not knowing why and everybody cheered.

"What!" she cried, throwing her head back and showing off those expensive teeth. In the English cold, so foreign to her Florida, she'd clutch her jaw whenever she went outside. Each and every one of the little while hills in her mouth were wired straight into her jaw. They were all fake. "My teeth just weren't made right," she'd said, and you could kind of tell. At the gum lines, it sort of showed. The cold froze those wires, she swore it, and she couldn't even walk from the tube to the office without it feeling like her jaw was frosting up, so she'd stumble up the four stairs to our building with mittened hands clutching her face.

I don't know why we kissed that day, but it was something—something—to feel besides Ezra's too-familiar lips that were starting to fit between my teeth like they were stick-out *Simpsons* drawings.

But Katie, she went home. It was Nicholas and I who closed down the party, outlasting even the drunkard Harry. Nicholas and I who took the half-empty bottles from the pub, the waitress whose name we both knew chasing us halfway down the block to get them back. We'd paid for them, hadn't we? Nicholas and I who ended up on the office steps when it was getting dark, but the blackness came so early now. He'd forgotten his keys at the pub, but screw it. We gathered close on the steps, passing bottles and letting our fingertips touch until they were all empty.

"What are you doing?" he asked me bluntly, fingering a label edge that was pulling away from the glass.

"Nothing," I said. Like he thought I was hoarding a nip and not sharing.

"Not now," he said. Even in my drunkenness, I could hear the slurs. "With—you know what I mean. With him."

"Ezra?" I asked. Had Nicholas ever even met him? Or had I just talked about him? What all had I let fly from my innards all those nights we were drunk?

"Yeah," Nicholas said. "You don't love him, everyone can see it. Why are you battening down your life like this?"

I despised Nicholas in that moment, for luring me into him with fast smiles just to nail down my palms and feet to demand truths.

"He's a good guy." It's all I could come up with.

"You should . . . you should go for more." He should know. Nicholas had told all of us his coming out story, how when he was fifteen he had a girlfriend who was a lesbian and it was devastating breaking up with her. She threatened to tell everyone he was gay if he did, and since he couldn't prove she was a dyke, he believed her. Thought he had no blackmail of his own. He stayed with her for a year, taking her to dances, until her military dad scooped her away to a base in Japan. It was then that he told his parents, balling up all his everything for those two words. His mom immediately stood up from the table, went rustling in the back room, and came back with a photo of Nicholas at four, flamboyant with jazz hands while on a swing.

"We've known for *years*," is all she said. And that was it. When Nicholas met his husband in grad school in London, they were supposed to be roommates. And they both just knew, like that.

But I was scared. I didn't want to have to do this all over again, risk the chance of tripping right into another Ben who baited me with honey words 'til I got close enough so his fangs could fold out and sink in.

The next morning, emails were waiting for me to accompany a pounding headache. I'd tried to make Ezra jealous when I told him I was home so late and drunk because I was with Nicholas, but he didn't care. He knew he was gay. Anyway, when Nicholas came in after me, a rarity, he came up immediately with a scared look and whispered, "The bottles. We didn't pick up the bottles." We hadn't, but when I'd arrived they were gone already, our little night binge erased from the cobblestone street.

Amanda had filed for divorce, and it was for real. There was a defeat in her email, a clear step-by-step plan she wasn't going to waver from no matter what. *Chuck is going to pay for this*, she said. *You know when he was in that psych ward? One of the nurses, she took him home with her. Can you believe that?? Like some kind of female white knight syndrome. He's living with her now, her and her six kids. Six effing kids. I can just picture it over there. I need someone ASAP. Someone that will make him jealous.* I just ignored that last part in my reply, could already see the years unfolding in front of her of mistake after mistake after mistake.

And Zadie. *I think I'm going to marry him.* That's all she needed to say. Maybe we could get married around the same time, plan our lives so they trotted along beside each other, just one race lane away.

That night, the hangover with its claws still in me, Ezra had found some D&D group online and was going off to hunker into someone else's basement flat for once. Some fat guy from Manchester is what he'd said, a guy he'd found on Craigslist. Their little fold had met up a few times, sometimes at pubs, but now they were getting cozy enough to ditch the veneers of a social gathering. All they really needed were their notebooks, big hardback guides, and one of them to volunteer to weave together some kind of life better than what they knew.

When I woke up at one in the morning, he was still gone. It wasn't the extra air in the room that jostled me up. It was the spider. An experiment when Ezra was deep in chemo had revealed something terrifying about myself—sometimes, rarely, I sleep with my eyes open. It lets in all these hideous nightmares, ones that are so much more than lucid dreams, my eyes pulling in all my surroundings and turning them into monsters. Always spiders. I'd figured it out one night when an enormous tarantula was perched just a foot above my head. It was too big and, I just knew, too fast for me to move. I couldn't stick my head under the blankets like it was a poltergeist in a hotel room. I had no choice but to just keep watching it. I kept my eyelids peeled open until my corneas burned and, slowly, it turned into a wall bracket that was holding up the makeshift headboard. In total awareness and clarity, I moved from the dream world to the real world with both eyes wide open.

The same thing happened here, months since the last time. I saw a gigantic spider legging across our white comforter that almost glowed in the dark and it felt so, so real. That's when I realized he was gone.

Where are you? I texted him. Waited one minute. Nothing. I called, and it just rang endlessly before the bored sounding British voicemail recording picked up. Again, three times, four. Finally I left a voicemail, could hear my mom's shaky voice in my own over the wires, but knew it was pointless.

I sent him twenty-four texts that night, each one shorter and madder. What if this wasn't what I thought? What if he was hurt, dead, bleeding out in some black park? But my phone held no answers. We didn't get Wi-Fi in the basement, didn't even have it set up. And I couldn't even begin to guess at the English version of 911. It was past five when I finally heard the keys in the front door.

"What the hell?" I hiss-yelled to him. The landlord had the flat right next door.

"Sorry," he said. "Lost track of time."

"I was freaking out, I—you know what? I don't believe you." The words settled in the gray room's light with all the bearings of truth.

"Don't be stupid," he said. Not even offering up an excuse.

Venice. What about Venice? I think I always knew I'd never go.

I got up, got dressed, went to work and wasted the day looking up how much it would cost to just go home early. Skip Italy, maybe fly straight to Georgia and let Zadie tell me what to do. I looked at ads for teaching English in South Korea, looked at the nonprofit job boards in Portland. But there were no beacons pointing anywhere. Katie, swaddled tight in her old ballet leggings, asked if I wanted to drink after work and didn't even act surprised when I said no.

No. I wanted to punish myself. For all the stupidness I'd done.

I knew when I left that morning, Ezra ignoring me as he brushed his teeth, that I wasn't coming back. I didn't take my heaviest coat, but tucked my passport into my pocket. Grabbed a book, my acne cream, the fold-up travel toothbrush and all the cash we had buried deep inside the littlest suitcase. Not that it was a lot. Not that it could get my anywhere, but my credit cards could.

As soon as Harry left the office, I was two minutes behind him. Left the heavy, wrapped new Oxford Dictionary on the table where we all did the games pages every day. One of the games, you had to come up with more complicated words than what you were presented—Harry always said we failed because the cheap paperback dictionary in the office wasn't comprehensive enough. That was my gift to them, what I'd leave behind. A big, thick volume of words I mostly didn't understand.

And I walked. For miles, for hours, past all the places I hadn't gone or wanted to redo without Ezra. Buckingham Palace and the guards, Big Ben, Parliament and Tottenham Station where the famous *An American Werewolf in London* tube scene was filmed. That werewolf always got to me the most, the way the transformation scene was so fake it had to be real. When it was dark, too dark to keep on. When the rains began. When it felt like I had walked my hip bones into dust, I picked a well-lit, safe looking station and let the cold, slick walls hold me up. In minutes, the freezing ground turned me numb. Eleven at night.

Where are you? Ezra's text flashed on my phone. I had three quarters of a battery. Ten minutes later when it began to vibrate, I silenced it and watched his name flash across the screen over and over again. *Ezra, Ezra, Ezra.*

You there?

Pick up

??

Are you trying to get even with me???

"Can't sit here." The cop was on me, looking serious in his fitted uniform, but I was beyond caring. "Station's closing."

"Okay," I said, pushing myself off the cement. I hadn't noticed the stain, probably urine, that I had planted my thighs right on.

"Miss?" he said to my back.

"Huh?"

"King's Cross."

"What?"

"King's Cross station. They're closed but have a covered area with a bench. It's open all night." He was trying to be kind. He felt sorry for me.

"Isn't that where the bombs went off?" I couldn't help it, those were the words that labored through my teeth.

"'Twas," he said. *'Twas.* So proper.

Ezra texted and called 'til one, then gave up. He'd drained most of the battery siphoning the bars away as I walked through the storm to the station. I wondered if he was sitting, mad and boiling, flipping through his childish books but not digesting the words. Maybe he really had gone to sleep. I wondered if he'd go to Venice alone, use my empty seat as a place to put his grubby backpack or the desserts from the prepacked foods when he found them too sweet. By the time the King's Cross bench shone before me, I didn't care what he did anymore.

There was just enough battery, probably, to make a call. I didn't even know how calling direct to other countries worked, but I knew the American country code from all those work calls I had to place to US universities. I didn't know how much was on my prepaid phone, couldn't recall the last time I'd topped up. If it cost a dollar, five dollars, twenty dollars a minute, I didn't care. I only knew a scattering of numbers by heart, most imprinted into my brain years ago when my feet didn't look just like my mom's and my thighs hadn't rubbed together so hard they'd created some kind of permanent callous. My passport shoveled into the soft perch above my hipbone as I leaned over the cheap little phone, the one I'd never give back to the office. Let them buy another.

I'd forgotten how soothing the familiar dial tone was, how much better it was than the strange British one. It was early on Friday morning back there, and I didn't know if they'd be up. Be busy, not recognize the number and miss me altogether. Two rings, three. Outside the small cove covering, the British flag flapped madly in the wetness, looking exposed and confused. It was put there after the explosions. Four rings. The book I'd taken that morning had pages bleeding together, words melting and crashing into one another. Bits of it was already sloughing off onto my jeans. Five rings, come on. *Come on. Come on.*

"Hello?" The voice, so familiar, blossomed like spring across the ocean and steadied my anxious heart.